He had never wanted a woman as much as he wanted this one.

Amanda Sutherland was intelligent and sassy and exciting as all get-out. At work, she was also absolutely fearless, which sometimes scared the hell out of him. But, hell, the truth was, he flat out adored everything about the woman—her sharp mind, her wicked tongue, that gorgeous face, those dynamite legs.

Reilly rolled a peppermint around in his mouth thoughtfully. What cinched it, though, what really grabbed him in the gut, was that flash of vulnerability he'd glimpsed....

Sucking on the peppermint, Reilly maintained his indolent pose, but a determined smile curved his lips.

Amanda had done a good job of evading him for over a year and a half.

Not that it was going to do her any good.

For, however long it took, he would win....

Dear Reader,

Welcome to Silhouette *Special Edition* ... welcome to romance.

Last year I requested your opinions on the books that we publish. Thank you for the many thoughtful comments. Throughout the past months I've been sharing quotes from these letters with you. This seems very appropriate while we are in the midst of our THAT SPECIAL WOMAN! promotion, as each of our readers is a very special woman.

This month, our THAT SPECIAL WOMAN! is Lt. Callie Donovan, a woman whose military career is on the line. Lindsay McKenna brings you this story of determination and love in *Point of Departure*.

Also this month is *Forever* by Ginna Gray, another book in the BLAINES AND THE McCALLS OF CROCKETT, TEXAS series. Erica Spindler brings you *Magnolia Dawn*, the second book in her BLOSSOMS OF THE SOUTH series. And don't miss Sherryl Woods's *A Daring Vow*— a tie-in to her VOWS series—as well as stories from Andrea Edwards and Jean Ann Donathan.

I hope you enjoy this book, and all of the stories to come!

Sincerely,

Tara Gavin
Senior Editor

QUOTE OF THE MONTH:

"I have an MA in Humanities. I like to read funny and spirited stories. I really enjoy novels set in distinctive parts of the country with strong women and equally strong men.... Please continue to publish books that are delightful to read. Nothing is as much fun as finding a great story. I will continue to buy books that entertain and make me smile."

—T. Kanowith, Maryland

GINNA GRAY

FOREVER

Silhouette®

SPECIAL EDITION®

Published by Silhouette Books

America's Publisher of Contemporary Romance

SILHOUETTE BOOKS

ISBN 0-373-09854-5

FOREVER

Books by Ginna Gray

Silhouette Special Edition

Golden Illusion #171
The Heart's Yearning #265
Sweet Promise #320
Cristen's Choice #373
Fools Rush In #416
Where Angels Fear #468
If There Be Love #528
Once in a Lifetime #661
A Good Man Walks In #722
Building Dreams #792
Forever #854

Silhouette Romance

The Gentling #285
The Perfect Match #311
Heart of the Hurricane #338
Images #352
First Love, Last Love #374
The Courtship of Dani #417
Sting of the Scorpion #826

*The Blaines and the McCalls of Crockett, Texas

Silhouette Books

Silhouette Christmas Stories 1987
"Season of Miracles"

GINNA GRAY

A native Houstonian, Ginna Gray admits that since childhood, she has been a compulsive reader as well as a head-in-the-clouds dreamer. Long accustomed to expressing her creativity in tangible ways—Ginna also enjoys painting and needlework—she finally decided to try putting her fantasies and wild imaginings down on paper. The result? The mother of two now spends eight hours a day as a full-time writer.

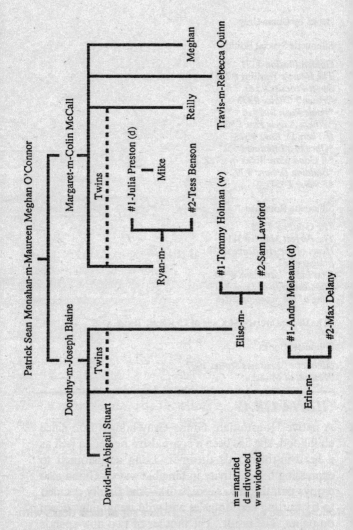

Patrick Sean Monahan-m-Maureen Meghan O'Connor

Dorothy-m-Joseph Blaine

Margaret-m-Colin McCall

David-m-Abigail Stuart

Twins

Twins

Ryan-m-

#1-Julia Preston (d)

Mike

#2-Tess Benson

Reilly

Meghan

Travis-m-Rebecca Quinn

Elise-m-

#1-Tommy Holman (w)

#2-Sam Lawford

Erin-m-

#1-Andre Meleaux (d)

#2-Max Delany

m=married
d=divorced
w=widowed

Chapter One

Amanda Sutherland spied the letter the moment she entered the newsroom.

For a fraction of a second her steps faltered, a hesitation so brief it was nearly indiscernible. Almost without breaking stride, she resumed her usual self-confident saunter through the maze of desks. Only the fluttering pulse at the base of her throat betrayed her disquiet.

All around, the Channel 5 KLUX-TV newsroom bustled with activity and sound. The click of a dozen computer keyboards created a muted castanet rhythm against the hum of PC monitors and the rustle of paper, the electronic chirp of telephones. Disconnected conversations blended together in a low rumble, punctuated now and then by a taunting call or a bark of laughter. Overlaying it all was the never-ending flicker and drone of the station's studio monitors.

Some of Amanda's fellow workers hurried about. Some stood in small groups, talking. Others sat at their desks with telephones cradled against hunched shoulders or banged away at computers.

They might have been on another planet for all the attention Amanda paid them.

Dropping her notepad onto her desk and her purse in the bottom drawer, she sat down and stared at the letter.

It lay atop the stack of mail in her In basket, ordinary and innocuous-looking, but the buff envelope with the tiny, precise writing was becoming all too familiar to Amanda.

Reluctantly she lifted the letter from the stack. As usual, it bore a Houston postmark but no return address.

After a brief hesitation, she slit open the envelope and removed the single sheet of paper.

Dearest Amanda,
You were wonderful Tuesday night at that oil refinery explosion. You're so beautiful and so brave. To watch you standing there, calmly reporting the facts with the fires raging in the background when everyone around you was panicking, made me so proud. No other woman can compare. You have spoiled me for anyone else. Only you fill my dreams and light up my life. I would do anything for you, my Amanda. Anything.

Amanda stared at the words. The uneasy niggle she experienced earlier had swollen into a hard knot that lodged just beneath her breastbone.

As always, the note was unsigned. The handwriting was so tiny and so painfully neat it almost looked as though it had been produced by a machine. The whole thing barely took up a fraction of the page.

The letters were arriving more frequently; it had been only four days since the last one. What bothered her even more, though, was their changing tone.

The first one had been merely a fan letter—a bit gushy perhaps, but harmless. Receiving fan mail was such a rarity for a roving TV reporter that she had been pleased at first.

The feeling had not lasted. With each succeeding letter the expressions of devotion had increased. So had the hint of possessiveness that she found so disturbing.

What on earth would make a man become preoccupied with a woman he didn't know, someone he'd never even met? It was downright spooky.

Amanda folded the letter and stuffed it back into the envelope. Tapping the edge against her desk top, she glanced toward the news director's glass-partitioned office at the far end of the room. Should she show him the letters? At the moment, the miniblinds were shut tight and the door was closed. Either Harry Kowalski was catching a little midafternoon snooze or someone was being called on the carpet. As a rule, Harry liked to keep an eye on his staff. In either case, he wouldn't welcome an interruption.

As she had in the past, Amanda quickly decided against bringing the matter to her boss's attention. The letters were in no way threatening, after all. What could she say? That they gave her the creeps? She could just imagine what Harry would have to say about that. He was forever griping that working women used the flimsiest excuse to scream "sexual harassment." Knowing him, he'd probably use the situation as an excuse to pull her out of the field. If that happened, she could forget any hope of a promotion or eventually getting a network job.

Enlightened, Harry was not. The old war-horse had cut his teeth in hard copy, working in his early days for several of the nation's leading newspapers, and he was chauvinistic right down to his nicotine-stained fingertips. As far as he was concerned, women reporters were fit to write only what he considered fluff—the society page, advice to the lovelorn, a cooking or decorating column. Maybe an occasional movie or theater review if she was exceptionally sharp. Fieldwork, especially investigative reporting, was strictly a man's domain.

"The old testosterone freak," Amanda muttered, and shoved the letter into her middle desk drawer with the other five.

Determined to push the matter aside, she reached for the other correspondence in her basket. The best way to handle the situation was to ignore it; eventually whoever was writing would tire of the whole thing and focus his attention elsewhere.

The thought had no sooner run through her mind than a pair of large hands clamped on her shoulders.

"Gotcha!"

"Aaagh!" Amanda jumped as though she had been shot and whirled around. Sagging in the chair, she closed her eyes and put her hand over her caroming heart. "Eric! For Pete's sake! Don't sneak up on me like that. You scared me half to death."

"Hey. Take it easy." Eric Paterson backed away a step, holding his hands up. His suave face reflected genuine puzzlement. "What's your problem, Sutherland? The way you reacted you'd think Jack the Ripper was attacking you in a dark alley or something."

Amanda winced. He was right. She was letting those stupid letters and her overactive imagination frazzle her nerves.

"Sorry. I, uh, I was a million miles away, that's all. Did you want something in particular?"

"Actually, yeah. You know, you're a hard woman to find. I've been trying to track you down all day."

"Crusher and Norman and I have been over in Beaumont covering the black-market baby trial. All you had to do was check with Harry and he could've told you where I was."

"Yeah, I did, finally. But only as a last resort. Mentioning your name to Harry is iffy at best. Today it was like lighting a fuse." Hooking one leg over the corner of her desk, Eric perched on the edge and waggled his forefinger at her. "You've been butting heads with him again, haven't you, Sutherland?"

Amanda put her hand over her heart and fluttered her lashes. "Me? Why, whatever makes you think that?"

"Oh, I don't know. Maybe because when I asked where you were, Harry launched into a ten-minute tirade about pushy women. Or it could be because all day he's been chomping on antacid tablets like they were candy. So, tell me, gorgeous, what was it this time?"

"Well...maybe we did have a teensy bit of a discussion about who would cover the trial. Harry wanted to send a man, but I felt since I had uncovered the baby-selling ring and broken the story in the first place, I should get to cover the trial phase, too. Harry finally saw it my way."

Eric rolled his eyes. "One shudders to think what method of persuasion you used."

"Actually, Harry was quite reasonable." That was after she had hinted that Bob Donaldson, the station manager, might view his refusal to allow her to follow through on the story as discriminatory.

Mr. Donaldson and the owners of Channel 5 were cognizant of the changing times and tried to provide equal opportunities. It had been Bob Donaldson, not Harry, who had given Amanda the assignment to cover a political powder-keg situation in the Middle East the summer before last.

Amanda had done a good job—an exceptional job, in her opinion. She had hoped that the assignment would bring her network recognition or, at the very least, a promotion with Channel 5, but so far, nothing. In her more pessimistic moments she wondered if Harry had deliberately sabotaged her chances with the network brass.

It rankled that Amanda had to practically beg Harry for every decent assignment, or else resort to veiled threats, as she had done that morning. Both methods were distasteful, but she had made up her mind years ago that she was going to succeed in her career. If that meant using whatever weapons were available to her and butting heads with a cantankerous, hairy-knuckled, stogie-smoking Neanderthal, then by heaven, she would. The Harry Kowalskies of this world were not going to stand in her way.

Not that Harry minded giving her the grunge jobs, or even potentially dangerous ones. At times she felt he did so deliberately to try to discourage her. But the truly important stories, the ones that could skyrocket a career, he always tried to give to the men.

"Harry? Reasonable?" Eric hooted. "Who're you trying to kid? C'mon, Amanda, what really happened? You can tell me."

Amanda merely smiled.

Eric was okay. Sort of. At least he wasn't a total jerk. However, as the station's director of community affairs, he often worked closely with Harry. The two had become drinking and fishing buddies, and Amanda wasn't about to fall for that "you can cry on my shoulder" routine.

Like every man who worked at the station, Eric knew to run for cover when Amanda gave that dangerous little smile. One or two, to their sorrow, had learned the lesson the hard way. With a few choice, sweetly spoken words, Amanda could cheerfully cut a man off at the knees. When she was truly annoyed, she smiled.

No fool, Eric backed off at once. "Okay, okay. Forget I asked."

He started to rise, and she cocked one eyebrow. "I thought you said you wanted to see me about something."

"Oh, yeah. I just wanted to know what time I should pick you up for our date tomorrow."

The reminder gave Amanda a jolt. She had forgotten that she had invited him to go with her to the housewarming party at Tess and Ryan's.

Cripes. She couldn't believe she had actually set herself up to spend the better part of a day in Eric's company. In the past she had always refused whenever he had asked her out. It was just her bad luck that all the other single men she knew were unavailable tomorrow.

Looking at Eric's cocky grin, she ground her teeth. Oh, Lord, was she really that desperate?

She thought about what would probably happen if she showed up at the party alone and sighed. Yes. Oh, yes.

"The party starts at three. Why don't you pick me up about a quarter to," she said with an utter lack of enthusiasm.

Eric didn't seem to notice. Leaning across the desk, he lifted her chin with his forefinger. "I could make it earlier and we could have our own party. Hmm?"

The lecherous gleam in his eyes set Amanda's teeth on edge, and she responded with another of her tight smiles. "Only if it's your wake, Paterson."

Eric's amorous expression wilted. "Okay, okay. I get the message. I'll see you tomorrow afternoon."

Watching him stalk away, Amanda rolled her eyes. She was tempted to break the stupid date and just stay home tomorrow.

She sighed. But of course, she couldn't do that. Tess McCall was her dearest friend in the world. They were like family to each other; closer, in fact, than many sisters.

A tender smile tugged at Amanda's mouth. Tess was the gentlest, nicest person she knew. In the past, life had dealt her friend some bitter blows. God knew she deserved the happiness she had found with her new husband. Tess was so excited about the home that Ryan had built for them and anxious to show it off. Amanda had no choice; she had to go to the housewarming.

Her expression turned sour again. She yanked a file from the top drawer and slammed it down on the desk with a *thwack* that drew the attention of several people around her. Paying them no mind, she flipped open the file and glared at the pages of notes. This whole thing was Reilly McCall's fault. If it weren't for the aggravating man, she would have gone to the darned party alone.

He was sure to be there; he was Ryan's identical twin, after all. He and all the rest of the McCall and Blaine clan were coming to help Tess and Ryan celebrate.

Shoot, Reilly was at his brother's home half the time, anyway, or at least it seemed that way to Amanda. She could hardly visit her friend without running into the big, good-looking devil.

Merely thinking about Tess's brother-in-law created a fluttery sensation in Amanda's stomach. She gritted her teeth. *Damn you, Reilly McCall, why won't you leave me alone?*

For more than a year, the man had been pursuing her. He called at least once a week to ask her out, even though she always said no, sometimes not too politely. He flirted with her outrageously whenever they encountered each other, which happened all too often since he was now part of Tess's family. Nothing Amanda did or said discouraged him. She didn't understand it.

Amanda liked men. She enjoyed their company, enjoyed teasing and flirting with them, enjoyed the attention they gave her, but until now she had always been the one in charge. She had never before had any difficulty keeping a man at a safe distance or even in sending one packing...not until Reilly.

"The man has the hide of a rhinoceros," she muttered. What's more, he was driving her nuts. Otherwise, she would never have asked Eric to escort her to the housewarming.

Amanda didn't relish the idea of spending almost a whole day in Eric's company, but at least she wouldn't have to deal with Reilly. He was a determined man and bold as they came, but she doubted even he would hit on another guest's date. Who knew, he might even get the message that she wasn't interested.

Experiencing a twinge of conscience, Amanda wrinkled her nose. All right, all right. Maybe that wasn't precisely accurate. So maybe she was interested... sort of. Attracted, anyway.

But she didn't want to be! Just because her body went on red alert and her hormones began to bubble when she was around him didn't mean she was stupid enough to get involved with a charming womanizer like Reilly McCall. She was an intelligent, logical, ambitious woman. She made decisions based on sound reason and good judgment, not some crazy and totally inappropriate chemistry. Reilly McCall was all wrong for her, and that was all there was to it.

For a Friday afternoon it was quiet in the newsroom. Amanda made a few calls, but after a couple of hours she called it a day.

On her way out of the building, she ran into Crusher Williams, her favorite cameraman, and Norman Krupps, who was a trainee in the station's new apprentice program.

"Hi, fellas. You packing it in, too?"

"Yeah. Me'n Josie and the kids are spending the weekend at the lake. If I don't haul my tail home soon, that woman'll skin me alive."

Crusher held the door open for Amanda, and she sailed through, chuckling. The image was ludicrous. Josie Williams was a petite dynamo who weighed one hundred and ten pounds, tops. Her husband stood a hulking six foot seven and was three hundred pounds of solid muscle.

"How about you, Norman? Big weekend ahead?"

"Yeah, man, I bet a stud like you has a hot date all lined up." Crusher gave the young man a friendly cuff on the shoulder that sent him reeling. "Whoa, easy there." He caught Norman's elbow and hauled him upright. Frowning, Crusher flexed his huge hand around the young man's arm and looked him over, shaking his head. "Shoot, man, you need to put some meat on them bones. You're so skinny you'd fit through a mail slot.''

Turning red, Norman ducked his head and tucked a long hank of stringy brown hair behind his ear.

He was the most unprepossessing male Amanda had ever met. Gangly and scruffy-looking, he had a pock-marked face, protruding, watery eyes and a big nose.

Giving her friend a speaking look, Amanda slipped her arm through the younger man's. ''Don't pay any attention to the big ox, Norman. Everyone looks skinny to him.''

''Say, kid, you ever try lifting weights?''

''Crush*er*,'' Amanda warned.

''What? Whadisay?'' Crusher stopped in the middle of the parking lot and spread his massive arms wide, his ebony face blank.

''It's all right, Ms. Sutherland. I . . . ah . . . ah . . .'' Norman's watery eyes grew wider, and he groped in the back pocket of his jeans for a handkerchief. '' . . . Ah . . . ah-*choo!*''

''Bless y—''

''Ah-choo! Ah . . . ah-choo!''

''Mercy. You poor thing. You've been doing that all day. You must be allergic to something.''

''I think it's your perfume. The kid only has these sneezing fits around you.''

''What?'' Amanda's startled gaze shot to Crusher.

''Hey. Don't blame me. All I know is for the past couple of hours since we got back from Beaumont he's been fine. But let him get within three feet of you and his nose goes berserk.''

''Norman, is this true?''

''Well, I . . . ah . . . ah . . . ah-choo!'' Norman buried his face in his handkerchief and nodded glumly. ''But that's o-o . . . ka . . . hay. No pr-pr-problem. I don't mi-mi—*ah-choo!*''

''Don't be silly. Of course it's a problem. You can't go around like this.'' She patted his arm, then backed away from him. "Thank goodness it's easy to fix. I'll just switch perfumes."

Norman looked at her over the top edge of his handkerchief, his streaming eyes wide. "You'd do thad for me?"

"Of course. It's no big deal. Besides, we can't have our number-one apprentice photographer sneezing every breath, now, can we?"

Turning red to the tips of his ears, Norman began to back away. "Thangs, Midz Sutherland. Thad's really nidth of you. Well . . . I, uh, I gedth I'll see you Monday."

Bemused, Amanda and Crusher called so long and watched him scramble aboard his motorcycle and peel out of the parking lot. Crusher shook his head.

"Pitiful. Man, that is pit-ti-ful."

"Yes, he is painfully shy, isn't he?"

"Shy, hell. I'm talking about that giant-size crush the boy's got on you."

"You think so?" Crusher gave her a disgusted look, and Amanda made a face. "Well, don't worry, it won't last long. He can't be more than . . . what? Nineteen? Twenty? As soon as he meets some sweet young thing his own age he'll wonder what he ever saw in an old thirty-year-old woman like me."

"Yeah, but meantime it's gonna be a pain in the butt to watch him mooning around after you like a sick pup. Man, he's gonna be useless."

Amanda unlocked her little red fireball of a car. Standing in the wedge of space created by the open door, she paused and fluttered her eyes wickedly at Crusher. "Can I help it if I've got this fatal charm?"

Eric gave a low whistle the next afternoon when he turned into the Wildwood development on the northwest edge of Houston. "Nice neighborhood."

Amanda glanced around at the curving streets and elegant homes on half-acre wooded lots. "Mmm. Tess's husband and his brother are the developers and builders."

"Man, this place has the look of money. Your friends must be making a mint."

Amanda rolled her eyes. Trust Eric to see dollars signs instead of the magnificent job the McCall brothers had done of building a first-rate community while still preserving the natural beauty of the property. "They had a rough spell getting started, but things have picked up this past year, in spite of the economy."

Tess and Ryan's home was on the lake. When they arrived, the curved drive and the street in front of the house were already lined with cars. Amanda rang the bell and a few seconds later the door was opened by an attractive young woman with lovely aquamarine eyes, which lit up when she saw them.

"Amanda! Oh, how wonderful to see you again!"

"Abbey!"

Both women surged forward and hugged. When they broke apart, Amanda held Abbey at arm's length. Her gaze moved slowly down the other woman's ripening figure to the firm mound beneath the maternity dress.

"Why, Abbey Blaine. Just look at you." Her gaze raised to meet the glowing aquamarine eyes. "When?"

"Four months from now. In early July."

"David . . . a father?" Amanda made a wry face. "It boggles the mind."

David Blaine, Ryan and Reilly's cousin, was a rough-around-the-edges, ex-FBI agent who, until he'd met Abbey, had been a confirmed bachelor. No one in the family had expected him to ever marry, but he was thoroughly besotted by this bright-eyed slip of a woman.

Abbey giggled. "I know. And that's not all. Would you believe it's twins?"

"You're kidding!"

Abbey shook her head, and both women went into peals of laughter, clinging to each other for support.

"He's praying for boys," she sputtered between guffaws. "He says if he has to deal with two more females...I'll have to...have him committed!"

"I can imagine!" Amanda gasped.

David had spent much of his life looking out for his irrepressible twin sisters, Erin and Elise, bailing them out of one scrape after another, and so far, Abbey was turning out to be just as much of a handful.

Only when Eric began to loudly clear his throat did the women make an effort to recover their composure. Amanda apologized and made the introductions, and after congratulating Abbey again, she and Eric went in search of their host and hostess.

They found them circulating among the guests in the large family room. Her friend was radiant, her pretty, wholesome face aglow with happiness and excitement. Sticking close to Tess's side, his hand resting on her shoulder, Ryan watched his wife with pride and loving indulgence. The grimness and anger that had once etched his handsome features was truly gone, Amanda noticed as she and Tess exchanged a hug. Ryan now had the look of a man who had found complete happiness.

"Have you seen the family yet?" Tess asked once the introductions were over.

"Just Abbey. Wow. Twins."

"I know. Isn't it wonderful? Dorothy and Joe are on cloud nine. They're finally going to be grandparents."

"Yeah, and David's about to have a nervous breakdown." Rich amusement colored Ryan's deep drawl, which earned him a poke in the ribs from Tess.

"Shame on you. You're enjoying the poor man's misery."

"Damn right. When we were growing up he was Mr. Macho, always in control. Now he's either fretting over Abbey or walking around with that dazed look. I swear, I've never seen a man that proud and that terrified at the same time."

"Oh, pooh. David will be fine, you'll see." Tess gave Amanda's arm a squeeze. "Why don't you take Eric around and introduce him to the clan? They're all here, even Erin and Max and Elise and Sam. Let's see. I think I saw Travis and Rebecca just a minute ago over there talking with Reilly and his date."

"Date? You mean...you mean Reilly is here with a date?" For some reason, Amanda's chest was suddenly so tight she could barely breathe.

"Yes. Ah, there they are, right over there."

Amanda's head whipped around, her gaze zeroing in on the tall, dark-haired man standing by the fireplace...next to a stunning brunette.

Unable to help herself, Amanda stared. The woman was gorgeous—tall and slender, with exotic features and straight, shining black hair that swung around her shoulders like a silk cape.

"Well? Shall we?" Eric prodded, nudging her elbow.

"What? Oh." Amanda dragged her gaze away from Reilly and the woman, and with an effort focused on her own date. "Uh, sure, why not."

Perversely, she led Eric in the opposite direction, away from Reilly and the brunette. Working her way slowly around the room, Amanda introduced him first to the senior McCalls, Maggie and Colin, their youngest offspring, Meghan, and to Maggie's sister and her husband, Dorothy and Joe Blaine, the parents of David, Erin and Elise.

From there they moved on to a group that included the infamous twins and their husbands, Max Delany and Sam Lawford. David was in the next group, along with the youngest McCall brother, Travis, and his wife, Rebecca. When at last they had worked their way around to Reilly, he and the brunette were on their own.

His blue eyes twinkled as he watched their approach. Amanda had the feeling he knew she had been stalling and was amused.

"Hello, Reilly," she said, lifting her chin.

He looked fabulous. She was accustomed to seeing him in jeans or work clothes, but today he wore dark slacks and a loose knit, blue turtleneck that exactly matched his eyes. His wavy black hair had been ruthlessly brushed into submission and his strong jaw had a freshly shaved look, with only the faintest hint of a shadow beneath the skin.

Fascinated by his newfound sartorial elegance, Amanda ran her eyes over him, only to have the image shattered when her gaze reached his feet—and encountered shiny black cowboy boots.

She fixed him with a droll look and cocked one eyebrow. The twinkle in his eyes told her that he knew exactly what she was thinking, but, as usual, Reilly was unflappable. He merely returned the favor.

Taking his time about it, he looked her over and grinned—that slow, sizzling grin that made her insides melt. "Hi, Mandy. I was beginning to wonder if you were going to get around to me," he drawled.

"I had to introduce my date. He doesn't know anyone here. And don't call me Mandy." Slipping her arm through Eric's, she deliberately inched closer and gave Reilly a defiant look.

Startled, Eric blinked. Then a cocky grin spread over his face. Quickly making the most of the opportunity, he rubbed his arm against the side of her breast.

"I'd like you to meet Eric Paterson. He works at Channel 5," Amanda said, digging her nails into Eric's arm. He winced and stopped instantly, and she slanted him a cool smile. "Eric, this is Reilly McCall. He and Ryan are twins."

"Uh, yes. So I see," he said, and prudently eased away, putting a couple of inches between himself and Amanda.

Reilly's gaze shifted to the other man, his expression as affable as ever. If he felt so much as a twinge of jealousy it didn't show, and as the two men shook hands, Amanda experienced a spurt of irritation. *Why should he be,* she thought sourly, *when he's got a busty babe hanging on him?*

"Man, it really is uncanny how identical the two of you are," Eric said, staring with unabashed fascination at Reilly. "I thought at first that our host had made a quick change of clothes." He glanced at Amanda. "How on earth do you know who's who?"

"It's not so difficult, once you get to know them. They're really very different."

Actually—though she had never given the matter any thought before—Amanda suddenly realized that from the moment she and Tess had met them she had never had any trouble telling the brothers apart.

Like their cousins, Erin and Elise, Reilly and Ryan were almost mirror images of each other. They had the same rugged good looks and both were tall and broad-shouldered, with the muscular build of a man whose job involved physical labor. Each had thick black hair and vivid blue eyes, which were set off by a deep tan acquired during long hours spent outdoors.

Yet . . . there was something about Reilly. . . . Something intangible that she instinctively recognized. Why, Amanda had no idea, but she had the unsettling feeling that she would be able to pick him out blindfolded.

"Yeah, I'm the nice one," Reilly quipped, and grinned at Amanda's unladylike snort.

Slipping his arm around the brunette's waist, he drew her forward. "I'd like you to meet a friend of mine. This is Brandy Alexander."

Amanda almost laughed aloud. What a ridiculous name. It couldn't possibly be real. What parents would name their baby after a cocktail, for heaven's sake? She sniffed. The woman was probably an exotic dancer or a porno queen.

Which, of course, was no more than she expected from Reilly. The lecherous oaf.

"I'm so pleased to meet you both," the woman purred in a throaty voice that grated on Amanda like fingernails on a chalkboard. Both men, however, seemed to find it enchanting. "Especially you, Amanda. I see you on television all the time. I enjoy your work very much. You're very good at your job."

Amanda gave her a tight smile. "Thank you." *I'll bet you're good at yours, too,* she thought snidely.

"What is it you do at Channel 5, Eric?" Brandy asked in her come-hither voice, and Amanda gritted her teeth. She could almost see Eric's chest puff up.

He promptly launched into an expansive explanation of his duties as director of community affairs. He droned on for five minutes or more, time that Amanda spent trying not to look at Reilly.

Watching him and Brandy, she experienced a welter of strange emotions that she could not define, but that she definitely did not like. There was an easiness between the two that spoke of long acquaintance. She could see it in their body language, the looks that passed between them, the familiar way the woman touched his arm to get his attention. This was not someone new in Reilly's life.

The thought made Amanda furious. Obviously, for more than a year and a half, all the while he had been chasing her, he'd been involved with this woman.

Amanda's eyes narrowed on Reilly. This merely proved that she had been right about him all along. Reilly McCall was a shallow, no-good, womanizing playboy who was incapable of any kind of real depth of feeling or commitment. She had been right to rebuff him.

"Would you like something to drink?" Eric asked during a lull in the conversation.

It took a second and the expectant stares of the others for Amanda to realize that the question had been addressed to her. "Uh, yes. Thank you. A ginger ale would be nice."

"That's a good idea. I could use a refill myself," Brandy announced, rattling the ice cubes in her otherwise empty glass. "I think I'll go with you. That is, if you don't mind?"

Mind? Eric? Now there was a foolish question. The man had hardly taken his eyes off Brandy's bosom for the past ten minutes. Amanda could just imagine him objecting to having her company all to himself for a while.

Actually, she was relieved to be rid of both of them. Already, she'd had more than enough of Eric's company and everything about Busty Brandy irritated her. As the pair walked away toward the bar across the room, Amanda watched the provocative sway of the woman's hips, and her lip curled. God, how she hated exotic brunettes.

"Brandy's a great gal," Reilly commented casually, drawing Amanda's attention.

She slanted him a look and saw that he was watching the couple, too. Was he jealous of Eric? If so, good. Served him right.

"Mmm. Have you known her long?"

"Oh, Brandy and I are old friends. We go way back."

"I see. And what does your friend do for a living?" she asked, placing subtle emphasis on the word *friend*.

"She's an orthopedic surgeon."

Amanda snorted. "Uh-huh. Right. And I'm the Queen of England's long-lost daughter."

"Now, darlin', would I lie to you?" Reilly drawled.

"Does a goose go barefoot?" Amanda responded sweetly with one of her patented little drop-dead smiles.

Reilly chuckled, a rich, warm sound that created a flutter in Amanda's stomach, which only increased her ire.

One of the things that irritated her most about the aggravating man was his damned insouciance. In her experience, a flippant remark accompanied by a go-to-hell smile made a man back off quicker than any vituperative tongue-lashing ever could. The tactic had worked like a charm on every man she'd ever known . . . with the maddening exception of Reilly.

The louse didn't even have the sensitivity to know when he was being insulted, she fumed.

"Ah, Mandy, darlin', you are a delight. By the way, have I mentioned that you look beautiful today? Downright scrumptious, in fact, in that sexy outfit."

"Sexy? This?" Amanda couldn't believe her ears. For the afternoon party she had teamed an old-fashioned, high-necked, long-sleeved blouse of cream silk and lace with a coffee-colored velvet pantsuit. It was the least provocative outfit in her wardrobe, and she had deliberately chosen it because she knew Reilly would be there. To go with the demure outfit, she had pinned up her thick mane of streaked blond hair in a modern version of the Gibson girl. "You're crazy. There's nothing in the least sexy about this outfit."

That electrifying chuckle came again, sending a ripple of goose bumps down her spine. "Ah, sugar, that's what I love about you. For a sophisticated woman, you don't know beans about men. Don't you realize that prim little number just makes a man itch to find out what's under it? Besides, you look more delectable than my mama's peach parfait in all that lace. Tempts a man to carry you off and gobble you up."

He paused to glance around as though checking to be sure no one was in earshot, then leaned close. Suggestively fingering the lace-edged jabot on the front of her blouse, he whispered, "Just say the word, darlin', and I will."

Between her skittering pulse and her temper, Amanda felt as though she would burst into flame at any second, but somehow she managed to hold on to her composure. Raising one eyebrow, she said in her frostiest voice, "Aren't you forgetting something?"

"What's that?"

"Your little friend. Bootsie."

"Brandy," he corrected, grinning.

"Whatever. She's the one you brought to the party. Remember?"

His grin widened. "Why, Mandy, you sound jealous."

It was too much for Amanda. Her eyes narrowed into slits. "In your dreams, McCall," she said with sweet venom.

Predictably, Reilly laughed. Amanda whirled and stalked away.

"Where you going, sugar?"

"To the kitchen to help Tess. And I told you, don't call me Mandy! And *don't* call me sugar!" she snapped over her shoulder.

Chapter Two

Reilly absently fished a peppermint from the pocket of his sweater. He unwrapped the candy and popped it in his mouth, his gaze all the while focused on the enticing sway of Amanda's hips as she headed for the kitchen. Man, oh, man, he did love the way that woman moved—all feline and fluid. Just watching her was a feast for the eyes. Even when she was angry, there was nothing jerky or abrupt about Amanda's gait. She walked with the sinuous grace of a lioness.

That was what she reminded him of—a beautiful, alluring jungle cat. It was more than just the seductive way she moved. There was that tawny mane, and those slumberous, slightly slanted amber eyes.

Reilly chuckled. What a woman. Amanda Sutherland lit a fire in his burner like no woman he had ever known. She was beautiful and intelligent and sassy and exciting as all get-out. When it came to her work, she was absolutely fearless, which often scared the hell out of him. She was also the only woman he knew who could be sultry and cool at the same time.

Reilly rolled the peppermint around in his mouth thoughtfully. Sultry. Yeah, that was the best word to describe her. Most blondes looked cool and aloof, but not Amanda. She was hot and enticing.

Hell, the truth was, he flat-out adored everything about the woman; her sharp mind, her wicked tongue, that gorgeous face, her swimsuit-model body. And man, oh, man...those endless, dynamite legs..

He'd had some pretty erotic fantasies about those legs. Her sexy, hip-swiveling walk nearly drove him crazy and kept him awake at night.

He got a kick out of the way she had of looking at a man so that he was never sure if she was flirting with him, laughing at him, or consigning him straight to hell. Shoot, he even loved that little killer smile of hers.

What cinched it, though, what really grabbed him right in the gut, was that flash of vulnerability he'd glimpsed every now and then. Other people would probably think he was nuts. On the outside Amanda was sexy and smart and self-assured, but he had a hunch that underneath that sleek sophistication and flippant banter was a scared child.

Sucking on the peppermint, Reilly maintained his indolent pose and carefree expression, but as he watched Amanda disappear into the kitchen his insides twisted with longing. He had never wanted a woman as much as he wanted this one.

At first he'd thought he was experiencing just the usual physical attraction for a beautiful woman, but it was more than that; he knew that now. After all this time, with any other female the enchantment would have waned or he would have become bored or disillusioned and moved on. With Amanda, the longing that was eating him up grew stronger every day.

Over the past year and a half he'd come to realize that Amanda's sophisticated, slightly flirtatious manner was pure sham, something she used to keep men off balance. From what he'd been able to wheedle out of Tess, Amanda avoided serious relationships like the plague. She'd sure as hell done a good job of avoiding him for more than a year and a half.

A determined smile curved his mouth. Not that it was going to do her any good. He was a patient man. However long it took, he would eventually win her over.

Her reaction to Brandy was encouraging. He'd been looking forward to this party, hoping to use the chance to make some headway with Amanda. Thank heaven, Tess had tipped him off that she was bringing a date.

He'd told himself that she was just using the guy as a shield, but he had to admit, deep down he'd been uneasy. When she had walked in with that slick dude—Paterson—he'd had a few uneasy moments...until he'd seen them together up close. If there was so much as a spark between those two, he'd eat his new handmade ostrich-skin boots.

Looking across the room to where Eric and Brandy were standing in front of the bar, Reilly's eyes narrowed. Even so, he didn't care for the lecherous gleam in loverboy's eyes or the way he kept putting his hands on Amanda. The creep used the slightest excuse to touch her.

Thank God he'd decided to fight fire with fire.

Reilly smiled and his gaze softened when it settled on Brandy. She was an old and dear friend. And the only woman he knew who was a match for Amanda.

He watched Eric and Brandy leave the bar and head back his way. Studying the gorgeous brunette, Reilly shook his head. The chemistry between a man and a woman was a mystery. Brandy was every bit as beautiful and intelligent and interesting as Amanda, but not even during their brief affair, years ago, had she ever given him this giddy, tied-inknots feeling or turned his knees to mush the way the mere sight of Amanda did.

The sex had been pleasant, but the spark hadn't been there. It hadn't taken them long to figure out that they were much more suited as friends than lovers. And that was exactly what they had been for ten years; the best of friends.

Brandy—bless her—had been more than happy to help when he'd told her about the situation.

"Where's Amanda?" Holding a drink in each hand, Eric stopped beside Reilly and looked around, his expression puzzled.

"In the kitchen helping Tess. I guess she forgot about her ginger ale." *And you,* he added silently with a smirk.

"Oh, too bad." Brandy linked her arm with Eric's. "Why don't I show you the back garden and the view of the lake from the patio? You don't mind, do you, Reilly, honey?"

"Not at all. I have to find Ryan and talk to him about a client, anyway."

"Well . . . I guess if Amanda is busy. . . ."

"Come on. You really must see this. Tess and Ryan have done a great job with the garden."

Reilly watched Brandy lead Eric toward the French doors that led out onto the patio. "Have fun, you two," he called after them.

Smiling, Brandy looked back over her shoulder and winked.

"Of all the egotistical, insensitive, disgusting leches," Amanda muttered under her breath. "Carry me off and gobble me up, indeed." She shoved the kitchen drawer shut and sent a sizzling glare in the general direction of the den. "You wish, McCall."

She stalked over to where Tess was arranging a tray of dip and raw vegetables and slammed the silverware down so hard the stacks of plates on the counter rattled. "The man is nothing but a two-timing flirt. It'd serve him right if I told his old friend Brandy."

The microwave dinged. Amanda jerked open the door, snatched out the platter of cheese puffs and slammed them down on the counter beside the dip.

"All right. That's it. I can't take any more of this. Neither can my dishes. What on earth is wrong with you?"

Amanda opened her mouth to speak but Tess held up her hands, silencing her. "No. Wait, let me guess. You've had another run-in with Reilly, haven't you?"

"That man is driving me crazy," Amanda fumed. "He's a pest, a cretin, a two-timer, a . . . a shallow, arrogant, mannerless, macho Neanderthal!"

"Oh, dear. What has he done now?"

"He had the nerve—the *nerve*—to ask me out again."

Tess gasped. "The beast. You're right. He ought to be horsewhipped."

"Very funny. But I'm serious, Tess. I can't believe he did that, not after all the times I've turned him down in the almost twenty-one months I've known him. And with his date right across the room, yet. Can you believe the unmitigated gall of that man?"

"My, my. Isn't it interesting that you remember exactly how long it's been since you met?" Tess added more celery to the tray and slanted her a teasing smile.

Amanda sniffed. "The only reason I remember is because it was the day I helped you move into the apartment next door to Ryan's, as you know perfectly well. And will you quit chuckling? This *isn't* funny."

"Okay, okay. I won't tease. But I don't understand why it bothers you that Reilly is interested. You should be accustomed to that sort of thing. Ever since we were kids males have been drawn to you like bees to honey. Shoot, even those obnoxious five-year-old boys in our kindergarten class weren't immune. They trailed after you like adoring puppies. I mean, really, Amanda, you've had plenty of prac-

tice fending off males. You've always been able to captivate
men and hold them at arm's length all at the same time.''

"Don't think I haven't tried—to fend him off, that is.
Anyone else would have gotten the message long ago, but
not Reilly. The blockhead doesn't have the brains to know
when to give up.''

"You're wrong, you know. Reilly is a very intelligent and
sensitive man. It's true he's laid back and easygoing and a
terrible tease, but when he really wants something, he simply keeps after it until he gets it.''

"Oh, gee, thanks. That's just what I needed to hear.''

"Amanda, Reilly is a truly nice man. If you'd just give
him a chance, I promise you'd like him.''

"Huh.''

"No, really. If you'd bend a little and go out with him just
once, get to really know him, you might be surprised. Come
on now, admit it. Aren't you just the teeniest bit interested?
Hmm?''

Amanda wasn't about to admit anything of the kind. Not
to anyone—not even Tess.

The powerful attraction made her furious—with Reilly
and with herself. The instant they'd met, she had felt the
wild chemistry that arced between them. She had been
fighting it ever since. Amanda was no fool; she recognized
trouble when she saw it.

"He's not my type. And there's no way I'm going out
with him. I'd sooner lick a toad.''

"But why? Reilly is sweet and fun. And God knows, he's
good-looking and sexy as all get-out.''

"Humph. Of course you'd say that. He looks just like
Ryan.''

"So? It's still true. What's more, Reilly really likes
women.''

"Oh, yes. He does that, all right,'' Amanda scoffed.

"What's that supposed to mean?''

"Nothing. Forget it.''

"I swear, sometimes I don't understand you at all. What've you got against Reilly?"

Avoiding Tess's demanding stare, Amanda fixed her gaze on the relish tray and needlessly rearranged the carrot and celery sticks. "I just don't like him, that's all."

"Why? Has he been rude to you?"

"No."

"Hurt your feelings?"

"No."

"Has he lied to you, or been obnoxious, or...or been too forceful or aggressive? What?"

"No. No, of course not. You know he's not that type."

"Then what's the problem? What terrible sin has Reilly committed to make you dislike him so?"

Amanda gritted her teeth. She hated to be backed into a corner, but she knew Tess. When she got that look you might as well surrender, because hell would freeze over before she would give up. "If you must know, he reminds me of my father."

"What?" Tess nearly dropped the jar of olives she was holding. She stared at Amanda, her face blank with shock. "I can't believe what I'm hearing. Your *father?* How could you say that? Reilly is nothing at all like Kyle Sutherland."

Glaring at Amanda, Tess poked herself in the chest for emphasis. "Don't forget, *I* was there. *I know* what kind of man Kyle Sutherland was, and no doubt still is. I'm shocked that you would compare a nice man like Reilly to him. They're not at all alike."

Tess was the sweetest tempered person Amanda knew. The fierceness of her outburst spoke volumes about her feelings toward her brother-in-law and roused a pang of guilt in Amanda, but she stubbornly ignored it.

Shifting, she fingered the stack of napkins, her expression sulky. "Oh, no? You have to admit, they're both too handsome for their own good. And just like my father,

Reilly hasn't an ounce of ambition or drive, or the least sense of responsibility in that big gorgeous body of his.''

Shiftless and utterly charming, Kyle Sutherland had bounced from one dead-end job to another—when he had bothered to work at all, which had occurred only sporadically when her mother's tearful pleading and prodding could no longer be ignored.

Most of her father's adult life had been spent avoiding work and beguiling gullible women. Aimless and self-indulgent, he had never given a thought to the future, or to the wife and child who had depended on him. Kyle Sutherland went where the wind blew him without a care, as though his sole purpose in life was to enjoy himself. A jazzy car, afternoons on the golf course, evenings at the ball game or in a bar with a pretty female on his arm were all her father had ever needed.

Amanda had been thirteen when he had met a woman who was younger and many times richer than her mother— one who did not pester him constantly about getting a job and paying bills or making something of himself. He had promptly left. Neither Amanda nor her mother had seen him since.

Tess stared at her in amazement. "How can you say that? Reilly is a hard worker. Let me remind you that he and Ryan founded R & R Construction together on practically nothing and built it into a profitable business. Does that sound like a shiftless man to you?"

"Okay, okay. So maybe Reilly isn't lazy," Amanda conceded. "But you have to admit, he is an incurable, glib-tongued flirt. He sails through life completely without purpose or goals of any kind. Face it, Tess. All he really cares about is enjoying himself."

"Just because he likes to have fun, that doesn't mean—"

"Fun! Tess, the man doesn't have a serious bone in his body. To him the world is just one big playground. To tell you the truth, it wouldn't surprise me if Ryan were the sole driving force behind R & R Construction. If the whole business were to collapse around their ears tomorrow, I doubt that Reilly would turn a hair. He's content with the status quo, no matter what it is."

"Well . . . it's true that Reilly has a unique ability to take life as it comes and enjoy it, but some people would see that as a plus."

"Tess, for heaven's sake…" Amanda groaned. "The man is totally lacking in ambition and drive. I swear, if I tried, I couldn't imagine anyone more unsuitable for me than Reilly McCall."

"We're not talking marriage here, you know. Just a simple date."

"Well, good, because marriage doesn't fit into my plans right now. In fact, I'm not sure it ever will."

"Oh, Amanda, don't say that." Tess's face clouded with concern, her irritation forgotten. "Don't deny yourself that special happiness just because your father—"

"It's not that."

Tess shot her a skeptical look, and Amanda grimaced.

"All right, maybe that's part of it. But not all. Marriage just isn't a high priority for me right now. I'm determined to make it to the top in my career. I can't even think about making a commitment to a man until my long-term goals are at least within reach.

"And, of course, even then, the man would have to be steady and serious and as dedicated to his career as I am to mine. Ideally, he would be someone in broadcast news. I would certainly never be foolish enough to fall for a lightweight womanizer like Reilly who drifts through life on his looks and charm.

"Not that Reilly is husband material, mind you," she added quickly when Tess gave her a strange look.

"Oh, I don't know. I think when he's ready to settle down he'll make a wonderful husband."

"Oh, yeah. Right. Trust me on this one, Tess. Reilly is just not marriage material."

Tess sighed and threw up her hands. "I give up. I think you're wrong, but I know there's no use talking to you. When it comes to your father—or any poor man you suspect of being like him—you're impossible. Let's change the subject, shall we?"

That suited Amanda just fine. Talking about the man made her almost as edgy as being near him. "You got a deal." Leaning back against the counter, she filched a carrot stick and bit off the end. "So... how is my goddaughter?" she asked, munching noisily. "And where is she, by the way? And Mike? I haven't seen either of them since I got here."

"Molly's still napping. Mike is upstairs with her. He'll bring her down when she wakes up."

Amanda grinned. "He's turned out to be a heck of a baby-sitter, hasn't he? I knew as soon as we met him that he was one good kid."

Amanda was fond of Ryan's son from his first marriage. The fifteen-year-old was funny and smart, and he had the good sense to adore having Tess for a stepmother.

In the beginning, Amanda had had reservations about Tess marrying Ryan. Theirs had not been a love match, at least not on his part. At the time, he had been a cold and embittered man, but Tess had changed all that. Ryan now loved Tess deeply, and anyone who didn't know would think that Molly was his.

"Mmm. Mike's crazy about Molly and vice versa," Tess said absently, loading the food onto trays. "He's forever toting her around and indulging her every wish. Between him and his father, they're spoiling her rotten. I have a nineteen-month-old tyrant on my hands."

Amanda laughed. "She's not spoiled. She's merely an intelligent female who knows her own mind, like her Aunt Amanda."

Tess gave her a dry look. "The next time she throws a tantrum, suppose I call you to deal with it."

"Go ahead," Amanda said with airy confidence. "Molly and I understand each other. She's always a perfect angel for her auntie."

Tess retrieved a box of colored toothpicks, stuck them into a cut-crystal holder and added it to the tray, and Amanda dumped a sack of chips into a bowl.

"Reilly's date is certainly beautiful," Amanda said casually.

"Mmm."

"She seems friendly, too."

"Uh-huh. She is." Tess hefted one of the trays and headed for the den.

Amanda picked up the other one and followed. "By the way, do you happen to know what she does for a living?"

Pausing with her hand on the swinging door between the kitchen and den, Tess looked back over her shoulder. "Brandy? Oh, she's an orthopedic surgeon."

Amanda stumbled and nearly dropped the tray. "You're kidding, right?"

"Not at all. From what I hear, she's an excellent surgeon and highly regarded by her peers."

Tess pushed through the door. Amanda followed more slowly, her mouth agape.

During the remainder of the afternoon, while the guests enjoyed the buffet and sat around talking, Amanda managed to avoid Reilly. She visited with all of the McCalls and Blaines, joining in when they teased one another, as they always did when together.

David, in particular, came in for more than his share this time because of his impending fatherhood and the way he clucked over Abbey like a fussy mother hen. He weathered the razzing with grudging tolerance and only an occasional snarl, but he continued to hover over his wife.

When Mike joined the party carrying Molly astraddle his hip, Amanda almost had to wrestle the toddler away from the boy, and even then, he wouldn't let her out of his sight.

Amanda spent an hour playing with Tess's daughter and bantering with Mike before Maggie McCall claimed her newest grandchild and carried her off. After that, Amanda retreated to the kitchen where she kept busy washing dishes—anything to avoid Reilly.

Around eight, the guests began to leave, and finally it was time to go. Relieved, Amanda went in search of Eric.

She had seen little of him since arriving, just glimpses now and then from across the room. Most of the time he had been with Brandy, she'd noted. Not that Amanda had minded; she'd been grateful that she did not have to entertain him—or worse, have to fend off his advances, as had happened earlier in the day.

It must have been some kind of macho male pride, Amanda decided. Despite her warning of the day before, when Eric had arrived at her condo to pick her up, he'd made a pass, and Amanda had been forced to deliver a sharp rebuke. All the way on the drive over he had sulked like a child.

Amanda had searched through every room downstairs when she literally bumped into Reilly.

"Whoa, sugar." He grasped her shoulders and held her at arm's length. "What's your rush?"

"Have you by any chance seen Eric?"

"Not recently, no. But I could probably make a guess where you'll find him."

"Where?"

"You sure you want to know?"

Something in his tone put Amanda on alert. She did not care for the gleam in his eyes or the faint air of smugness about him. Her eyes narrowed. "Where is he? So help me, McCall, if you've said something to make him leave, I'll strangle you."

"Me? Hey, don't blame me. I haven't even spoken to the guy since right after you two got here." He was the picture of wide-eyed innocence and wounded dignity. Amanda didn't trust him one bit.

"Then where is he?"

"In case you haven't noticed, he's spent most of the day with Brandy. My guess would be they're down by the lake."

"The lake? I know the weather has been mild lately, but it's still cold by the water, especially at night. What on earth would they be doing down there?"

The slow grin that spread over Reilly's face was positively wicked. "Probably making out."

"What!" Her jaw dropped, but one look at Reilly's expression and she quickly snapped it shut again. "Oh, don't be ridiculous. This may come as a shock, McCall, but not all men have a one-track mind like yours. I can't speak for your girlfriend, of course, but Eric has too much class and manners to do something like that."

"You sure about that?"

She wasn't sure at all, especially considering the way Eric had acted earlier, to say nothing of his smarting pride. And he'd certainly seemed enthralled with Reilly's date. Amanda would bite off her tongue, however, before she admitted as much to Reilly.

"Certainly. Eric is a gentleman. He would never—as you so crudely put it—try to make out with a woman while on a date with someone else."

"Hmm. Well, since you're so certain, whaddaya say we make a little wager on it?"

"What do you mean?" Amanda gave him a suspicious look.

"We'll go down to the lake. If I'm wrong, I'll stop pursuing you."

"And if I'm wrong?"

The wicked smile returned, full force. "Then you have to go out on a date with me, just the two of us."

"In your dreams, McCall."

"Okay, I understand." Reilly spread his hands wide and shrugged. "If you don't have any faith in the man, I certainly won't force you."

Of course, she had no faith in Eric. Zero, zilch, zip. But she couldn't let Reilly know that. She had her pride, after all.

Amanda lifted her chin. "All right. You've got a bet."

Reilly solicitously fetched her cape and led her out onto the patio.

They took the winding path down to the lake. Neither spoke nor made a sound, but when they reached the shore, Amanda gasped and came to an abrupt halt.

There, not twenty feet away, stood Eric and Brandy, locked in a passionate embrace, sharing a hot, hungry, open-mouthed kiss.

Flustered, Amanda looked away, only to encounter Reilly's gaze.

His vivid eyes sparkled with amusement and triumph, and tiny laugh lines crinkled the corners.

"What time shall I pick you up tomorrow night?"

Chapter Three

"I don't know about you guys, but I'm ready to call it a day," Amanda said from the back of Channel 5's remote van.

"Day, hell, I'm ready to call it a week," Crusher replied. "And I'm sure enough ready for a little R and R. Kowalski's sent us on every garbage assignment that's come up lately. Probably to get even with you for forcing his hand on that baby-selling trial last week. Woman, next time you lock horns with the boss, do me a favor and ask for another cameraman, will ya? I've had it with these dirt jobs." He snorted. "A damned hog-calling contest clear over in the next county. What the hell kind of story is that for a primo crew to cover?"

Amanda laughed. "One meant to keep us humble, I expect. *And* to take us—or rather me—down a peg. And, Crusher, sweetie, you know I'd never ask for another cameraman. You're the best."

He growled and shot her a dark look in the rearview mirror. "Don't try buttering me up, woman. That sweet talk of yours may work on the other men around here, but it don't cut no ice with me," he said in the gruff, gravelly voice that terrified most people.

Amanda was unfazed. Just the sight of Theotis "Bone Crusher" Williams struck fear in the hearts of the toughest macho males. During his college days, while studying TV production and cinematography, he had supported himself as a professional wrestler, which was how he'd earned his nickname. Yet for all his fierce demeanor and imposing size, Amanda knew that Crusher was a marshmallow—at least when it came to females. She also knew that he was secretly pleased.

They had worked together for more than seven years, ever since she had joined the Channel 5 staff. From the start, Crusher had taken her under his wing. He treated her with the same gruff affection and protectiveness he would one of his own daughters, of which, at last count, there were five, ranging in age from four to seventeen.

That number would most likely go up in a few months, however, since Josie was pregnant again. Crusher adored his daughters but he was hoping for a son this time. Just to razz him, Amanda had been taking bets at the station that the new little Williams would be a girl.

She met his scowling reflection in the mirror with a saucy grin. "Pooh. You know you love working with me."

"Humph. Why should I?"

"Because I'm the best." She fluttered her eyelashes and added in a simper, "And because I'm so sweet and easy to work with. Not to mention, adorable."

Crusher made a rude sound. "You're good, all right. I'll give you that. But damnation, woman, you push it so hard and take so many fool chances, a man takes his life in his hands going out on assignment with you."

"That's ridiculous. I never take unnecessary risks."

"Lordy, Lordy." Clenching the steering wheel, Crusher craned his head and looked up at the night sky. "If lightning don't strike us for that whopper it'll be a miracle. Woman, you'd rush right into hell itself if you could get an interview with the devil."

"I'm just doing my job, that's all."

"Hmm. Mebbe so. But I think you oughta know that the camera crews are talking about petitioning for hazardous duty pay when we have to go out with you on assignment."

"Bunch of lily-livered wimps," Amanda muttered with a sniff, but she had to bite her lip to keep from laughing.

"I think Ms. Sutherland shows a lot of grit, covering dangerous stories the way she does," Norman said tentatively.

Crusher rolled his eyes and groaned.

Giving him a quelling look in the mirror, Amanda reached over the seat and patted the younger man's shoulder. "Why, thank you, Norman. You're a sweetie pie."

Norman ducked his head, and even in the dim interior of the van she could see a blush spread all the way up to his hairline.

Other than grunts and occasional one-syllable responses to Crusher's orders, it was the first time he had spoken since they'd left the station almost four hours ago. In the eight or nine months that Norman had worked at Channel 5, Amanda had become so accustomed to his long silences, when he did speak, it startled her.

"Boy, mind your tongue," Crusher growled. "This wild woman don't need encouragement."

Norman immediately ducked his head lower and hunched down in the seat. Crusher was his hero. The young man's ambition was to become a top-notch field cameraman exactly like the gruff black man. The least criticism from Crusher, even comments made in jest, Norman took hard.

Feeling sorry for him, Amanda changed the subject. "Since it's Friday night, how about we file our story and head over to The Station House for a pizza?"

Crusher wheeled the van into Channel 5's parking lot and brought it to a halt in the reserved space. "Sounds good to me." He climbed out and slid open the cargo door and assisted Amanda out. "Josie's having one of those X-rated lingerie parties tonight. Says pregnant ladies need pretty things to cheer them up."

"I know, I got an invitation. Didn't you remind her that wearing that sexy stuff is what got her in that condition in the first place?" Amanda teased.

A wide grin split Crusher's ebony face. "Hell, woman. My mama didn't raise no fool."

"Macho pig," she muttered affectionately, and turned her attention on the younger man.

"How about you, Norman? You coming with us?"

"I guess," the boy mumbled, busying himself with gathering up the equipment.

"Great. I'll just—" Amanda turned toward the station, took two steps, and came to an abrupt halt.

Less than twenty feet away, leaning against the hood of her car, thumbs hooked in the belt loops of his jeans, outstretched legs crossed at the ankles, was Reilly.

"Holy—" Crusher almost cannoned into her back. Only a quick, stumbling side step prevented him from knocking her down. "Jeez, woman, what'd you do that for? At least give a man warning when you're gonna stop like that. I coulda flattened you."

"What are you doing here?" Amanda demanded, barely aware of her friend's comments. Her heart banged against her rib cage. Just the sight of Reilly, so big and bold and utterly sure of himself, made her tingle all over.

One look at Amanda's expression and Crusher's eyes narrowed. Frowning, he followed the direction of her gaze. "You know this dude?"

"I came to see you," Reilly replied pleasantly. "They told me inside that you were out on assignment, so I figured I'd just wait for you."

"You shouldn't have come here. I—I can't talk to you right now. I, uh, I've got to file my story."

"No problem. I'll wait."

Amanda wanted to scream. Didn't the man ever give up? He had called her every day for the past week, trying to set up a date and collect on the bet. She had put him off with a variety of excuses—she already had a date, she had to work late, she had aerobic class, a headache, it was her night to clean her fish tank—anything, no matter how flimsy. She had hoped that eventually he would tire of trying and give up. She should have known better.

"No, you can't. That is—"

"Is this guy bothering you, Amanda?" Crusher took a step forward, assuming an aggressive stance.

He was an intimidating mountain of a man. His voice rumbled like thunder, his head was shaved and his biceps were the size of small trees. A gold skull-and-crossbones earring swung from one ear, and he wore a T-shirt with the words C'mon, Sucker. Make My Day emblazoned across a chest that made Arnold Schwarzenegger look anorexic. His menacing scowl alone would have sent most men scurrying for cover.

Reilly grinned.

"The name's Reilly McCall," he said, extending his hand. "I'm Amanda's date."

"What!" Amanda squeaked. "Why, that's—you—"

Crusher's frown eased a bit, but he was far from mollified. He studied Amanda's flustered expression, then turned his suspicious gaze back on Reilly. "Date, huh? Well, now, if that's true, that's good news. This stubborn woman doesn't date near often enough, you ask me. But, I gotta tell you, mister, she sure doesn't look too happy to see you."

Reilly winked and grinned. "Ah, well, there's a reason for that. You see, the truth is, she doesn't really want to go out with me," he confided in a man-to-man way that totally disarmed Crusher and infuriated Amanda. "But we had this bet and she lost, so she has to. Only now she's trying to welsh."

"That's not true!" Amanda lied huffily.

"No? Well, hey, that's great. So, where would you like to go?"

"Uh, that is, I . . . I didn't mean tonight. I . . . I can't possibly make it tonight."

"Oh? Why not?"

"Well . . ." She darted a desperate look at her two coworkers. Both were watching the exchange with the concentrated interest of spectators at a tennis match, their heads swiveling back and forth between Amanda and Reilly. "I— I've already made plans. I promised to stop off for pizza with Crusher and Norman before heading home."

"Hey. No big deal," Crusher said. "Shoot, we can do that anytime. Me'n Norman, we don't wanna muck up your social life. Do we, boy?"

Norman shrugged and stared at the pebble he was pushing around with the toe of his sneaker.

"No, no. A promise is a promise. I wouldn't dream of going back on my word. Reilly and I will just have to go out some other time." If she was lucky, about three hundred light-years from now.

"Aw, hell, I don't feel right about this." Crusher gave Reilly another piercing look. "Look, man, I know it's not the same, but why don't you join us?"

Horrified, Amanda gaped at her friend. "But . . . but—"

"Thanks. I'd love to," Reilly said with an infuriating grin before Amanda could stammer out an objection.

"Good. C'mon inside with us. Soon as Amanda files the story and we stow our equipment, we'll be on our way."

Simmering with frustration, she looked from one man to the other. Finally, clamping her jaws together, she whirled away and stalked toward the station.

Inside, Amanda marched straight through the newsroom to Harry Kowalski's office. She didn't bother to look back to see if Reilly was following. Crusher invited him; let him look after the aggravating man.

The news director was an old misogynist with a bald pate, a pot belly and ulcers. Harry had the face of a pit bull and the disposition to match, but at the moment Amanda much preferred his company. She was spoiling for a fight, and Harry could be counted on to say something thoroughly obnoxious. At the moment she would welcome any excuse to vent the charged emotions roiling through her.

Amanda was one of the few reporters with the station who was not terrified of Harry, which had earned her his grudging respect, if not his admiration.

She tapped twice on the door of the glass office and shoved it open without bothering to wait for an invitation, then slammed the door shut behind her, so hard the mini-blinds rattled. "Here's your hog-calling." She slapped the video down on Harry's cluttered desk. "It was a fascinating experience," she drawled.

"So? Don't tell me." Harry waved a meaty hand in dismissal. "Go take it to editing and see if Stuart can use it on the ten o'clock news."

"How long are you going to keep sending me out on these asinine assignments? You know that Stuart's not going to use one foot of this tape. You're wasting my time and the station's money sending me out on these piddling stories."

Harry looked up at her over his horn-rimmed glasses. His smile was nasty. "You don't like your work, you can always get another job, you know, missy."

"You'd like that, wouldn't you?"

"I wouldn't cry," he admitted.

"I'll bet. Well, forget it. I'm not going anywhere, no matter how much you try to discourage me, or how many dumb assignments you send me out on."

"Yeah, yeah. That's what they all say." Harry gave a derisive chuckle and waved her toward the door. "Go on, get outta here. I got work to do."

Amanda ground her teeth. Why tonight, of all nights, did Harry have to be in one of his more tolerant moods? She needed to cut loose in a toe-to-toe, nose-to-nose, good old-fashioned shouting match. She glared at the top of his shiny head and simmered. Finally, making a frustrated sound, she pivoted on one heel and stormed out.

She stalked across the newsroom, flopped down in her chair and began to drum her fingers on the desk top. Her agitation was so great, almost a full minute passed before she noticed the buff envelope among the mail in her basket.

Her anger drained away in a rush, leaving her with a vague, shivery feeling in the pit of her stomach.

Buried halfway down in the stack, only a corner of the envelope was visible, but Amanda knew with sickening certainty what it was. The way her luck was running, what else could it be? She stared at the small triangle of pale tan paper as though it were a snake poised to strike.

She was tempted to ignore it, even to throw it in the trash unopened, but the uneasy feeling in the pit of her stomach wouldn't let her. With two fingers, she grasped the corner of the envelope and pulled it from the pile.

The tiny script came as no surprise. As usual, there was no return address. She turned it over slowly, looking at it from every angle, but other than the Houston postmark, there were no other marks on the envelope.

With a feeling of dread, Amanda ran her thumbnail beneath the flap and removed the single sheet of paper.

My dearest Amanda,

As the weekend gets closer I get more and more depressed. I hate those two days when you are off. Hate them, hate them! I spend the whole time waiting for Monday when I know I might see you again. You are the most important thing in my life, my sweet Amanda. You are everything to me. You were meant to be mine. I know it. I can feel it. And I know you can, too. It is fated. Soon... soon, Amanda, we will be together, as we were meant to be.

A shiver rippled through Amanda. She dropped the letter and rubbed her forearms. All along she had thought the writer was a little weird, but it was worse than that. The man was obviously unstable.

Amanda felt shaken. Taking risks for the sake of her career was one thing. That was her job, and the choice was always hers. But this... this was different. This was personal. Somewhere out there was a disturbed man who was obsessed with her, and she had no control over the situation. None. Amanda folded her arms over her midriff and hugged herself tightly. It was creepy.

"You about ready?" Reilly murmured in her ear.

"Aaagh!" Amanda jumped and clutched her throat with one hand.

"Hey. What's the matter?" He leaned down, bracing one palm flat on her desk and the other on the back of her chair. A frown tugged his dark eyebrows together. "Damnation, you're as white as a ghost. What the hell has happened?"

"Nothing," she said quickly. With fumbling fingers, she folded the single sheet of paper and stuffed it back into the envelope. "I... I was just, uh, just thinking about a story that disturbed me. That's all."

She shoved the letter into the middle desk drawer and locked it. Grabbing her purse, she looked at him pointedly, willing him to move and let her up. "I'm ready."

Reilly didn't budge. "Amanda, are you sure there's nothing wrong?"

"Of course. I told you, everything's fine," she insisted in a brittle voice. "Now, shall we go?"

He searched her face, feature by feature, delving deep into her eyes. Amanda stared back defiantly. After what seemed like an eternity, Reilly straightened and stepped back.

Amanda marched out ahead of him with her face set, but the show of resentment was pure sham. As much as she wanted to, she couldn't seem to whip up her usual angry defense against him. At the moment, her problem with Reilly seemed insignificant.

The Station House, an unpretentious little club located only a few blocks from the Channel 5 studios, was a favorite gathering place for the station's employees, especially the news staff. Arnie Potello, the owner, was a retired Houston policeman, and a valuable source of inside information for the reporters.

The club was a family affair. Arnie tended bar and his wife, Teresa, and mother-in-law, Angelina Gianno, cooked the delicious Italian food for which The Station House was known. The Potellos' daughter, Anna, and two sons, Tony and Frank, waited tables.

"Hey, Amanda. Can I get you anything else?"

Blinking, Amanda glanced up at Tony Potello with a distracted look. "Uh, no, thanks. I'm fine."

"Okay. Just holler if you want anything." The young man hurried away at a fast clip, carrying a loaded tray high.

Amanda slid her glass from side to side on the shiny acrylic finish of the wooden table, watching the trail of condensation beneath it elongate.

"Where'd you meet that guy?"

It took a second for the mumbled question to register. Amanda turned her head and looked at Norman. "Tony?"

"No, Reilly."

"Oh. Well . . . about a year and a half or so ago, my best friend moved in next door to his twin brother. Tess and Ryan eventually got married." Amanda shrugged. "Since Reilly is a part of Tess's family now, I often bump into him when I visit her."

"But you don't go out with him?"

"Heavens, no."

Amanda propped her chin on the heel of her hand and looked at Reilly. He and Crusher stood about fifteen feet away. Absently, she watched the play of muscles in Reilly's back as he drew back his right arm, slung it forward and let a dart fly.

"Ah, man," Crusher groaned when the point pierced the edge of the bull's-eye. "That's another game to you."

Reilly laughed. "Blame it on my misspent youth. Me and my brothers and my cousin David must have played ten thousand games of darts when we were growing up. Tell you what. Next game, I'll spot you twenty points."

"Hey, watch it, Irish! Don't do me no favors. I'm gonna take you this time, so watch out."

"Big talk," Reilly hooted, giving Crusher a cuff on the shoulder.

Men. Amanda rolled her eyes and made a face. For the past three hours she'd been watching the disgusting display of male bonding.

Crusher had started warming to Reilly during dinner. Over a giant pizza and a pitcher of beer the two had chatted and joked with increasing ease. By the time they had finished eating, you would have thought they were old bosom buddies.

Under normal circumstances, Amanda would be furious, but she was too preoccupied. She couldn't stop thinking about the letters. Each successive one had become more intense and possessive. The latest was especially disturbing. Was that nut case really going to try to make contact with her? A little frisson ran down her spine, and she shivered.

At the moment, Amanda simply did not have the energy or the concentration to stew over Reilly.

Throughout dinner she had said little, but her aloofness had been due more to distraction and nerves than anger. Actually—though she would cut out her tongue before admitting it—inside she was relieved and grateful to be there. She was too on edge to be alone. Tonight, even Reilly's disturbing company was preferable to going home to her empty condo.

"Crusher sure seems to like the guy," Norman grumbled.

"What? Oh." Amanda glanced at the young man and felt a stab of pity. He sat hunched in the opposite corner of the booth, his expression woebegone. He looked as though he'd lost his best friend.

With an effort, she roused herself and reached across the table and gave his hand a pat. "Hey, don't pay any attention to those two. They're on a macho kick, showing off to each other like a couple of overgrown kids. But they don't have anything in common. Trust me, by tomorrow they'll have forgotten each other's name."

Norman grimaced and shifted on the seat, but she'd seen the hopeful look in his eyes.

The dart game, though closer than the others, went to Reilly, which drew an agonized groan from Crusher and a string of boastful taunts from the winner.

"Okay, Irish. You beat me at darts, but how good are you at a real man's sport?" Crusher challenged as the pair headed back to the table.

"Like what?"

"Like basketball?"

"I do okay."

"Yeah? Prove it. I got a hoop set up in the driveway at my place. Come over in the morning and we'll go a little one-on-one."

"Deal."

Both men grinned like fools and gave each other a high five before sliding into the booth.

Reilly unwrapped a peppermint and popped it in his mouth. He turned to Amanda with a smile, which she pretended not to notice.

"So…what time should I pick you up tomorrow night?"

That got her attention.

"What!" She shot him an appalled look. "What do you mean, pick me up?"

"For our date."

"Forget it, McCall. *This* is our date. I'm not going out with you again tomorrow night or any other night. As far as I'm concerned, we're square."

Reilly sighed and shook his head. "Mandy, Mandy, Mandy," he said reproachfully. "There you go, trying to welsh again. You can't expect me to accept tonight as payment of the bet. I'm here at Crusher's invitation. If you'll recall, the terms of our wager were that if you lost, you would go out with me alone, just the two of us. And, my sweet Mandy, I'm going to hold you to that. You owe me a date."

Amanda gave him one of her mean little smiles. "In your dreams, McCall."

Something hot leaped into his eyes. His gaze lowered to her mouth. "Mandy, sugar, if you only knew what kind of dreams I have about you," he said in a sexy rumble that only she could hear.

The words shot a tingle through Amanda, but she pretended indifference. "No, thank you. I'm not interested." She tried to imbue her voice with frost, but it came out weak and a little wobbly, which infuriated her. "And don't call me Mandy. Or sugar. And I'm *not* going out with you again, so just forget it. You wanted a date, and you've had one. That's it."

"I hate to say this, but I gotta agree with Reilly on this one."

"What?" Amanda's head whipped around. "Crusher, you can't mean that!"

"Hey, I didn't set up the terms. But a bet is a bet. If you agreed to go out with the man alone, then I don't think you ought to try to wiggle out of it."

"But—"

"You did agree, didn't you?"

"Well . . . yes. But—"

"Then you owe him a date. Anything less and you're welshing."

Amanda shot both men a furious look and reached for her purse. "Okay. Fine. I'll go out with you tomorrow. You can pick me up at seven. Are you happy now?"

Reilly grinned. "You bet."

"Sounds good to me," Crusher agreed.

Norman scowled.

"Good. Now, would you mind letting me out? I'd like to go home."

"Hey, you're not leaving us so early, are you? It's the shank of the evening. Besides, I can't go home yet. That sexy underwear party is still going on over at my place."

"What kind of party?"

"Lingerie. It's a lingerie party, McCall," Amanda snapped, unreasonably irked by the way he suddenly perked up. "As for you," she added, aiming a venomously sweet look Crusher's way, "I'm sure Reilly will keep you company. You two seem to be hitting it off so well."

"Uh-oh. Sounds like we're in trouble. What's the matter, sugar? Have I neglected you tonight?"

She smiled again. "I wish."

Reilly laughed.

Gritting her teeth, Amanda elbowed him until he slid out of the booth. She quickly followed, but before she could tell them good-night, Reilly spoke up.

"I'm afraid Norman will have to keep you company, Crusher. I'm going to follow Amanda and make sure she gets home all right."

"Don't be ridiculous!"

"Hey, man. No problem. Me'n Norman'll kick back with another cool one. Maybe even shoot some stick."

"Reilly, I'm a big girl. I don't need anyone to see me home."

He cupped her elbow, settled his Stetson on his head and nodded to the two men in the booth. "I enjoyed it. And I'll see you in the morning, Crusher."

"Come prepared to take a whuppin', man, cause I'm gonna stomp your sorry butt," Crusher called after them.

"Yeah, yeah." Without looking back, Reilly lifted his hand and waved.

"Reilly, will you stop?" Amanda commanded under her breath, but he marched her across the room and out the door. "I don't need an escort home, for heaven's sake. I go home by myself every night."

"Well, now, sugar, I'm real glad to hear that. But tonight you're with me, and my mama taught me to always see a lady home."

Amanda didn't doubt that for a second. Maggie and Colin McCall were salt-of-the-earth types who had instilled in all their offspring the old-fashioned values of decency, honesty and chivalry.

"Oh, all right," she muttered with decided bad grace, and allowed him to hustle her through the parking lot.

At her car he held his hand out for her keys. Making an exasperated sound and rolling her eyes dramatically, she fished the ring out of her shoulder bag and slapped it into his palm. Unfazed by her show of bad manners, Reilly unlocked the door and held it open for her with a flourish, his twinkling smile full of indulgence and wicked charm.

Once seated behind the wheel, Amanda cut her eyes up at him and drawled in a voice that dripped sarcasm, "You're a regular Sir Galahad, McCall."

"Yeah, I know. Just one of my many virtues." He made the statement with such a comic lack of modesty that she had to fight back a chuckle, but then he leaned down and gave her a steady look that sobered her instantly. "I may not sweat the small stuff, Amanda, but when you get to know me better, you'll learn that I take great care of what's important to me."

The sincerity in his voice stunned Amanda and left her with an odd feeling. Before she could think of a reply, he gave her a half grin and turned away to climb into his battered old truck, which was parked next to her red sports car.

On the drive to her northwest Houston condo, Amanda tried to sort through her feelings. On principle, she had felt obligated to protest, but if she was absolutely honest with herself, she was really relieved. Her nerves were frayed, and no matter how hard she tried she could not seem to shake the uneasiness that niggled at her deep inside. For the first time in her life that she could recall, she was apprehensive about being alone. As much as she hated to admit it, it was comforting to see Reilly's headlights in the rearview mirror.

Of course, she would choke before telling anyone, especially Reilly. The man was impossible as it was.

Amanda had barely brought her little fireball of a car to a halt in the parking garage of her building when Reilly pulled his truck into the adjacent slot. He climbed out and was beside her door before she could remove her key from the ignition and gather her purse.

"Sugar, I don't know if anyone's mentioned it before, but you drive like a bat outta hell. Lady, you were going ninety back there on the freeway."

"I happen to be an excellent driver," she said in an offended voice.

"Hey, I don't doubt it for a minute. Sugar, you could give A. J. Foyt lessons. Not to mention heart palpitations."

Amanda started to protest, but she was distracted when he began to walk beside her.

"Reilly, you don't have to walk me to my door. Honestly, I'll be fine from here on my own."

"Save your breath, darlin'. I never do things halfway." He slanted her the same tolerant smile she'd seen him give his nephew, placed his hand against the small of her back and nudged her toward the elevator.

Their footsteps echoed through the garage, reminding Amanda of how alone they were. Inside the elevator, the deafening silence vibrated with tension. She was certain he could hear her heart thudding.

She fixed her eyes on the floor indicator above the door. Every nerve ending in her body hummed and twitched. She couldn't recall ever being so aware of a man before.

From the corner of her eye she saw his hand, braced against the paneled wall of the elevator. Suddenly she was acutely conscious of how large that hand was, how utterly and beautifully masculine. She saw the faint sprinkle of dark hairs across the back, the clean, trimmed nails, the broad wrist that protruded from the sleeve of the sweater, and for some idiotic reason her stomach went woozy.

Her heart rate kicked up another notch, and she barely stifled a groan. She could smell his cologne, mixed with the heady scent of male. Oh, Lord, she could even feel his heat. Quelling the urge to fidget, Amanda stared at the panel of numbers above the door and willed the ride to end.

When the doors finally opened, she shot out into the hall like a cork out of a bottle and headed for her apartment without waiting to see if Reilly followed.

He caught up with her at the door. Her hands shook so badly she could not fit the key into the lock. On the third try, he reached around her, put his hand over hers and guided it home.

Amanda froze. She could not have moved if the building had suddenly burst into flame around her. Eyes closed, she stood in the small amount of space between the door and Reilly, barely breathing, her heart caroming crazily. She felt hot and cold all at once.

His hand was warm and dry. Against her smooth skin she could feel the calluses that ridged his palm, and the sensation was incredibly erotic. Except for his hand, he wasn't touching her, but all across her back she sensed his presence, his heat. She felt surrounded by him. Engulfed by him.

He turned the key and the tumblers in the lock clicked loudly in the silence.

For what seemed like an eternity, neither of them moved. Then Reilly gripped her shoulders and gently turned her around. Amanda pressed back against the door and looked up into his face, her heart pounding painfully against her rib cage. He stood so close she could see each of his eyelashes, the crystal quality of his blue eyes. She could smell peppermint on his breath, and just a hint of beer.

He was going to kiss her; she could feel it with every cell in her body.

He hovered over her, his slumberous gaze glittering in the dim light of the hallway, trailing over her features one by one. His naughty half smile promised seduction. Awareness and anticipation throbbed in the air between them.

Reilly's eyes grew heavy-lidded. He braced his palm against the door frame and leaned closer.

Breathless, trembling with unwanted excitement, Amanda felt her stomach drop and her knees go weak. Helpless to resist the pull between them, she closed her eyes and lifted her face.

With painful anticipation, she waited for his lips to claim hers. Instead, something whispered across her cheek.

Her eyes flew open to face twinkling blue ones and a knowing grin. Slowly, Reilly trailed his forefinger down to the corner of her lips. "Good night, Mandy," he whispered.

Before Amanda could gather her senses, he strode down the hallway and punched the elevator button. The doors opened at once, and as he stepped inside he called over his shoulder, "I'll pick you up at seven tomorrow night."

Chapter Four

Amanda spent a restless night. She tossed and turned, alternately fretting over the disturbing letters and her foolish reaction to Reilly.

However, she was never one to stay down long; by morning her innate confidence and determination had begun to reassert itself. She dismissed her fears regarding the anonymous fan; she had been overly tired and as a result had let that stupid letter rattle her.

Dismissing Reilly was not quite so easy. When Amanda thought of the way she had practically melted and run all over him, she wanted to kick something—hard. Preferably Reilly.

Deep inside, she knew it was a mistake to go out with the man.

Amanda tried her best to always face reality head-on. It was her job; she had been trained to be objective and clearsighted. Much as she disliked it, no matter how unacceptable and foolish it was, she had to acknowledge that the physical attraction between Reilly and her existed and that it was powerful and highly combustible.

The most intelligent way to handle it—the *only* way to handle it—was to stay as far away from him as possible. If she'd needed proof of that, the previous night had done the trick. All he'd had to do was get near her and she had practically gone up in flames. He hadn't even kissed her, for heaven's sake! Lord help her if he ever did.

She had managed to evade him for more than a year and a half, but now, thanks to that stupid bet, she was trapped.

Reilly had played on her weakness. The sneak. He had been around her enough to know that she would not be able to back down from a challenge. She suspected, also, that he'd spilled the beans about their wager because he knew Crusher would never let her live it down if she reneged. The man was a scheming, manipulating, unconscionable louse.

Whipping up her anger was the only means Amanda had of allaying her misgivings, and she diligently applied herself to the task for the rest of the day. By the time Reilly rang the doorbell that evening she was back in fighting form.

Determined to remain aloof, she opened the door and met his grin with a cool stare.

It wasn't easy. He looked so darned gorgeous and sexy he took her breath away. Big, vital, and utterly masculine, he stood with one hand braced against the door frame and the other propped on his hip, his gray suede sport coat casually shoved back out of the way. The stance exposed a magnificent chest, a taut abdomen and trim waist and hips. He wore dark charcoal slacks, a blue silk shirt and a blue and silver tie.

"Hi," he said softly. He had recently shaved. He smelled of soap and masculine cologne, and when he spoke she caught a whiff of peppermint.

Her eyes made a sweep of him, and one corner of her mouth twisted when they reached the floor. "For heaven's sake. Don't you ever wear anything on your feet but cowboy boots?"

"Not if I can help it," he replied cheerfully. He pushed his pearl-gray Stetson to the back of his head and looked her over. A warm gleam lit his eyes. "Ah, Mandy, sugar, you look like a million bucks."

"Thank you," she said stiffly. She took her purse and shawl from the coatrack beside the door. "Shall we go?" Amanda knew it was rude not to invite him in, but the thought of Reilly in her apartment was too unsettling.

"I think you'll enjoy the restaurant I've chosen," Reilly said, heading his truck toward the Sam Houston Tollway. "It's owned and operated by two old friends of mine."

Amanda turned her head and raised one eyebrow. "You have friends?" She sat pressed against the door of the old dilapidated truck, as far away from him as she could get.

Reilly laughed. "Yeah. Quite a few."

"Are you as high-handed with them as you are with me?"

"High-handed? Me? Darlin', you wound me deeply. How can you say that?"

"Easy. You pester me constantly, you refuse to take no for an answer, you make a nuisance of yourself, you pump my friend for information about me, and when all that fails, you trick me into a bet, just so I'll have to go out with you. Then you spill the beans to Crusher to make sure that I do. *That's* high-handed. Not to mention manipulative."

"Oh, well, if you're going to be picky..."

Amanda rolled her eyes.

"Anyway, haven't you ever heard the expression 'all's fair in love and war'?"

Amanda turned her head slowly, and from beneath half-lowered eyelids she seared him with a droll stare. "Have you ever heard the expression 'kiss off'?"

He glanced her way, his eyes sizzling as they zeroed in on her lips. "Funny you should mention kissing..."

"Oh, pul-leeze."

"Easy now, darlin'. You don't have to beg. We'll get to it before the evening's over."

"We'll—" Amanda gaped. Then her eyes narrowed into slits. "In your dreams, McCall."

"Oh, yeah," Reilly agreed with a fatuous smile. "All the time."

Shooting him a withering look, she folded her arms and looked out the window, but Reilly didn't turn a hair at the silent treatment. He withdrew a peppermint from his pocket and unwrapped it.

The crackle of cellophane drew Amanda's attention and she turned her head in time to see him pop the candy into his mouth. Sensing her gaze on him, Reilly gave her an apologetic look. "Sorry. Would you like a peppermint?"

"No, thanks," she said, frowning. "Are you addicted to those things? You eat them all the time."

"Sorta, I guess. It's something I picked up when I quit smoking. Ever since my cousin David married Abbey she's hounded all of us to kick the habit. I swear, looking at her, you'd think she was a docile little thing, but that woman's about as malleable as Attila the Hun when it comes to her beliefs, and she's dead set against smoking. My family found out real quick it was easier to just quit the weed than to have Abbey after you."

"So you traded one addiction for another? Not smart, McCall. That stuff'll make you fat."

"Nah. I never gain weight. Besides, I'm told it makes for sweet-tasting kisses." He grinned and waggled his eyebrows at her. "Wanna give it a try?"

Amanda flashed him one of her killer smiles. "No, thanks. I don't like sweets."

The rest of the drive went much the same, with Reilly baiting Amanda shamelessly and her peppering him with tiny barbs.

She reacted to his flirting with scorn, but on some remote level she was aware that she was enjoying herself.

Matching wits with Reilly was somehow stimulating and fun. Inexplicably, he made her feel fizzy and keyed up—more alive than any man she knew.

Amanda had thought he would try to impress her by taking her somewhere ostentatious, but he surprised her. The restaurant he chose was one that she had never heard of, a supper club called The Velvet Rose, tucked away among the office buildings in Houston's Greenway Plaza area, southwest of downtown.

It was an elegant little place with a refined, intimate atmosphere. Discreet, dark-suited waiters moved soundlessly among the candlelit tables and alcoves, and a mellow combo played soft music while couples glided around the dance floor. It was a place where people could relax and dine, and talk privately. It was a place for lovers.

As they were escorted to a secluded table in a window alcove overlooking the lights of the city, Amanda experienced another flash of misgiving.

This was madness. Sheer madness. What was she doing here? *Lord, Sutherland, how could you have been so stupid to have gotten yourself trapped in this situation?* It was crazy to play with fire, and that was exactly what she was doing, going out with Reilly. After all, an intelligent person knew better than to strike a match around gasoline.

Once they were seated she searched for something to say, anything that would take her mind off her jittery nerves. "This place certainly seems to be popular. I wonder why I've never heard of it."

"It's kind of low-key. But I'm surprised that Tess and Ryan haven't mentioned it to you. This is one of their favorite places."

"Really?" Amanda felt oddly hurt.

"Yeah, but the folks who frequent the place are the kind who appreciate a tranquil atmosphere. I suppose they figured you wouldn't be interested."

Amanda lowered her menu partway. "Was that some kind of a crack, McCall?"

"Heck no, sugar. It's just that you seem to thrive on the breakneck pace you keep. You're always racing around town after a story, or flitting all over the globe reporting on military coups and border skirmishes. They probably thought, after all that, this place would be too mild for you."

"I've only been on one overseas assignment in my entire career, and that was over a year and a half ago. Besides, it's not that I particularly enjoy the frenetic pace—it simply comes with the job."

She raised her menu, then lowered it again and shot him an annoyed look. "And I *don't* flit."

Reilly laughed, but then he reached across the table and covered her hand with his. His eyes smiled warmly at her in a way that made her heart give a little bump.

"What do you say we call a truce and just relax and enjoy the rest of the evening? Hmm? After all, the whole purpose of this date was so I could prove to you that I'm not the slimy maggot you think I am. I can't do that if we're constantly sparring, now can I?"

Amanda experienced a pang of conscience at the description. She didn't really think he was a maggot; just a charming, feckless flirt, exactly the kind of man she had long ago learned to avoid at all costs.

She studied him warily, then sighed. "All right. I'll agree to a truce if you'll tell me one thing."

"Shoot."

"Why are you doing this? I mean, I haven't given you any encouragement. In fact, I've made it perfectly clear that I don't want to start anything with you. Yet from the moment we met, you've been after me like a hound after a fox. I can't for the life of me imagine why."

"Don't you believe in love at first sight?"

"No."

He didn't miss a beat. "How about lust at first sight?"

Try as she might, Amanda could not quite quell the smile that tugged at the corners of her mouth. "Now *that* I believe. But you're wasting your time. It's not going to happen, McCall. We're not right for each other."

"Maybe, maybe not. You can't know that for sure until you give it a chance. That's what tonight is for, to let us get to know each other better."

Flashing another of his confident smiles, he gave her hand a pat, then released it and picked up his menu. Amanda gazed at him. His unperturbed air left her speechless.

Finally she sighed. "Oh, all right. For the sake of peace, I suppose I can be civil for a few hours."

But she still intended to keep her distance. No matter what he said, she had her future all planned, and there was no place in it for a man like Reilly McCall.

Amanda soon discovered, however, that remaining cool and aloof around Reilly was not easy.

Throughout the meal he continued to surprise her. Despite his plea for a truce, she had expected him to flirt and make sly propositions and innuendos, but, other than occasional intense looks, he was a perfect gentleman ... and surprisingly easy to talk to.

She had assumed that, like many handsome men, he would be self-absorbed. However, throughout the meal he kept the conversation centered on her, asking endless questions.

Despite herself, Amanda was flattered by his interest. Without even realizing it, she soon began to relax and respond to his questions with an ease she would not have thought possible only a few hours before.

With a shock, she realized that there was a warmth and sincerity about Reilly that tugged at something inside her, that drew her like steel shavings to a magnet. He had a way of looking at her, of listening—really listening—to what she had to say as though he found every word fascinating.

"So ... have you always lived in Houston?"

"Actually, I was born in Big Springs, but my parents moved to Houston when I was barely four."

"Is that when you met Tess?"

Amanda paused in cutting her Veal Oscar and smiled softly. "Yes. She lived three doors down from the house my folks rented near Rice University. The day we moved in, Tess came over and invited me to play on her backyard swing. We've been best friends ever since. From kindergarten on, we went all through school together. We were even roommates in college."

"Wow. That's a great friendship. Not many last that long."

"I know. I value my friendship with Tess more than anything else in my life. We're more like sisters than friends. We've always been there for each other. Until she married, we were all either of us had."

Reilly picked up a roll and buttered it. "What about your families?"

"We were both only children. I don't know if Tess has told you, but her parents were both killed in a car accident while we were away at college."

A look of profound shock and compassion came over Reilly's handsome features. "No. No, she hasn't. But then, I guess I shouldn't be surprised. Tess is such an upbeat person she rarely mentions anything unpleasant or tragic." He shook his head. "God. She really is a survivor, isn't she? First she loses her parents, then after only a few years of marriage her husband dies and she's left all alone and pregnant." He looked up into Amanda's eyes and smiled again. "Thank goodness she had you."

"And Ryan, don't forget. Your brother was there for her when she needed help most." Amanda shuddered delicately. "It still terrifies me to think about what could have happened if he hadn't been there to deliver Molly during that hurricane."

"Are you kidding? No one could have kept Ryan away from Tess once we knew that storm was heading our way. He was already in love with her by then, even though he wouldn't admit it."

"You're kidding. But... but she was seven months pregnant when she moved into the apartment next door to his and Mike's. And he was a dyed-in-the-wool woman hater."

Reilly grinned. "Yeah, I know. Ain't love grand." He scooped up a forkful of potatoes. All the while he chewed, his eyes twinkled at Amanda's flabbergasted expression.

"So, tell me about your parents," he said, catching her off guard.

She lowered her eyes and reached for her wineglass. "My mother passed away last year. For the last five years of her life she lived in a retirement village in Arizona."

"And your father?"

Slowly, her gaze lifted. She stared across the table at him. "What about him?"

"Is he deceased, also?"

"I have no idea. Nor do I care. He walked out on my mother and me when I was thirteen. I haven't seen or heard from him since." Frost coated her clipped words and her set face would have silenced most people.

"Did he leave the two of you for another woman?"

Amanda's eyes widened. His astuteness amazed and angered her. So did his questions.

She had no idea why she had told him as much as she had. Usually she never discussed her father with anyone but Tess. When people probed for information about him, she either sidestepped the issue or told them bluntly to mind their own business.

But who knew? Perhaps once Reilly learned the whole story he'd realize he was wasting his time.

"Yes. One ten years younger than my mother, with a hundred times more money. You see, my father didn't like responsibility. He especially didn't like to work for a living.

He was, and no doubt still is, shiftless and utterly charming. Women love him, and he loves them. When he found one who could keep him in style, he latched onto her."

"Is that why you've never married? Because you're afraid you'll end up with someone like your father?"

Amanda experienced a little jolt. There it was again, that uncanny ability he seemed to have to put his finger right on the crux of a problem.

Yes, her father's desertion had taught her some important lessons. One of them was to never fall in love with a charming womanizer like Kyle Sutherland...or Reilly McCall.

"I haven't married because wedded bliss isn't high on my list of priorities. I want to concentrate all my energies on my career. Also, I haven't met a man to whom I would want to make that kind of commitment."

"Mmm. Then again, maybe you have, but you just didn't notice him because you were so busy."

"Maybe. But I doubt it. Anyway, it's not important. Frankly, I really don't care whether or not I ever marry."

Amanda experienced a pang of conscience. All right, all right. So there were times when she secretly longed for a home and family of her own so much it was painful. And there were times when she found herself envious of the love between Tess and Ryan and their joy in their children. So what? She was always able to squelch the foolish emotions and focus on the goals she had set for herself. It was nonsense, anyway. She wasn't the domestic type.

"I see," Reilly murmured. "So, what made you choose journalism as a career?"

"Well...I was always good with words. By the time I graduated from high school there were already a few women reporters in top network positions. I began to realize that broadcast journalism was a field that was open to promoting women. So...here I am."

"I see. What are you shooting for? The anchor position on the evening news?"

"That's certainly a step in the right direction."

Reilly's eyebrows rose. "Only a step? That sounds like you have big plans."

"I do. I would have been farther along already if I hadn' had a world-class chauvinist for a boss these past few years But Harry is due to retire soon, and the way I figure it, once he does I'll have a shot at the anchor desk at Channel 5 Eventually I'll move on to the network—maybe in Washington, D.C., or New York, or maybe even overseas—at least for a few years. One day, though, I intend to be a prime-time network anchorwoman."

She had made herself that promise years ago.

From the time she was a little girl, when she had first realized what kind of man her father was, she had sworn never to be like him, sworn that somehow, some way, she would make something of herself. She had also sworn that she would not let a charming womanizer ruin her life the way Kyle Sutherland had ruined her mother's.

Even though her mother hadn't seen him in years and he had abandoned her for another woman, Amanda knew that Margaret Sutherland had never stopped loving her father When she died the year before, the last word she spoke had been his name.

The thought of something like that happening to her made Amanda shudder.

No, she definitely did not need Reilly McCall in her life She didn't *want* him in her life. No matter how attractive and irresistible she found him, he was all wrong for her. Just as she was wrong for him.

Why couldn't he see that? She was ambitious—some said driven—while he was anything but. She was intense about whatever she did; he took almost nothing seriously. He came from a large and stable family; she'd grown up an only child, abandoned by her father and forced, at the age of thirteen, to assume the role of parent and protector of her emotionally shattered mother. She and Reilly were opposites.

"I see," Reilly murmured. He gave her a long look, then adroitly changed the subject.

Throughout the rest of the meal their conversation bounced from one subject to another. They talked about the latest antics of Reilly's big and boisterous family, his and Ryan's plans to begin stage two of the planned community they were developing, amusing incidents that had happened to Amanda while filming news reports.

Much to her surprise, they discovered they liked the same kind of music and movies, they shared the same general political philosophy, they both liked to ski and they were both rabid Houston Oiler fans, though they argued vociferously over who the team's next draft pick should be. They even discovered that they both had a weakness for cheesecake.

By the time they reached the coffee stage, Amanda was feeling relaxed and mellow, and when Reilly asked her to dance she was caught off guard.

She glanced to where the other couples were gliding to the music and experienced a prickle of misgiving but immediately squelched it. What could happen on a dance floor, after all?

Besides, she hadn't danced in ages.

"All right," she said, rising.

The instant she turned into his arms, Amanda knew she had miscalculated. What could happen to her on a dance floor? Plenty.

Reilly did not just hold her; he embraced her. He did not just dance; he made love to music.

Pulling her close, he cradled her against him and wrapped his strong arms around her. She had no choice but to rest her forearms against his chest.

"Uh, Reilly, I don't think—"

"Shh. Just relax, sugar," he murmured in that sexy rumble. She felt his moist breath feather against her ear and shivered.

Relax? How? All at once her heart was beating ninety to nothing and every cell in her body tingled.

A bit panicky, Amanda realized there was something deeply comforting and pleasurable about being cuddled against Reilly's powerful body, surrounded by all that masculine strength. The urge to nestle her head against his chest and give herself over to his keeping—just for a little while—was almost irresistible.

Amanda fought the yearning, but the matter was taken out of her hands a second later. Reilly simply tightened his hold and tilted his head until his jaw rested against her temple. Somehow Amanda found her face nestled against the side of his neck, fitting into that notch between his jaw and collarbone as though it had been sculpted for that express purpose.

She held herself stiff at first, but with every breath she inhaled his scent—a mix of soap, cologne, and a marvelous musky maleness that made her head spin. Her body gravitated toward his of its own accord, and little by little her muscles lost their rigidity. Finally, with a shuddering sigh, she gave up and relaxed against him.

From her knees to her hairline, his heat seared her. The solid hardness of his body cushioned her softness in an utterly natural way that felt good, so good. Amanda sighed with pleasure.

The slight friction of their bodies moving together to the slow music was the most erotic sensation she had ever experienced. Her nipples hardened into pebbles. A knot coiled in her belly.

Amanda wondered if Reilly could feel her reaction. Vaguely, she knew she should pull away, perhaps even be incensed, but she simply could not whip up even a shred of indignation; the voluptuous sensations felt too wonderful.

Releasing another sigh, she closed her eyes, pressed her face closer against his neck and inhaled deeply.

That she was obviously having an equally powerful effect on Reilly was a balm to her pride and squashed any lingering misgivings. With every movement, she felt the hard evidence of his desire pressing against her belly.

For a big man, he moved with surprising grace. His entire body swayed fluidly to the rhythm of the music, while his hands roamed her back, rubbing and flexing against her flesh through the thin silk of her dress in a way that felt so good she almost groaned.

She felt trembly and on fire, almost feverish. Oh, Lord. It wasn't fair. It simply wasn't *fair*, she wailed silently, even as she snuggled closer and slid her arms around his waist beneath his jacket. She was no shy virgin. She'd kissed dozens of men in her time. She'd even made love with one of them. But none of that even came close to the erotic pleasure of merely being held in Reilly's arms.

And the really pathetic part was, she didn't regret it.

Not now, at any rate. Dancing with Reilly was a sensual experience not to be missed.

The song came to an end, and Amanda felt a pang at the thought of relinquishing the heady delight, but she had not reckoned on Reilly. He kept right on dancing through the few seconds of silence between numbers and glided them into the rhythm of the next dance without missing a beat. Docile as a lamb, Amanda followed his lead; the thought of objecting never entered her head.

Amanda had no idea how long they danced. It could have been minutes; it could have been hours. Not until reality intruded in the form of a disembodied voice over the microphone was she aware of anything or anyone but Reilly.

"I'm sorry, sir...ma'am. But it's closing time."

They blocked out the remote voice.

"Uh, sir. Sir, I'm afraid you'll have to leave now."

It took a second for the words to penetrate, and a second longer for them to realize that the music had stopped and the musicians were packing up their instruments. Even then, when Reilly loosened his embrace and eased back, Amanda groaned a protest.

"Sorry, sugar," he whispered. "God knows, I don't want to stop, either, but I think they're throwing us out."

Slowly, their feet ceased moving. Slower still, they drew apart. Only when Amanda turned, blinking, and saw the amused expression on the face of the man at the microphone did she fully comprehend.

He gave them a regretful look and spread his hands. "Sorry, folks, but it's closing time."

A tide of embarrassment surged up inside Amanda, sending a flush sweeping over her from the tips of her toes all the way to her hairline. She was sure her whole body was glowing. Even her ears felt hot.

Oh, Lord. What had come over her? They had practically been making out on the dance floor like a couple of randy teenagers, for heaven's sake.

Not in the least flustered, Reilly merely grinned at the band leader and escorted Amanda over to their table to retrieve her purse. With his hand at the small of her back, she swept out the door with her flaming face held high.

All the way home Amanda remained silent. Reilly cast a few glances her way, but he made no effort to initiate a conversation or draw her attention. He simply popped a peppermint in his mouth and drove with his usual casual competence.

She was shaken. She had known it was a mistake to go out with Reilly. From the instant she had met him, every instinct she possessed had screamed "Run!" And her instincts had been right on target. One dance, one touch, and every rational thought had flown right out of her head.

Reilly McCall was a dangerous man, a threat to her emotions and her plans.

Yet, even knowing that, she couldn't shake off the fizzy excitement, the floating-on-air feeling that had held her entranced all evening. She had only to glance at him and the knot in her stomach tightened.

The feelings intensified between the parking garage and her condo. By the time they reached her door, every nerve ending in Amanda's body was twanging like a plucked string on a cheap guitar.

She was not going to invite him in; she had already behaved foolishly enough for one evening. And she would not—absolutely would *not*—let him kiss her good-night, she told herself firmly. A handshake, a polite "Thank you for a lovely evening," and it would all be over. The bet would be paid and they would go back to the way they had been, she vowed, turning the key in the lock with shaking fingers.

Yet when she swung around to face him, the words would not come. His vivid blue eyes glittered down at her, slumberous and hot beneath heavy lids. Amanda's heart began to beat so loudly the heavy thuds reverberated in her ears. When his head began its slow descent, she lifted her face and her eyes drifted shut.

The touch of his lips against hers, so soft, so warm, stole what little breath she had left. The kiss was potent, just as she had known all along it would be. His mouth caressed hers with an aching tenderness that made her tremble.

He raised his head a few inches, and when Amanda's eyelids fluttered open, he was looking at her with a smile in his eyes. He took her face in his hands and tipped it up at a more accommodating angle and kissed her once again.

This time his mouth was as firm as his body, as hard, as sensual, as thoroughly, unapologetically male. His tongue swirled in her mouth, and she tasted peppermint and coffee and a hint of wine. The combination was unbelievably erotic.

Amanda's knees went weak. She clutched the lapels of his jacket for support.

His lips left hers and strung a line of nibbling kisses across her cheek, his breath trailing hot and moist over her skin. Amanda's head lolled back, eyes closed.

"Say you'll see me again," he murmured against the side of her neck.

"No...I...I...can't."

He nipped her lobe. "Why not?"

"Be-because it won't work. We're...all..." She gasped and shivered as his tongue traced the swirl of her ear, then made a darting foray inside. "...All wrong for each other."

"No, we're not. We're perfect together." As he spoke he mouthed the tender skin at the juncture of her neck and shoulder and his arms slipped around her. He pulled her close, rocking her hips ever so gently against his. "We got along this evening, didn't we?"

"Yes...but—"

"And you enjoyed it, didn't you?"

"Ye-yes."

His fingertips played over her spine, and Amanda gave a helpless little groan. "You see." He ran his open mouth back over her cheek, leaving a moist trail on her skin. His tongue probed the corner of her mouth. "Go out with me again, sugar. I just want to be with you. You can pick the place and the time. We can go somewhere public where there're other people, if that'll make you feel better. Anything you say."

He strung tiny kisses around her mouth, tantalizing her with the promise of more. Nearly mindless with wanting, Amanda sought his lips but he evaded her, nibbling her cheek, her eyelids, the tender underside of her jaw. "C'mon, Mandy," he urged in a husky voice. "Give us a chance."

"Well...th-there is...the station's annual picnic coming up," she gasped as his fingers found the sensitive spot on the nape of her neck.

"When?"

"Next...next weekend."

"Great. So, are you asking me to go with you?"

"I...I..."

His tongue traced a tiny circle on the tender skin behind her ear, then he blew gently on the moist flesh. Amanda shivered. "Hmm?" he prodded.

"Yes. Yes!" Making a desperate sound, she grabbed his hair with both hands and pulled his mouth to hers. A deep chuckle of masculine triumph rolled from Reilly's throat as their lips met.

Chapter Five

The next morning, Amanda was appalled when she opened her morning newspaper and found a picture of her and Reilly. It had been taken while they were locked in each other's arms on the dance floor. Accompanying the embarrassing photo was a breezy little piece in the gossip column, full of innuendo and speculation.

The newspaper was owned by Channel 5, and the instant Amanda arrived at work she marched into Harry's office and demanded that he call the editor with a complaint. Not only did he refuse to intervene on her behalf, he tore a strip off her for bothering him.

Amanda's call to the columnist accomplished nothing. The woman informed her that, as a local celebrity, Amanda was fair game, and better they printed the picture than rival newspapers.

She called Reilly but he had brushed the incident aside with a laugh and a casual, "Don't let it rattle you, darlin'. Nobody reads that stuff, anyway."

When she hinted that perhaps they should forget about the picnic, he argued and cajoled, and before she knew it, she had succumbed to his persuasive charm. However, Amanda approached the outing with something less than enthusiasm.

The picnic was held about twenty miles west of Houston at the Bar S Ranch, home of Oliver Stanton, Channel 5's major shareholder. Except for a skeleton crew, all of the station's employees and their families were there.

The first person they ran into was Crusher. The way he and Reilly greeted each other, you would have thought they were brothers.

"Hey, Reilly! My man! Good to see you," Crusher bellowed, giving him a high five.

Reilly's affable personality made him a hit with both sexes. Within thirty minutes he was on a first-name basis with almost everyone who worked in the newsroom. However, it was not until after lunch when the softball game began that she learned just how enthralled some of the women were.

Amanda was standing on the sidelines when Reilly came up to bat. He stood and stretched, then hefted several bats. He selected one and took a few practice swings. Amanda's gaze followed every move. When he bent over to pick up a handful of dirt and rub it between his palms, her gaze zeroed in on his rear end. She stared at that tight tush, her breathing suddenly shallow.

She was so mesmerized, at first she didn't notice the two women sitting on a blanket on the sideline, just a few feet away—not until they started talking.

"Oh, mercy. Be still, my heart." Ellen Keyes, a fortyish divorcée who worked in the station's accounting department, sighed and fluttered her hand over her chest. "Now I ask you, have you ever seen such a hunk in your life?"

"Never." The dreamy agreement came from Joan Howe, the station's receptionist. Propping her chin on the heel of her hand, she watched Reilly take a few practice swings before stepping up to the plate. "He's absolutely gorgeous."

"Mmm. And built, too. Look at those shoulders, that chest. Not to mention that cute butt. I sure wouldn't kick him out of my bed."

"Oh, Lord. Can you imagine what kind of lover he'd be?" Joan speculated breathlessly.

"Or what he'd look like naked?"

Both women groaned. Neither was aware of Amanda.

It had not been her intention to eavesdrop. She could not help but overhear the remarks, however, and they caused a peculiar sensation in her chest.

Amanda blamed it on simple disgust. Foolish, man-hungry twits, she thought irritably.

Still, she supposed she couldn't blame them. Reilly was a stunning male animal.

Like a moth to a flame, her gaze drifted back to him.

Dressed in cut-off denim shorts and a muscle T-shirt, he stood over home plate, his legs braced wide, the bat held at the ready, high over his right shoulder. For once he had forsaken his boots for athletic shoes.

Shifting his weight slightly from one foot to the other, he called good-natured taunts at the pitcher while making feint practice swings. Amanda's mouth went dry as she watched the play of muscles in his back.

His arms and shoulders bulged with muscles that were the result of physical labor, not hours spent in a gym. Above the T-shirt his flesh had a bronze hue, but Amanda knew the tan extended at least to the band on his cutoffs. Several times while visiting Tess in her new home in Wildwood, she had seen him at one of the nearby construction sites working alongside the men in his crew, stripped to the waist. More than once, the sight had stopped Amanda in her tracks.

His flesh gleamed with a sheen of sweat. Dark hair peeked over the top of the scooped neck on his T-shirt. More dusted his forearms and muscled legs. He looked so strong, so uncompromisingly masculine, not to mention drop-dead gorgeous, he took her breath away. That he had a similar effect on her female co-workers was certainly understandable.

Joan heaved a wistful sigh. "I've been trying to attract his attention for the past two hours, but I don't think he's even noticed me."

"I know what you mean. I pretended to trip and practically fell into his lap earlier. He helped me up and asked if I was okay, but when I said yes he just smiled and walked away. It's maddening.

"Lord, I hate to see a prime specimen of a man like that wasted on Amanda. He needs a real woman, one who knows how to ring his chimes. She's too wrapped up in her career to even know what to do with a hunk like that. Why, I'd bet a week's pay she hasn't gone to bed with him yet," Ellen continued.

"You think so? Really?"

"Of course. Have you ever known Amanda to get serious about a man? Oh, she talks a big game and drives them all wild with her flirting and that sophisticated air of hers, but it's all for show. No man is as important to Amanda as her career, and that includes Reilly McCall. As far as I'm concerned, that makes him fair game."

Joan exhaled a wistful sigh. "I don't know how she can resist him. If he were my date, I'd jump his bones the first chance I got."

Ellen laughed. "You got that right. And I intend to get the chance."

Fury nearly choked Amanda. Her eyes narrowed and her lips tightened into a thin line. The devil with being understanding. She'd had enough of these two poaching cats. Just because she wasn't willing to make a lifelong commitment to Reilly didn't mean she would stand for this. There was such a thing as propriety and fair play, after all.

She started for the women but she had barely taken two steps when she caught herself.

Good grief! What on earth was she doing? Hadn't she been trying for ages to get rid of Reilly? Here was the perfect opportunity.

Not for a moment did she believe he would resist either of the women's advances. Not a ladies' man like Reilly.

The thought of him with either Joan or Ellen gave Amanda a sick feeling, but she battled it down. Gritting her teeth, she pivoted sharply on her heel and stalked away from the two women. If they wanted him, they could have him. And good riddance, she told herself.

Unaware that Crusher and Josie called her name, or that they stared after her with puzzlement and concern, she marched right past them without seeing them. For some reason her eyes stung and her throat ached as though she had swallowed an apple whole, which only served to make her more furious. She set her jaw and marched for the tennis courts. Her roiling emotions demanded an outlet, and a hard game of tennis was just what she needed.

Amanda spotted Norman slouched behind the fence that enclosed the courts. As always, he was alone.

Good, she thought, confident she could talk the malleable young man into giving her a game. She waved and headed toward him, but he must not have seen her because he turned and shuffled away in the opposite direction.

Halting, Amanda stared after him and gave an exasperated sigh. Oh, well, it was just as well, she supposed. A loner like Norman probably wouldn't know how to play tennis, anyway. Besides, he was a sweet kid. He didn't deserve the trouncing she intended to mete out. With a determined gleam in her eye, she looked around for another victim.

Then she spotted Eric... and smiled.

Standing outside the chain-link fence that surrounded the tennis courts, Reilly crossed his arms over his chest and shook his head, a bemused expression on his face. Lord have mercy, that woman was something else.

Amanda was running poor Eric ragged. She played with the ferocity of a Tasmanian devil, as though she were trying to annihilate the ball *and* her opponent.

Sweat drenched Eric's body and he huffed like a steam engine. His face was the color of a ripe tomato.

Amanda tossed the ball up and whacked it hard enough to knock the cover off, and slammed another ace across the net. On the next serve, Eric managed—barely—to stumble across the court and lob the ball back, but Amanda raced back and attacked it. With a two-handed backhand, she sent the ball zooming over the net like a missile.

"Tha-that's it. Eee…ee…nough." Dropping his racket, Eric bent from the waist, propped his hands on his knees and gasped for breath. His clothes stuck to his body, emphasizing the slight spare tire around his middle. Sweat dripped from his face and soaked hair. "I've had it. Go tor-torture someone else."

Amanda wiped her forehead with her arm. "What's the matter? Can't take it?" she taunted, breathing hard.

Eric waved a hand. "I don-don't care anymore. I…quit. You're…you're a demon."

Reilly almost laughed aloud at the smug look that came over Amanda's face.

Eric straightened painfully and hobbled away, his chest still heaving. Dismissing him with one last contemptuous look, Amanda turned and headed for the sideline. Halfway there, she spotted Reilly.

Her steps faltered but she recovered quickly and kept coming, her expression a mix of wariness and defiance that tugged at his heart. Lord, she was such a contrary blend of emotions.

Her clothes and her hair were sweat-soaked. Flushed and shining from her exertions, her face had long since lost every trace of makeup. She looked exhausted and worn…and utterly beautiful.

Behind the quick, truculent glances she darted at him, he saw that flash of vulnerability he'd noticed before, and he ached for her. He had always known that she was afraid of the chemistry between them. He just hadn't known why—not until their date the week before. She was afraid to love, afraid to trust. And who could blame her?

Damn that sorry father of hers! Reilly was slow to anger and basically a peaceable man, but if he could have gotten his hands on Kyle Sutherland at that moment he would have cheerfully broken every bone in the bastard's worthless body.

He wanted to take Amanda in his arms and comfort the abandoned child in her, to soothe away all her pain and fear and hurt pride, but he knew she wouldn't welcome the move.

Eventually, though, he would win her trust. No matter how long it took, he could wait. He was a patient man.

"What are you doing here, McCall? I thought you were playing softball." Amanda picked up a towel from the player's bench and buried her face in the thick folds.

"Game's over."

"Did you win?"

"Nah. They clobbered us."

She lifted her face from the towel. "It doesn't seem to bother you much." Flipping up her thick French braid, she looped the towel around her neck.

"Nope. Why would it? It's just a game."

"Maybe so, but the point is to win." She shot him a disgusted look. "Are you always so nonchalant?"

He grinned. "Yep. Pretty much. Are you always so competitive?"

"Yes," she snapped.

Reilly threw his head back and laughed at her pugnacious expression. "Well, don't worry about it, darlin'." His eyes twinkled at her. "I think it's kinda cute."

"Funny, McCall."

Casting him a sour look, she picked up her gear and headed for the dressing rooms located between the courts and the pool. Reilly fell in step beside her. "So what are you doing here?" she demanded rudely. "I'm sure there must be other activities you could enjoy."

"I came over to see if you'd like to go for a swim."

"You've already been swimming today."

"So? Are we limited to just one dip?"

"No. Of course not. I just thought that—"

"Yoo-hoo! Oh, Reilly!"

The trilling voice halted them. They turned to see Ellen strolling their way.

Ignoring Amanda, she sidled up to Reilly and gave him a coy look from beneath her lashes. "We were about to get together a volleyball team," she purred. "I thought maybe you'd like to join us." She paused and licked her lips, and slid her gaze over him. "I know I'd just love to have you." Her meaning was unmistakable. The woman even had the nerve to walk her fingers up over his chest while she made the outrageous statement. Reilly cast a sideways glance at Amanda and bit back a curse. Her face looked set in stone.

Dammit, he could cheerfully throttle the man-eating female. He'd been dodging her all day but she just wouldn't take the hint. He had half a mind to tell her straight-out that he wasn't interested.

Reilly gritted his teeth and sighed, knowing he wouldn't. It simply wasn't in him to be rude to any woman or deliberately hurt her feelings, no matter the provocation.

Catching her wandering hand, he gently but firmly removed it from his chest. "Sorry, uh, Elaine, was it?"

"Ellen," she corrected with a pout.

"Right. Ellen. Sorry, I'll have to pass. Amanda and I are about to go for a swim."

For the first time, she acknowledged Amanda, slanting a sly look her way. "Oh, I'm sure she wouldn't object. Would you, dear?"

"Of course not. Don't mind me."

Amanda started to walk away, but Reilly hooked his arm around her waist and hauled her back against his side. He looked warmly down into her tight face.

"Ah, but *I'd* mind, sweetheart. We haven't spent nearly enough time together today to suit me." He turned a polite smile on the other woman. "Thanks for inviting me, Ellen, but I'll pass."

Amanda started. She looked sharply at Reilly, then at Ellen. Clearly, she had expected him to accept. Sadness and a touch of hurt settled in his chest like a rock.

The other woman made a pouting moue, but it did not disguise the flash of annoyance in her eyes. He felt Amanda relax beside him. Sneaking a quick peek at her, he saw that she was pleased, though she tried hard not to show it.

"Are you sure you wouldn't rather play volleyball?" Amanda asked when she and Reilly were several feet away. "You seem to have made a conquest."

"I'm positive. So you might as well quit trying to palm me off on someone else."

Startled, she glanced up at him. He saw the guilt in her eyes and knew he'd guessed correctly.

Outside the dressing rooms they stopped, and he grasped her shoulders, holding her in front of him. He looked deep into her eyes and heard the little catch of her breath. "Listen to me, Amanda. The only woman I want to be with is you," he murmured with every ounce of feeling in his soul. "Just you. No one else."

Amanda stared back at him. Surprise, doubt, and what looked like hope warred in her expressive eyes. She swallowed hard, her throat working. Finally she gave an abrupt nod, then pulled out of his grasp and quickly scuttled away into the dressing room.

Amanda gazed into the mirror, her heart hammering painfully. Oh, Lord. How was she supposed to resist a man who said things like that?

For the first time in her life she had been left speechless. No matter how she struggled, she had not been able to think of a single cutting remark to refute his claim and shatter the spell that had enfolded them.

Sighing, she made a face at her reflection. The trouble was, deep down she wanted so desperately to believe him.

From the first instant their eyes had met she had known that Reilly McCall was a threat to her plans and her peace of mind. If she entered into a relationship with him, it wouldn't be a casual one. There was no way. He was too earthy, too potently male, too overwhelming, and the chemistry between them was simply too high-voltage to hold in check. Even now, a giddy excitement filled her and the urge to hurry and rejoin him churned inside her.

She was being torn in two, her heart and her traitorous body pulling her one way, her brain and common sense the other.

She ought to march out there and tell him she was ready to go home, nip this thing in the bud right now, before it was too late. *That's* what she ought to do.

When Amanda emerged ten minutes later wearing her tiny orange bikini, she found Reilly waiting for her.

He didn't say a word; he didn't have to. His gaze swept over her with slow thoroughness, from her coral-painted toenails to her bare shoulders, missing nothing.

Amanda had always considered herself to be unflappable. She was accustomed to men ogling her leggy figure. Most of the time she never even noticed their slack-jawed reaction, but Reilly's silent inspection made her blush like a schoolgirl. The look in his eyes was so hot and so blatantly amorous her nipples puckered in reaction.

It didn't help that she couldn't seem to tear her eyes from his body. She stared at the tiny strip of blue spandex that stretched across his narrow hips and her breathing grew shallow. Why, it was downright indecent, Amanda thought with a touch of panic. The scrap of cloth exposed a shocking amount of that magnificent body and clung to him in a way that left no doubt as to his potent masculinity.

An inverted triangle of dark hair covered his massive chest and arrowed downward over his taut belly, swirling around his navel and disappearing beneath the scrap of blue material. Even his bare feet were sexy, she thought irritably, long and narrow and well-shaped, with the faintest sprinkling of hair on his toes and the high arches.

Amanda tried to swallow, but her mouth was so dry she couldn't manage it. With an effort, she at last tore her gaze from his body, only to encounter Reilly's amused eyes. That he had known the drift of her thoughts was obvious. Brazening through, she cocked one eyebrow and tried for a look of bored sophistication, but the flush that warmed her face spoiled the effect.

Reilly stepped closer, his eyes still twinkling at her. She braced herself for a teasing remark, but he merely touched her cheek with his fingertips and murmured, "I like what I see, too, sweetheart."

His voice was deep and resonant with feeling, and a delicious tingle rippled through Amanda. She swayed toward him. He leaned closer, and excitement spiraled through her.

She closed her eyes, expecting to feel his arms close around her. Instead, he grasped her shoulders, turned her toward the pool and slapped her bottom.

"Last one in buys dinner."

Amanda's jaw dropped. She blinked twice.

Then she tore after him. "Reilly, you rat! No fair!"

Reilly McCall was a sorcerer. A down-home spellbinder. By the end of the day Amanda was sure of it. With his good natured teasing, his sexy body and outrageous flirting, he beguiled as effortlessly and surely as Svengali.

Only when the festivities ended and she trudged beside him toward the pickup, tired but oddly mellow and happy, did it occur to her how easily he had coaxed and cajoled his way past her defenses. Under the spell of his potent charm she had forgotten her misgivings and her prickly mood had dissolved like soft clay in a driving rain.

Casting him a disgruntled look out of the corner of her eye, Amanda sighed. The pathetic part was, she didn't even mind, nor did she feel the least guilt over her easy capitulation.

After today, she was convinced that no healthy, red-blooded female could possibly resist Reilly for long—especially when he fixed those blue eyes and that mischievous grin on her. The man was sexy, charming and funny, and a delightful companion. And she had to admit, she had enjoyed herself thoroughly.

A smile tugged at her lips at the memory of that wild frolic in the pool. They had swum like otters, racing up and down the pool, playing games of tag, splashing and dunking one another with merciless glee. Of course, Reilly had taken outrageous advantage. He'd used every opportunity to touch her, rubbing up against her, running his hands down her slippery arms and twining his legs with hers as they tread water. He'd even stolen a few quick, hard kisses.

Though she had pretended otherwise, she hadn't been able to work up any real anger. How could she, when each time the touch of his lips had sent a thrill streaking through her?

They reached the pickup, and Reilly tossed their things into the back and dug into his pocket for his keys. When he pulled them out, a slip of paper came out with them and drifted to the ground.

"What the heck—?"

"You dropped something." On reflex, Amanda stooped and snagged the scrap of paper before it fluttered away in the breeze.

Reilly frowned as she handed it to him. "That's funny. I didn't have anything in my pocket but my keys," he muttered to himself as he unfolded the paper. "What the devil is—oh, hell."

"What's the matter? What is it?" Amanda cast an idle glance over his arm, and stiffened. Written on the slip of paper in a neat, feminine hand was Ellen Keyes's name—beneath it, a telephone number.

The mellow glow that had filled her only moments before vanished. She turned to Reilly with a smile that did not touch her eyes. "Well, at least the day hasn't been a total loss for you."

"Dammit, Amanda, I'm not interested in that woman, and I sure as hell didn't ask for her phone number. She must have slipped into the dressing room and put that paper into my pocket while we were swimming." He met her suspicious gaze steadily, his expression resolute and forthright, without a trace of guilt or evasion.

Her stiff posture relaxed fractionally, but when she spoke, her tone was only slightly warmer. "You're probably right. Ellen is brazen enough to do something like that."

She was willing to concede that much, but the incident served as a sharp and timely reminder of why she had refused to become involved with Reilly all these months. He may not have encouraged Ellen, but that didn't mean he wouldn't take advantage of her offer. To think she had been sappy enough to let a few hours of fun soften her attitude toward him.

"Good. I'm glad you understand." Reilly unlocked the door and assisted her in. He rounded the truck, climbed behind the wheel and started the engine, but he made no move to drive away. Staring straight ahead, she felt his gaze on her. Finally he reached out and took her hand. "Here. Get rid of this for me, will you?"

Startled, Amanda stared at the slip of paper he had stuffed into her hand, then at him. "Are you sure you want to do this? You don't have to because of me, you know."

He stepped on the accelerator and sent the truck down the gravel drive, bumping over the first cattle guard before glancing her way. For an instant she thought she had angered him, but his eyes glittered with warmth and humor... and absolute honesty. "I don't have any use for it, darlin'. There's only one woman I'm interested in, and that's you."

In spite of all she could do, Amanda's heart gave a little skip. Was it possible? She had to admit, his behavior today had been exemplary, and God knew, he'd had plenty of opportunity to flirt with other women if he had wanted.

Amanda turned her head and stared out the window, confused and torn.

They rode for several miles without speaking. Reilly sat easy and relaxed, one elbow propped on the window opening, his other wrist draped over the top of the steering wheel. His gaze flickered to her now and then, his eyes glittering in the fading twilight.

A taut awareness pulsed between them. Desires that had been building all day hummed just below the surface, charging the air with an expectant feeling. Amanda's chest grew tight. She stared straight ahead and chewed on her inner lip. Soon, they would be back at her place...just the two of them.

"Uh, would you mind taking me by the station?" she blurted out. "I, uh, I want to check if any major stories have broken."

Reilly turned his head and looked at her, his smile faintly mocking. Amanda had a horrible hunch that he knew exactly what had prompted the request.

"You and all the other reporters have been wearing beepers all day. Don't you think you'd know by now if something had hit the fan?"

"I'd just feel better if I checked. Okay?"

"Okay, sugar. If that's what you want," he agreed amiably, but his amused look warned that the delaying tactic would not change what was about to happen between them.

Amanda clamped down on her nerves and ignored him.

The night staff was gearing up for the evening news when they arrived at the station. Most of them had come straight from the picnic, still dressed in their casual togs.

Harry's blinds were open. He never attended the picnic. He sported his usual rumpled look, his suit coat discarded, tie loose, shirt wrinkled and blowsy, the sleeves rolled up to his elbows. He had a pencil behind his ear and the few wispy tufts of hair on top of his head stood on end from raking his fingers through them.

He glanced up when Amanda walked in and sent her a sour look, then went back to scribbling something, one of his foul stogies stuck in his mouth. The wisp of smoke coming from the tip curled toward the ceiling.

Ignoring him, Amanda marched to her desk with Reilly at her heels. The first thing she saw was the buff-colored envelope propped against the stapler, right in the center.

Her heart gave a sickening lurch. Oh, no. Not again. Not now. She couldn't deal with this, too.

Sagging in her chair, she released a sigh and reached for the envelope with a shaking hand. She had no choice. She supposed she should have expected this, the way her luck had been going lately.

Amanda steeled herself as she removed the sheet of paper from the envelope and unfolded it, but the instant she began to read, she paled. By the time she finished, she was trembling.

"Amanda? Good Lord, what's wrong? You look like you've seen a ghost."

Only distantly aware of Reilly's questions, Amanda stared at the single sheet of paper as though it were a snake coiling to strike.

"Amanda! Look at me." He leaned over her desk and grasped her chin, tilting it up. Reilly's frown deepened. "What is it, sugar? C'mon, tell me."

Amanda blinked. Recalling herself, she struggled for control, but she could not seem to stop shaking. "Uh, nothing. Nothing's wrong." She tried to turn away, but his fingers tightened on her face.

"Don't give me that. I won't buy it—not this time. You look like you're about to pass out. Now tell me what's upset you." He glanced at the piece of paper. The tremor in her hand made it quiver. "Is it that letter?"

She pressed her lips together to stop their trembling. Instinct urged her to lie, but she was too upset to make the effort. In any case, the look in his eyes told her it would be a wasted one. With a despairing little moan, she nodded and handed him the letter.

Straightening, Reilly scanned the page. She watched his stern expression change to a scowl, then to shock.

You faithless bitch! Did you think I wouldn't find out? Well, I won't stand for it. Do you understand? You are mine, Amanda. Mine. You belong to me. I won't share you with another man.

I will have to punish you, of course. I don't want to—I love you—but you have been bad, and I must teach you a lesson.

Chapter Six

Hoping he had read it wrong, Reilly scanned the letter a second time, his gut knotting. When he reached the end, his gaze shot to Amanda. "Good God!"

"Exactly," she drawled, but the quiver in her voice exposed the fear she was struggling to deny.

"What the hell is this?"

"Believe it or not, a fan letter. Or at least . . . the first few were."

"The first few? You mean there've been others?" At Amanda's nod, he stared at her, appalled. "How many?"

"Seven. Eight, counting today's."

"Good Lord. No wonder you're upset. Why didn't you tell me?" He sat down on the corner of her desk and took her icy hands. Gently he rubbed them between his. "The letter wasn't signed. Do you know who wrote it?"

Amanda shook her head.

"Do you have any idea what the devil he's raving about?"

"Apparently this man has developed some sort of obsessive attraction for me." She made a face and shuddered. "For some reason, he seems to think that...well...that I belong to him. I—I guess that picture of us together in the newspaper set him off."

Reilly didn't like the sound of that—not one bit. "So what are the police doing about this?"

Amanda kept her eyes on their joined hands. "I haven't reported it to the police."

"What! You've got to be kidding! You don't have to be a psychiatrist to figure out that this guy's a real loony tunes. Hell's bells, sugar, he's threatening you."

"Actually, this is the first time he's done that. The other letters have just been a little weird."

"Dammit, Amanda, weird is bad enough. What are you going to do, wait until he attacks you to get help?"

"I don't need help. Eventually he'll get tired of the whole thing."

"And if he doesn't?"

"He will," she insisted stubbornly.

Reilly struggled for patience, something that he had never had to do before meeting this woman. "At least tell me they've taken some extra security precautions around here."

"No."

"*No!* Why the hell not?"

"Because I haven't told anyone."

"Good Lord, Amanda! You mean you haven't even reported this to your boss?"

Withdrawing her hands from his, she sat up straighter. Her chin jutted, and her expression turned mulish. "No. And I'm not going to, so don't waste your breath."

"The hell you say!" he roared, shooting off the desk. "Dammit, Amanda, if you think I'll just stand by and—"

"Keep your voice down, for Pete's sake," she hissed. "You're attracting attention."

A glance around proved her right. Several of her co-workers had stopped what they were doing and were staring, their expressions avid. Reilly cursed under his breath.

"Where are the letters?" he snapped.

"In my desk. Why?"

"Give them to me. We're getting out of here."

"Now look here—"

Bracing one hand on the back of her chair and the other on her desk, he leaned down and brought his face to within inches of hers. "Don't push me, Amanda. I don't get angry very often, but when I do, it's not a pretty sight. I'm just about a heartbeat away from losing it. Trust me, you don't want that to happen. Now give me the damned letters."

She stared up at him, her eyes wide. Her expression would have been comical if Reilly hadn't been so upset. Obviously she had never expected to see him in that state.

He was stunned, too. He couldn't remember ever being so furious before. He felt positively sulfuric. It wouldn't have surprised him if she had announced that smoke was coming out of his ears.

"Oh, all right." Flashing him a sour look, Amanda ungraciously withdrew the bundle of letters from her desk and slapped it into his hand. "There. Satisfied?"

"Not by a long shot. Now let's go."

Reilly grasped her arm, pulled her up out of the chair and hustled her toward the exit. Amanda practically had to trot to keep up. He derived a bitter satisfaction from knowing that she did not dare resist, not with every person in the newsroom watching.

Worry, however, nibbled at the edges of his rage. The very fact that she wasn't slicing him up with her wicked tongue and one of her mean little smiles revealed just how shaken she really was. That, and her ashen face.

The drive to Amanda's condo was made in silence. She sat huddled against the passenger door, her arms wrapped tightly around her waist, as though trying to physically hold herself together. Reilly stared straight ahead, his jaws clenched. He didn't know who made him angrier: Amanda or the creep who was bothering her.

Neither spoke until they reached her apartment. After unlocking the door, she turned to him, her expression stiff. "One way and the other, it's been a busy day, so I'll just say good ni—"

"Oh, no, you don't. You're not going to put me off that easy." Placing a hand on her arm, he propelled her inside.

"Now, see here—"

"Save it, darlin'. You're wasting your breath. I'm not going anywhere until I've read these letters. And when I finish, we're going to have a talk."

Leaving her sputtering in the tiny entryway, he marched into the living room and sat down on the sofa. Furious, Amanda followed and flounced down onto a chair. Drumming her fingers on the mauve upholstery and swinging one leg, she glared at him across the chrome-and-glass coffee table.

Reilly ignored her and slipped the rubber band off the bundle of envelopes. He examined each one carefully, noting the tiny handwriting and the Houston postmarks and the dates. After putting them in chronological order, he began to read.

The first seemed innocent enough—an ordinary, if somewhat overly enthusiastic fan letter. The obsessive tone of the second sent a curl of uneasiness through him. By the time he'd finished the third, he was scowling.

Each letter grew more disturbing, filled with declarations of abject devotion and love and references to a non-existent relationship with Amanda. Even more alarming was the possessive tone that escalated with each succeeding note. When he reread the latest, a chill trickled down his spine.

Fear and fury pounded through Reilly. That anyone would dare to threaten Amanda made him feel murderous. "How could you ignore this?"

Amanda shrugged. "I was flattered by the first letter. It isn't often that a television reporter gets fan mail. When the second arrived just a few days later, I was surprised. By the time the third one came, the novelty had worn off and the whole thing struck me as a bit sad and pathetic. The ones after that merely made me uneasy."

"Until today."

The reminder of her reaction earned him a resentful look, but he stared back, not giving an inch. After a moment she looked down at her tightly clasped hands and mumbled under her breath, "Yes. Until today."

"I think you should call the police."

Amanda's head snapped up. "No. I won't do that."

"Why not? You can't keep ignoring this loon."

"Yes, I can. I'm not calling the police."

Reilly wanted to shake her. She sat there looking at him with that calm expression, as though the whole thing were settled. Heaving a sigh, he shoved his hand through his unruly hair. "All right. All right. But at least say you'll talk to your boss. That way, security at the station can be beefed up and everyone will be on alert—just in case."

"No."

"*No!* What do you mean?"

The first glimmer of her usual sultry humor flickered in her eyes. "Exactly what part of no didn't you understand?"

"Dammit, Amanda, this isn't a joke. If you think I'm going to sit back and—"

"Oh, for Pete's sake, calm down, Reilly." She held up her hands, palms out. "Listen, I appreciate your concern. Really, I do. But you're making too big a deal out of this."

"He *threatened* you, dammit!"

"No. He threatened to punish me. For all we know, that could simply mean he won't write to me anymore. Please believe me, this will blow over soon. I promise. This sort of thing happens all the time to people who are in the public eye. Heavens, if we took them seriously we'd be in constant turmoil." She covered a yawn with her hand. Stretching, she pried off her sandals, tucked her legs beneath her and curled up in the chair as though she hadn't a care in the world.

Reilly glared. Her pallor had gone. Along with it, the fear in her eyes. She looked so confident, sounded so sure of herself, it was difficult to argue. But he wasn't convinced. "And if you're wrong?"

"I'm not. Trust me. The best way to handle this is to ignore the whole thing. If he gets no reaction from me, after a while whoever is writing the letters will get discouraged and give up."

Frustration hammered through Reilly. He wanted to yell at her. He wanted to kiss her.

His gaze zeroed in on her mouth, that luscious full lower lip, then slid down her body, skimming over the skimpy white shorts, her gorgeous long legs.

God, he wanted to take her in his arms and carry her to the nearest bed and make love to her over and over until he imprinted his image on her soul. He wanted to taste and touch and hold her so close nothing could ever harm her.

It was too soon, though, dammit. It'd taken him more than a year just to get this far. If he pushed, she'd slam the door in his face and he'd have to start all over.

But he'd be damned if he'd let her have it all her way. "I'll compromise with you. I'll forget about reporting this guy— at least, for now—if you'll promise to do one thing."

She cocked her head and eyed him suspiciously. "What?"

"We tell Crusher about the letters. That way he can keep an eye on you when you're out on assignment."

Amanda groaned, but he held up his hand. "Humor me on this, darlin'. Otherwise, I'll be forced to either follow you around myself or go to the police."

She glared. Reilly could almost see her weighing her choices.

"Trust me, sugar, that's the best offer you're gonna get from me."

"Oh, all right. I'll tell Crusher. Satisfied?"

"Well, now, I wouldn't say that, exactly," he drawled, sliding his gaze over her. He rose and crossed to her. Planting his hands on the arms of the chair, he bent and captured her mouth. The kiss was slow and hot and drugging. He felt Amanda's quivering response and smiled against her lips, pleased he wasn't the only one losing control. When he raised his head, he looked deep into her eyes. "But that will have to do for now." He kissed the end of her nose and straightened. "Night, darlin'. I'll call you tomorrow."

Amanda was not concerned about keeping her promise to Reilly. She was confident she could handle Crusher. All she had to do was give him a watered-down version of the whole thing. She'd make a joke out of it, especially Reilly's fears. Afterward, they would laugh it off.

With her plan set, the next morning Amanda strolled into the Channel 5 building, humming a jaunty tune. She'd planned to head straight for Crusher's cubicle, but when she entered the lobby the big cameraman was the first person she spotted. He stood in the corner beside a huge ficus tree, huddled in conversation with Reilly.

Amanda jerked to a halt. What in the—? She narrowed her eyes and headed for the pair. She had a strong urge to storm over there and tear a strip off of Reilly, but she'd be damned if she would let any man shatter her composure. Anyway, she had an image to protect. With a supreme effort, she pasted a look of mild surprise on her face and forced herself to maintain her usual nonchalant saunter.

"Morning, Amanda," Joan Howe said in her syrupy voice, but Amanda strolled right pass the receptionist's desk without acknowledging the greeting. She didn't even hear it—or notice the eager interest in Joan's face as the young woman's gaze cut back and forth between Amanda and the two men.

"Well, well, well. This is a surprise. What are you doing here, McCall?" Amanda drawled with a lethal little smile that would have sent most men—at least those with a healthy respect for their lives—running for cover.

Reilly didn't even flinch. He turned to her with a grin, his eyes warm, caressing. "Mornin', sugar. Damn, you look gorgeous."

The unexpected compliment snuck past her defenses, and even through her anger Amanda felt the flutter of pleasure. She shot him a pithy look and fought it down. "You're wasting your time if you think you can sidetrack me. I'm waiting for an answer."

He ran his callused forefinger down the line of her jaw. "You don't take compliments easily, do you, sugar? Ah, well, don't worry, you'll get used to 'em. And I wasn't trying to sidetrack. I was on my way downtown to pick up a permit, and since I was in the area I dropped by to tell Crusher about the letters." He rocked back on the run-down heels of his boots and grinned. "Like you and I agreed we'd do."

Amanda's smile grew tighter. He had her, and he knew it. "How...thoughtful of you," she said with saccharine sweetness. "But you really shouldn't have bothered. I was going to tell Crusher myself."

"Uh-huh!" Crusher snorted. "I just bet you were."

Unlike Reilly, her friend glowered at her, his expression as ominous as a roiling thundercloud.

"No, really, I was. Honest, Crusher. In fact, I was on my way to find you."

"Uh-huh. An' I had about as much chance of getting the straight skinny from you as a snowball has in hell."

"Crusher! How can you say that?"

"'Cause I know you, woman. So don't try that innocent act on me. If Reilly here hadn't clued me in you woulda done some fancy talkin' and glossed over the whole mess like it was no more'n a random call from a heavy breather.''

"Well, it isn't," Amanda protested, earning herself a threatening look.

Crusher stopped glowering at her long enough to give Reilly a grim nod and a clap on the shoulder. "Thanks, man. You did the right thing. And don't you worry none, I'll watch after her until they catch the creep."

"Oh, honestly. You two are making entirely too much of this," Amanda declared airily. Inside, she was a mass of jitters, but it wouldn't do to let these two know that. She gave a dismissive chuckle. "You're acting as though a crazed killer were stalking me with a meat cleaver. It was just a few letters from a pathetic man, for heaven's sake."

"A few sicko letters," Crusher corrected. "That ain' nothin' to mess around with. Even though you've done some harebrained things since I've known you, I always thought you were intelligent, but this is just plain stupid. If you were one of my daughters, I'd turn you over my knee and whup some sense into you."

"But, Crusher—"

"Hush up, woman. I'm not through with you. Now you listen up...."

Amanda grimaced and fell silent as, in his usual blunt manner, Crusher launched into a blistering lecture.

He did not intimidate Amanda, but she had learned that trying to stop him when he was on a roll was like trying to hold back an avalanche with your bare hands. Several times during the gruff harangue, she cut her eyes at Reilly, leaving no doubt as to whom she blamed for the reprimand.

"...And me'n Reilly talked it over and we agree that we ought to call the cops. And let Harry in on what's happening, too. You can't be too careful when you're dealing with a nut."

"What! Oh, no, we won't! Absolutely not! I won't hear of it!" She shot Reilly a furious look. "See what you've

done? I told you I wanted this kept quiet." She swept the
two men with a look that had even Crusher's eyes widen-
ing. "Not one word. Do you two macho studs understand
me? You are not to utter one word about this to anyone.
And I do mean anyone. You do, and so help me, I'll skin
you both alive and hang you out for buzzard bait."

After stabbing each man with an icy glare, Amanda pivoted on one foot and headed for the newsroom, her unhurried, fluid stride carrying her across the lobby with deceptive
speed.

The encounter left Amanda seething, and when she
passed the accounting department and spotted Ellen Keyes,
her anger found a target. Smiling, she walked up to the
woman's desk.

"Good morning, Ellen."

The woman blinked, surprise and wariness flickering over
her face at the unexpected gesture. She and Amanda had
never been particularly friendly.

"I wanted to return something of yours." Reaching into
her purse, Amanda withdrew the slip of paper that Ellen
had smuggled into Reilly's pocket and slapped it down on
the desk. "Reilly won't be needing this."

The look on Ellen's face filled Amanda with immense
satisfaction. Giving the woman another smile, she turned
and sauntered away.

Wiping a fleck of lint from the sleeve of her cocoa-colored
silk blouse, Amanda pushed the door of the ladies' room
open with her hip, stepped out into the hall . . . and nearly
jumped out of her skin when she bumped into Crusher.

"Oh!" She put her hand over her heart and closed her
eyes. "You nearly scared me to death!" She darted a look
around, then glowered at him and hissed, "For heaven's
sake, Crusher. You have to stop following me around like
this. People are beginning to notice. It's embarrassing."

Leaning against the wall beside the ladies' rest room, his arms folded over his massive chest, Crusher did not appear one whit concerned about office gossip. "Too bad. Let 'em yap. I promised Reilly I'd keep an eye on you and that's what I'm gonna do," he replied, giving her a bulldog look.

"While we're out in the field, yes, but not when we're in the station. No one is going to bother me here."

"You don't know that. You can't be too careful."

Making a frustrated sound that was close to a growl, Amanda spun on her heel and headed back toward the newsroom. Crusher fell into step beside her.

It was pointless to argue. For better than a week, ever since Reilly had ratted on her, the big cameraman had watched her with all the fierceness of a mother eagle with a newly hatched chick. She couldn't even escape to the ladies' room without her bodyguard.

It was ridiculous and embarrassing. And totally unnecessary. No amount of pleas or threats or reason had the least effect. Every morning she stepped out of the elevator into the parking garage in her building to find Crusher sitting in his car, waiting for her. He followed right on her bumper all the way to the station, and in the evenings he followed her home and watched until she entered the elevator again. In between, no matter where she went, he stuck to her like a cocklebur on an angora sweater.

And *that,* she fumed, struggling to ignore the whispers and sidelong glances that followed her and Crusher through the newsroom, was one more thing for which she had Reilly to thank. By the time this thing blew over he was going to owe her—big-time. The interfering, insufferable lout.

Telephones shrilled all over the newsroom. Across the way, Frank Dugan stood in the middle of an aisle with a receiver in each hand, alternately talking into one, then the other. Spotting Amanda, he paused and held both pressed against his chest long enough to holler, "Hey, Amanda. Ge that, will ya," when a telephone on her side of the room began to ring.

Crusher continued on to his cubicle as she detoured by the empty desk and snatched up the receiver. "Newsroom. Ron Heber's desk. Amanda Sutherland speaking."

Cradling the receiver between her shoulder and jaw, Amanda jotted down a message and added it to the others in the growing pile that awaited Ron's return to the station. By the time she worked her way to her own desk she'd had to stop and take three more messages for various people who were out sick.

It had been the same for more than a week now. A spring flu bug was running through the ranks of the Channel 5 employees like Sherman marching through Georgia. No sooner did one person recover and return to work than one or two others got sick. At any given time at least a quarter of the staff was laid low, both reporters and production people, leaving the newsroom woefully shorthanded.

Amanda had worked double shifts everyday, including the weekend, to help take up the slack. She had run herself ragged, darting from one location to another, trying to cover all the breaking stories. For a few days, while Gail Goodwin and her co-anchor, Ross Temple, had been laid low, she'd even gotten a chance to fill in on the anchor desk on both the six o'clock and the ten o'clock news.

The first thing Amanda saw when she reached her desk was the pile of message slips. "Oh, great. Leave for ten minutes and the phone rings off the hook."

She knew at a glance that the message on top was from Reilly. Doodled all around the edges were fanciful hearts and flowers and musical notes. Amanda picked up the slip of paper. In the center was written, "Reilly called. Said to tell you he misses you. *Sigh, sigh.*"

She cast a withering glance around, but everyone was hustling too much to notice, and she had to content herself with a grumbled, "Humph. You'd think, as shorthanded as we are, they'd knock off the childish artwork."

That type of thing had been going on ever since the picnic. Amanda hadn't set eyes on Reilly or talked to him since that morning in the lobby following the outing.

The hectic workload had left no time for a social life. For the past week she hadn't left the studio before eleven, and then most nights she dragged her exhausted body home, took a quick shower and fell into bed without bothering with dinner. The next morning she was always back at the station by seven.

Amanda had not really minded the heavy workload. As long as she was working eighteen-hour days she didn't have time to think about much else—such as what she was going to do about Reilly. She hadn't decided if she even *wanted* to do anything about him.

Which was truly pathetic and showed just how much she had weakened. A month ago she would have given him the boot without a qualm. Dammit. She'd known it was a mistake to let him get too close.

Amanda had not expected to miss Reilly. She was so busy by rights she shouldn't even have spared him a thought.

She had discovered, however, that Reilly did not have to be present to work his magic. Whoever coined the saying "out of sight, out of mind" obviously had never met the man. He had been sympathetic about the long hours she'd been keeping, but he had made certain that she did not forget him.

He called the station daily, usually missing her, but apparently charming anyone who answered her telephone—hence the cutesy artwork and unsolicited editorial comments on the messages he left.

He had also taken to sending her notes at the station—everything from a quickly jotted "Hi, darlin'. Miss you." to a teasing proposition, to a surprisingly touching love sonnet.

Every night Amanda trudged into her condo, bone-tired, to find the message light on her answering machine blinking. No matter how hard she tried to hold on to her pique, invariably her heart gave a little bump when she heard that deep, sexy voice drawl "Hi, darlin'."

Unlike most people, Reilly was not in the least self-conscious about conversing with a machine. He rambled on just as though he were there with her, often taking up the whole tape, his voice a velvety murmur, intimate and caressing and full of teasing devilment, which—no matter how hard she strove to remain detached—always made her heart flutter and brought a smile to her lips. The man was irresistible. A brawny Pied Piper in a Stetson and cowboy boots.

Amanda's gaze went to the vase of flowers on the corner of her desk. Only the night before she had returned to the station from the scene of a double murder, out of breath, depressed and frazzled, to find the bouquet. Nothing so common as roses or carnations or mums, but tiger lilies. "They remind me of you," the accompanying note had said. "Gorgeous and sultry, yet delicately feminine."

Remembering, Amanda reached out and touched one of the velvety petals, a faint smile curving her mouth. She sighed and shook her head. It wasn't fair. How was she supposed to stay angry with a man who did things like that?

The answer, of course, was she couldn't, which she was sure was exactly what Reilly was counting on. Even knowing that, Amanda found her anger toward him fading day by day.

The other women at the station loved it, of course. Amanda sighed. It galled her to admit it, but apparently she was just as susceptible to romantic gestures as the next woman.

Harry Kowalski stepped to the door of his office and bellowed, "Sutherland! Crusher! Haul butt! We've got an explosion at Dansa Petro Chemical in Pasadena."

Jerking to attention, Amanda sprang out of her chair and grabbed her purse and notepad. "I'm on my way!"

Crusher came barreling out of his cubicle with his camera on one shoulder and the equipment bag slung over the other, signaling to Norman to hustle. The trio met in the middle of the room and headed for the exit. They had almost made it when Harry yelled after them.

"Take the chopper and get me some live aerial shots. And be sure you get close! I damn well want to smell that smoke."

"Oh, great," Amanda muttered to Crusher. "Now he's trying to asphyxiate me."

Amanda couldn't believe it. She was actually leaving the station before dark. Even better, it was Friday and she had the whole weekend off. Two weeks. For two long, miserable weeks she had worked almost nonstop. Thank heaven, the crisis seemed to be over at last. Over the past few days most of the flu victims had returned and the workload at the station had settled down to its usual frenetic level. A good thing, too, Amanda thought wearily. She didn't think she could have kept up the pace much longer.

For the first time since the flu struck, she was actually going home at a decent hour, and by heaven, she was going to pamper herself. Amanda moaned in anticipation. Already she could feel her body sliding into a steaming tub of scented bathwater.

After a long soak, she intended to fall into bed and sleep the weekend through, even if she had to unplug the telephone and switch off her pager—something she had never done in her seven years as a journalist.

Her stomach growled, reminding her that she hadn't eaten since the doughnut and coffee she had gobbled down on her way to the courthouse that morning. With dragging steps, Amanda trudged across the lobby toward the heavy glass doors, debating whether it was worth it to stop somewhere for takeout.

"Hi, beautiful. What took you so long?"

The deep, drawling voice stopped Amanda in her tracks. Her head swiveled toward the man who stood next to a potted palm just a few feet away. His thumbs were hooked in the belt loops of his jeans; he had one knee bent, and the sole of one boot and his broad shoulders propped against the wall at his back. His Stetson was tipped low over his forehead.

"Reilly! What're you doing here?"

"Waiting for you."

He pushed away from the wall and strolled her way, his gaze taking in every inch of her. The look on his face set off a tingling warmth deep inside Amanda.

"God, sugar, I've missed you," he growled, coming to a halt in front of her.

He ran one callused fingertip along her jaw. Sparks of sensation sizzled along the line of that rough, tender touch. Amanda shivered. Reilly's pupils widened and his nostrils flared slightly, and she shivered again, her heart kicking into overdrive.

Ignoring her body's foolish reaction, she snatched at her composure and took a half step back. "Why were you waiting for me? And how did you know when I'd get off? No. No, let me guess. Crusher called you, didn't he?" Reilly grinned and she bit off a curse. "That rat! Wait'll I get my hands on him. I should have known something was up when he didn't follow me out of the newsroom."

"Don't be too hard on Crusher. I asked him to let me know when you finally had a night off. I figured since you've been working so hard, I'd take you to dinner and administer a little TLC."

"Reilly, I can't. I'm too tired to go out. All I want is a bath and about seventy-two hours of sleep."

"I appreciate that. But you've still got to eat. It'll be quicker and easier if you let me feed you."

"Reilly, no. Really, I can't."

"Sure you can. If ever I've seen a woman who needs a little caring, you're her. Now just relax and leave everything to me. You'll enjoy it, I promise you."

"Reil-ly," Amanda moaned, but he'd already taken her arm and was ushering her out the doors.

"Trust me on this, darlin'. It won't take any time at all. I'll follow you and we'll drop your car off at your place. Then we'll have a quiet dinner and I'll bring you straight back. I'll have you home by eight. Scouts' honor."

Amanda narrowed her eyes. "Were you ever a Boy Scout, McCall?"

"Sure. I even got a merit badge." He shot her a devilish look. "In CPR. I was real good at mouth-to-mouth. All through junior high and high school I practiced it every chance I got in the back seat of my old Chevy."

"I'll bet." Amanda drilled him with a withering look, but he merely smiled innocently and bundled her into her car. Before she realized his intent, he bent and planted a kiss on her lips, then straightened and shut the door. "See you at your place." He gave the top of her car a thump of farewell and strode away to his pickup.

He was as good as his word. He took her to a quiet little restaurant just a mile or so from her condo, stuffed her with spaghetti and salad, then took her home. In spite of the short distance, Amanda nodded off during the drive. The next thing she knew, Reilly was whispering in her ear.

"Mandy, sugar, wake up. You're home."

Amanda made a sleepy sound and snuggled her face closer against Reilly's shoulder.

He chuckled and stroked his hand over her cheek. "C'mon, darlin', let's get you upstairs."

"I told you I was too tired to go out," she grumbled as he helped her out of the truck. "I don't know why I let you talk me into it."

But she did know. Reilly, with his subtle wooing, had managed to take the heat out of her ire. She could barely recall exactly why she had been so irked with him two weeks ago. Worse, she had missed him dreadfully.

She had begun to look forward to his notes and sonnets, the exotic bouquets of flowers. And the sound of his rumbling voice on her answering machine talking to her so intimately every night when she got home was oddly comforting. He had stirred feelings in her that she didn't know how to deal with.

"Just lean on me, sugar. I'll have you upstairs in two shakes."

Amanda didn't argue. She was too tired. Anyway, her legs felt as though they might turn to rubber on her at any second. Leaning her head on his shoulder, she sagged heavily against his side and trudged with him for the elevators.

At the entrance to her apartment, Reilly took the key from her and unlocked the door. He swung it open and smiled with gentle affection at her sleepy expression. "I know you're beat, so I won't come in. I'll give you a call after you've had a chance to catch up on your rest." He took her face between his rough palms and tipped it up. She blinked at him owlishly as he lowered his head and captured her mouth. The kiss was slow and breathtakingly gentle . . . and so hot her toes curled inside her new Italian pumps.

Unable to help herself, she stepped closer and slipped her arms around his waist, returning the kiss with a sleepy passion. She felt as though she were caught in an erotic dream, and she gave herself over to the sensuous pleasure.

The distant ringing was only a slight irritation at first. When Reilly lifted his head, she made a distressed sound and tried to burrow closer. He smiled tenderly and murmured, "Your telephone's ringing, sugar."

"Telephone?"

"Hmm. Maybe you ought to answer it."

She blinked, and his smile grew. Taking her shoulders, he turned her around and guided her inside. As they stepped into the living room, the answering machine clicked on. The whisper that came from the speaker brought them both to an abrupt halt in the middle of the floor.

"Are you there, Amanda? Bitch! Whore! Did you think I had forgotten what you've done to me? I haven't. I never forget a wrong. You defiled what we had, Amanda, and for that you must pay."

Amanda stared at the machine, feeling sick. With each word, the chilling whisper became harsher, more edged with hysteria and madness.

The speaker paused, and into the taut silence came a choked sound, like a sob.

"Oh, God, Amanda. Why did you do it? Why? I loved you so. I would have done anything for you. You loved me, too. I know you did. Why did you have to go and spoil everything?"

He was crying now. Amanda could hear the gasps and low moans—like an animal in pain—and the sounds filled her with revulsion and pity. She pressed her balled fist to her abdomen and shuddered.

Reilly's hands squeezed her shoulders and he muttered something under his breath.

After a moment the snuffling sounds ceased, and when the caller spoke again, his whisper had turned vicious.

"You're a worthless slut. Soon, soon you will reap your punishment. Do you hear me, you faithless, two-timing bitch? Do you? I will make you pay. I swear I will!"

Chapter Seven

Releasing Amanda, Reilly strode across the room and snatched up the receiver.

"Now, you listen to me, you sick son of a— Damn!"

He slammed the receiver back into the cradle so hard it nearly bounced out again. A murderous fury glittered in his eyes when he turned back to Amanda. "He hung up."

His scowl turned to concern. "Are you okay?"

Amanda swallowed hard and nodded.

She took two shaky steps to the sofa. Her knees gave way as she reached it, and she sank down onto the cushion and clasped her hands in her lap to keep them from shaking. She stared at the geometric design on the rug and willed the terrible quaking and dizziness to stop. Fear and nausea roiled in her stomach.

"God, you're white as a sheet." Reilly cursed and crossed the room quickly. Sitting down beside her, he cupped her nape and forced her head down between her knees. "Take slow, deep breaths. That's it. That's it. Just take it easy, darlin'," he crooned.

Amanda closed her eyes and did as he ordered, feeling the blood pour back into her head as she sucked long drafts of air into her lungs. Beads of perspiration popped out on her face and upper body.

Reilly's hand left her neck. She felt the sofa cushions shift when he stood up, but she didn't move. Moments later he returned with a wet washcloth and sat down beside her again.

"Feeling any better?"

"Ye-yes. I think so." Chagrined, Amanda straightened slowly. Never in her life had she come that close to fainting.

"Good." Reilly gently wiped her face with the cool cloth, inspecting her closely as he did. Vaguely, Amanda considered objecting, but at that moment she hadn't the strength or the will ... or the desire. It was oddly comforting to have Reilly fuss over her.

When finished, he tossed the damp washcloth over a two-foot abstract crystal sculpture that sat on the coffee table. "Are you up to talking to the police yet?"

"The police?" Amanda looked at him in alarm. "What do you mean?"

"Surely it's obvious to you now that you have to report this nut to the authorities?"

"No. I told you before. I'm not calling the police."

"That was then." He gestured toward the telephone. "This changes things. We got ourselves a whole new ball game now."

"No. Not to me, it's not."

"Dammit, Amanda! You're acting as crazy as your stalker."

"Don't call him that!"

"What else would you call a delusional man who keeps tabs on your every move and makes threats? Face it, Amanda, you're being stalked."

"Stop *saying* that. You're just trying to scare me into reporting him, and I won't. I told you, if I ignore him, he'll go away."

Her nerves skittered wildly, and her uncertain stomach began to flutter again. Wrapping her arms around her midriff, Amanda hugged herself tightly. *Priorities. Priorities,* she repeated over and over in her mind. She could not let herself give in to fear. She had to focus on what was most important.

"Dammit, Amanda, will you use your head? For this guy to write to you at the station is one thing, but now he's getting too close. If he's managed to get your unlisted telephone number, it's only a matter of time before he gets your address. If he hasn't already."

Amanda felt herself pale, but she still shook her head. Reilly made an irritated sound and raked both hands through his hair. He looked away, the muscles in his jaw working. She could almost see him struggling for calm. When he turned back, his smile was strained.

"Amanda. Sugar, listen to me," he said gently. "Ignoring this sicko obviously isn't working. It's time to take action."

"You don't understand." Agitated, she twisted her fingers together and gave him a desperate look. "I have to think of my career."

"Your career? What does your career have to do with any of this?"

"Don't you see? I can't afford to call the police. There is no way we could keep it quiet, and the negative publicity might hurt my chances of ever landing a network job. Why would they want someone who attracts that kind of weirdo?" She shook her head. "No. No, I can't take that risk."

"That's it? *That's* the reason you won't report the creep?"

His appalled look made Amanda feel foolish and stupid. As a result, her expression turned sulky. "I knew you wouldn't understand. You have no ambition, no drive. You couldn't possibly know how much my career means to me."

"More than your life, evidently," he snapped.

"I keep telling you it won't come to that!"

"The hell it won't. You heard that guy. He's not stable, Amanda. You can't predict what someone like that will do. Nothing is worth taking that kind of chance."

"Maybe not to you. But nothing much matters to you, does it?" Amanda shouted, her nerves fraying.

"People matter to me, not things! Certainly not some stupid job!" Reilly bellowed back.

Amanda blinked, taken aback for an instant by the rare burst of fury. She had never seen Reilly so impassioned. She had not thought him capable of such intense feeling. However, fear and temper rode her, prodding her on like roiling spurs.

She bounded off the sofa, her hands curled into fists at her sides. The debilitating weakness of a few moments before might never have been.

"This is *not* some stupid job! This is my career we're talking about! Something I've worked and struggled and planned for ever since I was sixteen. I don't expect someone like you to understand, but reaching the goals I've set for myself is my number-one priority, and I won't let anyone ruin that for me! Not some pathetic, unhinged man and certainly not an aimless flirt like you!"

Reilly shot to his feet. "Dammit to hell! If you aren't the most stubborn, pigheaded, unreasonable, shortsighted—" He sputtered to a stop, his face dark with frustration and anger. "Hell's bells, I care about you, Amanda! And I'm trying to protect you!"

"I don't want your protection! I don't need it!"

"And my feelings? Are you saying you don't want them, either?"

She hesitated for a fraction of a second, her heart giving a little lurch. Then she jutted her chin. "If you'll recall, I tried for over a year to get you to leave me alone." The words hurt—much more than she had thought they would, like an iron fist closing around her chest—but not by so much as a flicker of an eyelash did she let the feeling show.

Reilly stared at her for several taut seconds. "Okay, fine! You want me to leave you alone? You got it, lady!"

Snatching his Stetson from the back of a chair, he crammed it on his head and strode out. A few seconds later the door slammed so hard the pictures on the walls rattled.

Amanda stood in the middle of the floor where he had left her, gazing at the empty doorway, her chin still high, but after a moment it began to wobble. The pain in her chest was crushing. She sniffed and blinked rapidly against the stupid tears that flooded her eyes.

"Well . . . good riddance," she said in a quavering voice. She was glad he was gone. She was! The last thing she needed in her life was an unreliable, shallow playboy like Reilly McCall.

Her throat ached and her nose burned. She pressed her lips together to stop their trembling. It was for the best. A relationship between them would never have worked, anyway. They were too different. Hadn't she always known that?

"Would you like chocolate pie or carrot cake for dessert?" Tess asked as she and Ryan cleared the patio table.

"Yeah, sure. That's fine," Reilly mumbled.

Ryan looked up from scraping the steak scraps into Gert's bowl and exchanged a concerned look with his wife.

His twin sat slouched on his spine in the padded wrought-iron chair, his legs stretched out in front of him and crossed at the ankles, his brooding gaze on his niece and nephew.

Babbling and crowing with delight, Molly toddled around the yard in pursuit of Gertrude, their new golden Lab puppy. Between fits of rolling on the ground giggling, Mike hovered over her, though whether he was protecting Molly from the dog, or vice versa, wasn't clear.

Ryan's shrewd gaze went from his brother to the children, then back. Personally, he thought his kids were adorable and utterly fascinating, but he knew it wasn't their antics that Reilly found so absorbing. His brother's mind was miles away. Ryan didn't need a crystal ball to know where.

He winked at Tess and cleared his throat. "Okay. Pickle with mustard it is. Uh, you want coffee or hemlock to drink with that?"

"Yeah, that's great," Reilly mumbled politely.

After exchanging another look with his wife, Ryan added the plate to the tray that she was about to carry inside, and sat down on a padded lounger next to his brother.

"All right, this has gone on long enough. Why don't you spit it out?"

"Mmm," Reilly replied. Three seconds later he turned his head, scowling. "What?"

"Why don't you tell me what's happened between you and Amanda?"

"What makes you think something's happened?"

"C'mon, man. This is me you're talking to. Remember? I can read you like a book." Ryan leaned back in the lounger and laced his fingers behind his head. "You've been in a blue funk for almost a week now. You haven't teased or cracked a joke. You've barely said more than two words to anyone, and when you do, you practically snap their head off. Hell, if you're not careful you'll run off our office help. You had poor Jan in tears the other day."

"I didn't mean to upset her," Reilly grumbled. "Anyway, I apologized, didn't I?"

"That's not the point. This isn't like you, Reilly. Don't you think it's time you told me about it?"

"Ryan's right," Tess said, slipping into the chair on Reilly's other side. "You're the most good-natured man I know. If something is bothering you this much, you really ought to tell us about it. Maybe we can help. Especially if it concerns Amanda. Remember, she's my best friend."

Reilly frowned and returned his gaze to the children. "I can't. It would betray a confidence."

Tess sat forward, her eyes wide with surprise and hurt. "You mean Amanda's told you something she hasn't told me?"

"She didn't want to worry you."

"*Worry* me!"

"Uh-oh. Now you've done it, bro."

"Has something terrible happened? Is Amanda ill? Is she hurt? Has she had a car wreck? What?" Tess reached out and grabbed her brother-in-law's arm, unconsciously digging her fingernails into his flesh. "Reilly, you've *got* to tell me."

"Calm down, Tess. Amanda's okay. At least she was the last time I saw her."

"*Rei-lly!* What are you saying? Is Amanda in some sort of danger? You tell me right now, or so help me I'll ... I'll fill your precious ostrich skin boots with cement."

Reilly shot his brother a pained look and tried to pry his sister-in-law's fingers out of his flesh. "Jeez, Hoss, can't you do something with this woman?"

"Nope. You might as well spill the beans, old son, because I promise she won't give you a minute's peace until you do." Ryan sent his wife a fond glance. "Tess may look like a fragile flower, but when it comes to those she loves she's tough and tenacious as a bulldog."

"You tell me, Reilly! Right this minute!" Springing to her feet, Tess grabbed a padded seat cushion and walloped him over the head with it.

"All right, all right," he yelped, raising his arms to fend off more blows. "But you've got to promise not to breathe a word of what I'm going to tell you to anyone. Especially Amanda."

"Yes, yes. We won't say anything. Just get on with it."

Reilly glanced at his brother and grimaced. "And I always thought she was such a docile little thing."

"Hey. I warned you."

"Reilly McCall, if you don't start talking—"

"Okay. Okay." He felt guilty as hell about breaking a confidence, but the raw anxiety in Tess's eyes overrode his conscience. Taking a deep breath, he reached for her hand. "You see . . . Amanda has been receiving these letters. . . ."

During the telling Tess turned pale, and several times her and Ryan's gasps and frantic questions interrupted his explanation. By the time he finished, both his brother and sister-in-law were incredulous.

"You walked out? You just left her alone to fend for herself?" Tess accused. "Reilly, how could you?"

"What else could I do?" he flared, stung. "She didn't want my help. Or me. She made that pretty damned obvious."

"Oh, Reilly, you know she didn't mean that. She's just frightened. The more afraid Amanda gets, the more pugnacious she becomes. That's how she bluffs her way through."

"I'm surprised you couldn't persuade her to get help," Ryan said. "You can usually charm most women into doing whatever you want."

Reilly gave his brother a sulky look. "Yeah, well . . . Amanda's not most women."

He shot up out of his chair and began to pace the terrace. "Dammit. What the hell is the matter with that woman? Her career? There's a psycho out there somewhere stalking her and she's worried about her damned career? Why can't she get it through that granite head of hers that some things are more important?''

And why the hell do I care so much? he asked himself for perhaps the hundredth time in the past week. He stopped and jammed his hands into the pockets of his jeans and stared beyond the children to the blue water of the lake at the bottom of the sloping back lawn. Amanda was more trouble than she was worth. He was well rid of her.

Reilly snorted. *Yeah, right, McCall.*

He'd been telling himself that all week, for all the good it had done him. He'd done everything he could to put Amanda out of his mind. He had even taken out another woman.

The memory of that debacle made Reilly's mouth twist wryly. Poor Sharon must have thought he was a jerk. He hadn't even been able to work up enough interest to kiss her good-night.

From the start he had known that the attraction he felt for Amanda was stronger and more desperate than any he had ever experienced, but he certainly hadn't expected to feel so . . . so . . . involved. So concerned.

He would sympathize with any woman who was being harassed by a nut case, but where Amanda was concerned his feelings went deeper and were a hell of a lot more primitive. The mere idea of some wacko fixating on her, maybe even harming her, put a knot in his stomach the size of a fist and made him feel murderous. The woman aroused protective instincts in him he hadn't even known he possessed.

Yeah, and she threw them right back in your face.

Reilly rocked back on his heels, his mouth grim, oblivious to the concerned looks he was receiving from Ryan and Tess. *Face it, McCall. The lady doesn't want you or your protection.*

"Reilly, dear, I know it seems to you that Amanda is being unreasonable," Tess said gently. "And I agree. But what you must try to understand is that success is not just important to her...it's necessary. Partly, it's a coping mechanism, and partly it's fear."

"What do you mean?"

"Well, you see, setting goals for herself, then working like a demon to achieve them was—and still is—Amanda's way of coping with the pain she suffered when her father abandoned her mother and her. She zeroes in on a goal and blocks out everything else.

"Amanda's father was not only a philanderer, he was lazy and shiftless, as well. I think she's terrified of being like him. When he left, she made a vow that she would make something of herself. No matter what it took, she was determined to prove to the world—but most important, I think, to herself—that she was a worthwhile person.

"So she knuckled down in school and consistently made the honor roll. She was valedictorian of our class. She earned a full scholarship to college, and, of course, she always made the dean's list. Whatever Amanda does, she gives it her all.

"For her, making it to the top is somehow validation of her value as a person."

"Let me get this straight. You're saying that Amanda's self-esteem is all tied up in getting this network job she talked about?"

"Yes. Exactly."

"But that's crazy! She has a great job, one that a lot of people envy. And she's damned good at it."

"It doesn't matter. To Amanda, success doesn't simply mean doing well, it means being the best, the one at the top. If she doesn't land a job at the network level, she'll consider herself a failure.

"Her sights are set on New York. When you tried to force her to call in the police on the man writing those letters, you were threatening her future. I'm sure her reaction was pure reflex."

Reilly sank back down in the chair, shaking his head. "Good grief."

"You might as well know it all," Tess said with an audible trace of sympathy.

"Oh, Lord, you mean there's more?"

"I'm afraid so. You see, once, about seven years ago, Amanda was engaged."

Reilly stiffened. "To whom?"

"It doesn't matter. The point is, he turned out to be just as much a womanizing jerk as her father. It nearly killed Amanda when she caught him with another woman. Since then, she's shied away from serious relationships." Tess paused and bit her lip, watching Reilly uncertainly. "Especially with men she believes are like her father."

It took a minute for her meaning to sink in. When it did, Reilly took offense.

"*Me?* You mean she thinks that I would treat her like her old man treated her mother?" he demanded in an outraged voice.

"You can hardly blame her," Ryan drawled. "Face it, bro. Where women are concerned, you don't exactly have a reputation for constancy."

"Only because I haven't met the right woman."

"Until now, you mean."

"What?"

At the look of confusion on his brother's face, Ryan threw his head back and crowed with laughter.

"Just what's so damned funny?" Reilly's scowl would have blistered paint, but his brother merely laughed harder.

"Oh, man, this is rich. You really are pathetic. You don't have a clue, do you? Probably because it's never happened to you before."

"Ryan, you're not being nice," Tess scolded, but both men ignored her.

"What the devil are you talking about?"

A look of unholy glee came over Ryan's face. With brotherly directness, and not a little relish, he drawled, "What I'm saying is, for the first time in your life you're in love, you blockhead. And you don't even have the sense to know it."

"Don't be ridiculous. That's crazy. I'm not in love. I can't be. I—I..." He swallowed hard and looked around, his face slack with confusion. Then he focused on his twin again. His eyes were wide and a little wild, and his voice came out in a croak. "Can I?"

Smiling wickedly, Ryan nodded.

He was enjoying himself tremendously at his twin's expense, but Reilly was too stunned to care. The idea that he could be in love—*really* in love—knocked him for a loop.

Although, come to think of it, that would certainly explain why he hadn't been able to put Amanda out of his mind this past week. Hell, she'd barely been out of his mind for almost two years now. It would also account for his gut reaction to those damned letters and that phone call.

Could it possibly be? Was he in love?

The notion intrigued him. He had to admit, there had been times during the past few years when he'd been vaguely envious of his brothers' and cousins' happy marriages.

He thought about what it would be like to spend his life with Amanda—to wake up beside her in the mornings, to love her and tease her and fight with her, to watch her body grow heavy with his child, to grow old with her—and a soul-deep pleasure filled him.

Reilly, like his father and his younger brother, Travis, was a man who truly liked women. He downright adored the little darlin's—young or old, pretty or plain, short or tall, skinny or fat, bold or shy, or anything in between—he genuinely liked them all. And he had to admit, he'd enjoyed his share of success with the opposite sex—more than his share, according to some.

Yet, analyzing his feelings, he realized that the thought of total commitment and fidelity to one special woman held no fear for him. He'd grown up in a happy home with parents who were—and remained, after almost forty years of marriage—totally devoted to each other. He couldn't imagine a better way to go through life.

A smile spread over his face. *Love.* How about that? The knot of tension and anger that had been lodged just beneath his breastbone for the past week dissolved, and a tingling warmth began to trickle through him, like effervescent champagne bubbles skipping and bouncing through his bloodstream.

He was in love with Amanda. Well, hot damn!

"The question now is, what're you going to do about it?"

His brother's dry inquiry returned him to earth with a thump. He shot his twin an annoyed glance, but he mulled the problem over, his lips pursed in concentration.

He knew what he wanted to do. He also knew it wouldn't be easy. Amanda was a stubborn, independent, ambitious woman who had her sights set on making it to the big time. She was also prickly and defensive. And she had him pegged—erroneously—as some sort of insecure Lothario out to carve notches on his bedposts.

It was a formidable list of obstacles, any one of which would have discouraged most men, but with the discovery of love, Reilly's natural optimism had kicked in again. The depression and anger that had sat on his chest like a lump of wet cement for the past week vanished. He felt jubilant and eager, ready to take on the world. Especially one feisty blonde. Hell's bells. So they had a few problems to overcome. So what? They would work them out somehow.

He turned to his twin and winked. "Why, shoot, Hoss, that's easy. I'm going to do what any sane, red-blooded male in my situation would do. I'm going courtin'."

Amanda waved goodbye to Crusher and stepped into the elevator. The instant the doors closed, she slumped against the wall. Leaning her head back, she closed her eyes as the cubicle began its slow ascent. Lord, she was weary right down to her bone marrow. And depressed. And lonely. And, yes, dammit, miserable.

The last made her grind her teeth and silently curse Reilly McCall.

She simply did not understand it. Work—total concentration on whatever job was at hand—had always been her panacea for pain. She had thrown herself into her duties this past week with even more intensity than usual. Still, she couldn't seem to get that beguiling man out of her mind. It wasn't fair. He obviously hadn't given her a thought.

All right, so she had practically thrown him out and told him to leave her alone. He could have at least had the decency to call to see if she was safe. That weirdo was still out there, after all.

Against her will, snippets of the chilling letter she had received only yesterday coiled through Amanda's mind, sending a shiver down her spine.

She sniffed and firmed her mouth. Obviously she had been right about Reilly all along; at the first sign of trouble, he had cut and run. He was nothing but a self-involved playboy, interested only in having a good time.

The elevator pinged and stopped and the doors opened. Amanda stepped out and trudged down the hall, digging into her purse for her key. She was almost there when she looked up and saw him.

Leaning against the wall beside the door to her apartment, his arms folded over his chest, feet crossed at the ankles, he watched her approach, looking like a man without a care in the world.

Her heart gave a leap and joy surged through her, sharp and sweet. The reaction annoyed Amanda, but at least she managed to control her expression.

She sauntered forward and swept him with a cool look, one haughty brow cocked. "What are you doing here, McCall?"

Her frosty tone only made his grin widen. He straightened away from the wall when she reached the door. Before Amanda could so much as blink, he swept her up into his arms and captured her mouth in a searing kiss that wiped every thought right out of her brain.

All she could do was hang there in his embrace, limp as a wet rag, absorbing the pleasure of it, her arms dangling at her sides. Her heart pounded, the sound roaring in her ears. The strap on her shoulder bag slid slowly down her arm and the purse hit the carpeted hallway with a thunk.

Reilly's tongue swirled through her mouth in an erotic dance, and his big hands swept over her back and shoulders and buttocks, pressing her closer, molding her to him. The feel of his hard body, his warmth crushed against her, made Amanda's nipples pucker and tingle, and sent heat zipping through her veins, straight to her feminine core. She throbbed and burned, and when at last he withdrew his lips from hers, a helpless little moan escaped her.

She continued to hang in his arms, her head lolled back, eyes closed, lips wet and parted. When at last she forced her heavy lids open, he grinned down at her.

"Hi, sugar. Miss me?"

Amanda blinked...then stiffened, turning scarlet. "Reilly, what...what do you think you're doing, grabbing me that way? Let go of me, you idiot," she sputtered, pushing out of his arms.

He grinned, not in the least perturbed. He picked up her purse and handed it to her. "Sorry, darlin', I couldn't help myself. I've missed you like sin."

Amanda's heart gave another flutter. *Oh, for heaven's sake, will you get a grip?* she berated herself, but the fizzy feeling would not go away. "Oh, sure, I'll just bet."

"Honest. I did, sweetheart. This has been the most miserable week of my life."

"Huh." Amanda dug into her purse and pulled out her key. She turned away to unlock her door, and Reilly stepped up close behind her and grasped her shoulders. She could feel his heat all along her back, and when his fingers began to massage her tired muscles, she almost groaned.

"Are you ticked off because I didn't call or come by all week?"

"Don't be ridiculous. Why would I be? I never even gave you a thought."

She felt the chuckle shake his chest before the rich sound rumbled in her ear.

"Liar." He gave her lobe a little nip in retaliation.

Amanda shivered and closed her eyes. His moist breath feathering her ear was turning her knees to mush.

"I wanted to. God, how I wanted to," he growled. "But I was afraid you might take a baseball bat to sensitive parts of my anatomy if I showed my face too soon."

She gave him an arch look over her shoulder. "Oh? And what makes you think I won't now?"

"'Cause you care about me?" he said hopefully, then laughed when Amanda narrowed her eyes. "All right, all right, I confess. I checked with Crusher, and he said that whatever burr you had in your panty hose at the beginning of the week was evidently gone now, because you'd stopped snarling at everyone."

"Oh, really? I'll have you know I *don't* snarl. And even if I did, what makes you think it would have anything to do with you?"

Burr in her panty hose, indeed. She stabbed the key into the lock, gave it a wrenching twist, and shoved the door open, but when she tried to shake off Reilly's hands, he tightened his grip on her shoulders.

"C'mon, darlin'. Don't be that way. Admit it. You know you care. Now don't you?" he wheedled, mouthing the tender skin behind her ear. "Just a little? Hmm?"

"Cer-certainly not," Amanda denied, but her voice came out in a breathless waver.

"You sure? I'm crazy about you," he whispered, nuzzling his face into her hair. "And I didn't forget about you, sugar. Not for a minute. Even when I wanted to wring your pretty little neck, I still called Crusher and checked on you every day."

"Re-really?"

"Uh-huh. And, just in case you hadn't forgiven me yet, I brought a bribe with me."

"Wh-what do you mean?"

Reilly pointed to the floor. Surprised and disconcerted, Amanda glanced at the two sacks of groceries propped against the wall; she had been so caught up in Reilly's sudden appearance she hadn't even noticed them before.

"I'm going to cook dinner for you."

"You can cook?" Her voice dripped skepticism, and Reilly feigned offense.

"Are you kidding? Honey, you just give me an hour. I'll whip you up a meal that'll make your taste buds moan with ecstasy."

"Reilly, that's very nice of you, but I'm tired and—"

"I know, darlin'. That's why I'm here. Crusher told me what a grueling week you've had." He turned her around, his eyes twinkling down at her. "You're not going to refuse me, are you, after I've gone to all this trouble? C'mon, sugar, let me spoil you a little. You won't have to do a thing, I promise."

"Well...." Amanda bit her lower lip. "I guess it's okay."

She had barely gotten the words out when he swooped up the sacks and nudged her inside. "Good. Now you go on and take a long hot soak, or whatever it is you do to relax, and leave everything to me."

He dropped a quick kiss on the end of her nose and strode toward the kitchen, whistling a jaunty tune.

"Reilly," she called softly, and he halted and looked back, one eyebrow cocked.

"Yeah?"

"I, uh, I haven't changed my mind about calling the police, you know."

"I know." He sighed, and his mouth twisted in a resigned half smile. "I still think you're wrong, but if that's the way you want to handle it..." Letting the words trail away, he shrugged, then continued on to the kitchen.

Amanda stared after him. He didn't seem in the least angry or hurt, and she had to admit he had every right to be both, after the way she had treated him.

A smile blossomed on her lips. It was amazing. And ridiculous. All week, right up to a few moments ago, she had been blue and miserable, and now suddenly she felt as though she were walking on air, all because of one impossible man.

Chapter Eight

Amanda considered the emerald green silk caftan, and felt a quick tug of temptation. She could just imagine what Reilly's reaction would be if she were to swirl into the kitchen in a cloud of clinging silk and seductive perfume.

For a brief moment she actually considered doing just that. Luckily, sanity returned in time and she shoved the sexy garment back into the closet and prudently opted for an old pair of pale peach sweats.

She might be feeling uncharacteristically reckless, even a bit eager and excited, but she was not quite ready to throw caution completely to the wind.

The only concession Amanda made to her giddy emotions was to don the outfit without a bra, but that was a practice she always followed when relaxing at home. Anyway, the baggy old sweats were so loose, Reilly would never notice.

Leaning in toward the mirror, she hurriedly touched up her makeup, but she was in too much of a hurry to do more than give her tawny mane a quick brushing. When done, she left it loose around her shoulders and headed for the kitchen, letting her nose lead the way.

"Something smells wonderful."

Reilly turned from the stove at her announcement. His gaze swept over her, zeroing in at once on her breasts. A smile played around his mouth.

Damn. He'd noticed.

Amanda quickly slid onto one of the stools beside the kitchen island and propped her crossed forearms on the top in front of her chest. Reilly's mouth twitched again.

"It's nothing fancy. Just steak, potatoes and a salad."

He had a dish towel slung over one shoulder and one of her frilly aprons tied around his waist. He should have looked laughable. What he looked was drop-dead gorgeous.

"Oh, and apple crisp for dessert."

"My goodness. You really *can* cook."

The amazement in her voice produced an expression of exaggerated affront. "I'm cut to the quick, sugar. Of course, I can cook. You've met my mother. Do you think she'd allow any slackers in her family?

"All us kids had to learn to cook—at least enough that we wouldn't starve when we left home to be on our own."

Amanda had already learned that in Reilly's family, the term *kids* meant not just the McCall offspring, but their cousins, Erin, Elise, and David, as well. They had all grown up together in Crockett, Texas, the two families living just minutes apart.

"Well...actually...come to think of it, Erin never really got the hang of it. But we all pulled kitchen duty when we were kids. Even David. Our mothers' policy was 'if you eat, you cook.'" Reilly flashed a prideful grin. "You might say Ma and Aunt Dorothy were ahead of their time when it came to women's liberation."

"Do you enjoy cooking?"

"Hmm. Sometimes. I guess if I had to do it every night, like a lot of women do, it might become a drag. When I get married, I expect to do my share of the cooking though."

The microwave dinged, and he turned away to remove the baked potatoes. Amanda watched him, feeling bemused and oddly unsettled. Somehow, she had never thought of Reilly marrying.

He lifted the steaks out of the broiler onto two plates and placed them on the table in the breakfast alcove. "Ta-dum! If you'll bring the salad, darlin', we're all set."

Amanda couldn't remember ever enjoying a meal more. The steaks were perfect, the potatoes fluffy, the wine delicious, the salad crisp, and the dessert scrumptious. Reilly, she discovered, had even made his own salad dressing, a concoction he'd invented himself.

It was a rare treat to have someone else cook for her, but Amanda suspected her enjoyment sprang mostly from the company. The thought both frightened and thrilled her.

She told herself she should not get all worked up over a man like Reilly. Yet she could not deny that it pleased her to be near him—to hear his voice, to watch that magnificent body move with such utterly masculine grace, to catch the occasional whiff of soap and woodsy cologne and maleness that emanated from him...along with the ever-present scent of peppermint. Even the sight of those big, callused hands deftly chopping vegetables made her stomach go woozy.

After dinner Reilly would not allow her to lift a finger. Amanda felt wonderfully pampered, sitting on the stool again, watching him clean up. He did a thorough job of it, too, which somehow surprised her.

When he finished, they retired to the living room with their coffee. Reilly built a fire in the fireplace and loaded the CD carousel with romantic music. Somehow, when she wasn't looking, he even managed to turn out all the lights.

"What do you think you're doing, McCall?"

Amanda shot him a censuring look as he joined her on the sofa, but he merely grinned and blithely replied, "I've always thought that fires were more enjoyable this way."

"Uh-huh." Her tone oozed cynicism and suspicion, but beyond narrowing her eyes at him, she did nothing. The trouble was, she thought so too, though, of course, she wasn't about to tell him that.

Falling silent, she stared at the dancing flames. Reilly popped a peppermint into his mouth and did the same.

Amanda toed off her sneakers and propped her feet on the coffee table. She was still tired, only now it was a good kind of tired. The hot soak had eased her aching muscles, but most of all, the tension and unhappiness of the past week had miraculously fallen away. She felt relaxed and sort of boneless, but underneath the pleasurable feelings ran a fine thread of excitement, that delicious, expectant sensation she always experienced around Reilly.

A yawn caught her unawares. "Oh, my." Flashing him a sheepish smile, Amanda leaned forward and placed her cup on the coffee table.

"Tired?"

"Mmm."

Reilly put his cup down, as well, and reached for her. "Come here."

Only the glow of flickering flames lit the room. In the background Julio Iglesias crooned softly of love. The mood was beautifully mellow and romantic, and when Reilly put his arm around her shoulders and pulled her close, it seemed the most natural thing in the world to Amanda to snuggle against his chest.

It felt so good to be in his arms. *Too good,* a tiny voice prodded.

"Reilly, we have to talk." The last thing she wanted was to talk, but since it had become painfully obvious that she could no longer resist him, the least she could do was set some ground rules.

"Sure, sugar. Whadda you want to talk about?"

Taking a deep breath, Amanda pushed out of his arms and sat up. She couldn't think when he held her. "About this relationship."

Reilly grinned slowly, his expression so full of tenderness that Amanda's heart flip-flopped. He touched her cheek with his callused forefinger. "Do you realize that's the first time you've admitted we *have* a relationship?"

"You haven't left me much choice." She shot him a sullen look as fear and excitement skittered through her. "But after you hear what I have to say, you may change your mind about wanting one."

"I doubt that. But go ahead, darlin'. Fire away."

"What..." She stopped and cleared her throat. "What is it you want from me, Reilly? What are your expectations?"

A great uprush of emotion swelled Reilly's heart. *Love. Marriage. A family. The works.*

The words hovered on the tip of his tongue but he saw the fear and uncertainty in Amanda's face and his gut told him now was not the time to reveal the depth of his feelings or his hopes for the future. "Oh, I don't know," he hedged, shrugging. "I guess mainly I just want you to give us a chance and see what develops from there."

"You do realize that I am dedicated to my career, don't you?"

"Yep. I pretty much had that figured out from the start."

"The hours are long and lousy, and often demanding, and leave little time for a social life. There will be periods like the last few weeks when I won't be able to see you."

"Understood. I can handle that...as long as I'm the one you turn to when you're free."

Amanda studied him. "I'm not good at permanent relationships. I'm not looking for one," she stated defiantly, and Reilly felt a rush of tenderness for her.

He didn't believe her for an instant. Amanda was good at putting up a front. Her sultry beauty drew men like flies, but she used cool sophistication and a droll, sometimes biting humor like a shield to keep them off balance and at bay.

He didn't doubt that the thought of love and marriage and children terrified her—particularly after what Tess had revealed about Amanda's past—but in unguarded moments, she had unknowingly given herself away.

Countless times he had seen the wistful look in her eyes when she witnessed the love and closeness between his brother and Tess. Amanda adored Molly and Mike, and there was aching longing behind every look and touch she gave them. Oh, yes, she wanted commitment and permanence and all that went with it, all right. She was simply too afraid to admit it.

Reilly could understand her fear of being hurt, but he thought her worry that she might turn out to be like her father was absurd. Amanda was hard-working and dedicated and as loyal as they came. Her lifelong friendship with Tess was proof of that.

"Also, if I reach my career goals—and that could happen at any time—I'll be leaving Houston," she continued baldly, in the same challenging tone.

That possibility *did* bother him, Reilly had to admit, but it was a chance he had to take. Hell, he had no choice. "Well, darlin'," he said cautiously, "I guess I'm willing to let the future take care of itself. I trust you to follow your heart, wherever it leads."

Amanda strove to look cool and in control, but Reilly saw the turmoil in her eyes. He knew she wanted to give in, but she seemed determined to first point out all of the obstacles.

"I'm not ready for intimacy," she blurted out with a pugnacious lift of her chin. "I'm not sure I will ever be. If you can't accept that, then you can just hit the road right now, because I won't be rushed."

Reilly threw back his head and laughed. "Ah, sugar, you're adorable. I'll admit, I want you. More than I have ever wanted a woman in my life. Shoot, it's a downright miracle I'm not a blathering idiot, I ache for you so much. But I can wait."

He reached out and hugged her close again. "Tell you what," he murmured against the top of her head. "I'll leave it up to you. When and if you decide the time is right, you let me know. All you gotta do is whistle."

She looked up at him, her eyes wide. "Are you serious?"

"You bet, darlin'. I don't ever want you to feel pressured or do something you aren't comfortable with."

Amanda searched his face, and after a moment she sighed and rested her cheek against his chest again. Reilly cupped her head with his free hand, absently rubbing, the silken strands of hair shifting beneath his touch. Emotion swelled his chest with a painful sweetness.

"Everything okay now?"

"Mmm." Amanda was dazed, but hope was beginning to creep in.

Shifting into a more comfortable position, she nuzzled her face against Reilly's shirt and made a satisfied sound. The smells of laundry starch and soap and male tickled her nose, and she breathed deeply of the intoxicating scents.

"Comfy?" he asked.

"Mmm."

"Good."

They fell silent again and time stretched out. The scrambler on the CD switched to an old song by U2, and after that, one by Rod Stewart. Over and over, Reilly's hand ran up and down Amanda's arm in a rhythmic caress. The calluses on his palm created a delicious friction against her skin.

Raising his other hand, Reilly pushed a stray lock of hair away from her face and tucked it behind her ear. His fingertips lingered against the velvety rim, and a shiver rippled through Amanda.

She felt a soft kiss on the top of her head, felt his moist breath seep through the strands of hair and warmly caress her skin, felt her scalp tighten in helpless response. Amanda made a soft, unconscious sound.

Reilly hooked his finger beneath her chin, and she offered no resistance as he tilted her face up.

His blue eyes glittered down at her in the wavering firelight, full of emotion and need and longing. Amanda watched him through half-closed eyes, her chest growing tighter by the second, her heart beginning to thump.

"Aw, Lord, Mandy," he whispered in a tortured groan as his head began a slow descent. "You're so damned beautiful."

His mouth closed over hers with a gentle hunger that drew a sigh from Amanda. Her eyes drifted shut and her hand curled against his chest. This, she realized, was what she had been waiting for all evening.

Her heart bumped at the first touch of Reilly's tongue against hers. She moaned softly, and responded with a gentle nudge of her own. It was all the invitation he needed.

Instantly, Reilly deepened the kiss. His tongue slid over hers and they twined together, teasing, enticing. He tasted of coffee and peppermint and passion. The quivery sensations in Amanda's belly grew stronger. Reaching up, she curved her hand around his nape, her fingers threading through the short hairs that brushed his collar.

With a low growl, Reilly turned her and pulled her across his lap, holding her cradled against his chest. He took possession of her mouth. The kiss was no longer softly seducing, but hot and hard, bordering on desperate. She could taste his hunger, his frustration. Desire slammed through her like a runaway train.

She yearned. Oh, Lord, she had forgotten how it felt to need like this. She wasn't sure she ever had. To crave a man's touch so much that nothing else mattered, nothing else existed, was divine torture.

She supposed on some level she had always known it would be this way between them. From the moment they'd met there had been a deep, visceral awareness that had drawn her to him, no matter how hard she fought against it.

A desperate want filled her, drove her. Sensations poured through her body, one after another—heat, hunger, helpless longing. The barrage left her weak and clinging. The need drove her to dive into the kiss and greedily take...and take...and take.

Reilly groaned in agony...in ecstasy. How long had he dreamed of this? Forever, it seemed. Her arms were around him, clutching, binding them together. Her mouth—ah, her mouth. So sweet, so hot. Oh, God, he couldn't get enough of it. He could feel the helpless tremors that rippled through her, hear her raspy breathing, the urgent little gasps and moans that tore from her throat. She was wound taut, quivering—for him.

A hard shudder shook his big frame. His hand slid down over her hip and tunneled under the soft knit top. He touched bare skin, warm and smooth as silk, and his breath caught. Reverently, his hand closed around her breast. He squeezed the soft flesh, swept his thumb across the pebbled peak, and Amanda made a mewling sound that nearly shattered his control.

He tore his mouth from hers and looked down at her in the flickering light, his chest heaving. She lay quiescent in his arms and stared up at him with feverish eyes. Her mouth was wet and puffy and the pulse at the base of her throat tripped like a jackhammer.

"I want to look at you, sweetheart." The words grated from his throat, his voice guttural and rough with passion.

Something hot flickered in Amanda's eyes, but she did not speak or move. She merely watched him, breathing hard.

Reilly released her breast. With a shaking hand, he grasped the hem of her sweatshirt. Slowly, with exquisite care, as though opening a precious gift, he pushed the knit pants down and the top upward. In silence, Amanda lifted to accommodate him.

Awed beyond words, Reilly stared. Her creamy skin glowed with a pearlescence in the firelight, reflecting the gold and orange of the dancing flames. Her breasts, two perfect round globes, were full and lush, the nipples small rosebuds thrusting impudently up at him.

"Oh, sweet heaven," Reilly whispered. Cupping his hand around one pillowy mound, he lowered his head. With agonizing slowness, he dragged his open mouth over the pearly slope to the tempting mauve nipple. She whimpered and arched her back. With a growl he closed his lips around the sweet nub...and Amanda's beeper went off.

The electronic chirps shattered the silence like a shrieking banshee.

"What the—" Reilly jerked upright.

Amanda's head came up like a startled doe's. "It's my pager."

"Ah, hell."

Scrambling out of his arms and onto her knees, Amanda groped through the semidarkness over the chrome-and-glass table that butted up against the back of the sofa. Bracing his elbows on his knees, Reilly held his head in his hands and cursed.

The sudden cessation of noise was almost deafening when Amanda shut off the device. Immediately she snatched up the telephone and punched out a number. Waiting for the call to go through, she fidgeted from one knee to the other on the sofa cushions and glanced around.

Only when she encountered Reilly's hot gaze on her breasts did she realize that the top of her sweat suit was still in a wad up under her arms and the pants were barely clinging to her hips at just below navel level.

Amanda flushed and snatched at her clothes just as Harry picked up the telephone at the other end, and barked, "Yeah, Kowalski! Whaddaya want?"

Reilly was on fire, his body shrieking in protest. At that moment he could have cheerfully strangled Harry Kowalski with his bare hands. He could hear the man's voice bellowing through the line but he couldn't make out the words.

As Amanda struggled to right her clothes and hold the receiver scrunched between her shoulder and jaw, he watched her expression change. The call took only seconds, but by the time she hung up, the blurry look of passion had vanished from her face and she was alert and tense, all business. He doubted that she even remembered the feverish passion she experienced only moments ago.

"I've got to go." She bounded off the sofa and stuffed her feet back into her sneakers.

"Go? Go where?"

"A train has derailed on the north side. Crusher and Norman are already on their way. I'm meeting them there."

"At this time of night?"

"News doesn't happen just between nine and five, Reilly." She propped one foot on the edge of the coffee table, retied the shoe, then reversed feet and tied the other.

"Can't they send someone else? It's after eleven, and that's a rough part of town."

"That sort of thing comes with the territory. And all the other reporters are out on call. Otherwise you can bet Harry wouldn't be giving me such a juicy assignment. It's my job, Reilly. Don't worry, I do this sort of thing all the time," she said absently, looking around for her purse. She spotted it hanging on the brass coatrack in the entry and headed that way. "Look, can you let yourself out? I've got to run."

"Aren't you going to change? Jeez, Mandy! You can't go out like that."

She stopped and looked down at the peach sweats. "Why not?"

"Hell's bells, sugar, you're not wearing a bra!"

"Oh, for—I don't have time for this nonsense. I've got to go."

Reilly came up off the sofa like an uncoiling spring. "Then I'm going with you," he announced, stopping her in her tracks.

"What? Don't be silly. Reilly, I'll be perfectly all right. Besides, I may be out half the night."

"I'm still going."

Amanda glared at him in frustration, but a glance at her watch sent her scurrying toward the door again. "Oh, all right! I don't have time to argue with you. Just stay out of the way."

Snatching her purse off the rack, she slung it over her shoulder, jerked open the door and took off down the hall at a run. She did not bother to look back to see if he was keeping up.

When the elevator doors failed to open immediately, Amanda plunged into the stairwell and loped down the fire stairs with the grace of a sleek cat. Reilly had the devil's own job keeping up with her. Between the squeak of her athletic shoes and the thudding clang of his boot heels against the metal treads, they made enough noise to wake the whole building.

She cut him no slack. Reilly managed to sling himself into the passenger seat of her car seconds after she started the engine, but the door was still open and his right leg had not cleared the concrete when she reversed out of the parking slot.

"Hell's bells!" he yelped as sparks shot off his dragging boot heel.

Amanda didn't bat an eye. He barely had time to yank his leg inside and slam the door before she rammed the stick shift into first and sent the little fireball of a car streaking down the ramp and out onto the street in a red blur.

Reilly had never ridden in a car going warp speed before, but that was the only way to describe the trip to the derailment scene. Amanda drove with a verve, cunning and skill that made the Indy guys look like pikers. Even at eleven at night Houston's traffic was horrendous, but she shot through the snarl with the precision and speed of a guided missile. All Reilly could do was hold on and pray.

The accident scene was pandemonium when they arrived. Fire trucks and police vehicles lined the road beside the tracks, their blue and red lights revolving eerily. Far back from the crash sight, behind hastily erected barricades, a crowd had gathered. A few were people who lived or worked nearby who had been evacuated, but most were simply gawkers or members of the news media.

Almost at once, they spotted mobile units belonging to two other TV stations. Swiveling her head from side to side, looking for Channel 5's distinctive green and navy logo, Amanda grumbled and all but gnashed her teeth at the possibility the competition had already beaten her to the story.

Finally she saw Crusher down by the barricade, towering over everyone around him. Norman hovered right behind him with the equipment case and battery pack slung over his skinny arms. Crusher had the mobile camera on his shoulder, aimed at the fire marshal and several other men who were huddled together in intense discussion.

Amanda brought the car to a screeching halt behind the KLUX mobile unit. Reilly shot forward against his seat belt, then bounced back.

"Mandy, darlin', you drive like a bat out of hell."

"You got here in one piece, didn't you?" Barely sparing him a look, she snatched up her shoulder bag and sprang out of the low-slung car.

"Dammit, Amanda, wait!" Reilly cursed and popped opened the passenger door. Because of his size, he had difficulty unfolding himself from the sports car. By the time he finally made it to his feet Amanda was already racing toward her camera crew, elbowing her way through the press of people.

Reilly bit off a curse and barreled through right behind her. He arrived at the barricade just in time to hear Amanda ask Crusher if he had learned yet what had caused the accident.

"No, they haven't released any informa—Reilly! What're you doing here, man?" Crusher grinned hugely and thumped Reilly's shoulder. Then he turned a hard stare on Amanda. "What's up? You been telling me all week that you and my man Reilly here were finished."

"We just had a little misunderstanding, that's all," Reilly replied before she could answer. "It's all patched up now, though."

"Aw *right!* Way to go, Irish. That's great! Ain't that great, Norman?"

Norman shrugged and tried to dig a hole in the dirt with the toe of one of his ragged sneakers.

Crusher winked and gave Reilly another cuff on the shoulder. "I guess you came to keep an eye on your lady, huh?"

"Yeah. It's a tough job, but I figure somebody's gotta do it," he answered with a male-to-male grin.

Crusher guffawed, but Amanda turned one of her cold smiles on Reilly and said sweetly, "I believed we agreed that you'd stay out of the way. Open your mouth again, McCall, and I'll tie a knot in your tongue."

Norman snickered, but the sound quickly choked off under Reilly's stare.

"Shouldn't they turn the hose on those cars, in case they've sprung a leak?"

"I don't think they know what they're dealing with yet," Crusher said, panning the camera over the destruction of twisted rails and toppled tank cars. "Until they do, they won't know whether to hose them down with water or chemical foam."

Floodlights had been rigged to illuminate the sight. On the opposite side of the tracks, in the weed-choked strip between the raised rail bed and the chain-link fence that surrounded some sort of storage yard and seedy metal building, five tank cars lay askew on their sides like giant dead buffalo. All along the right-of-way firemen stood by with hoses ready while others conferred with railroad reps.

"Why don't we shoot our intro tape while we're waiting?" Crusher suggested. Amanda made a disgruntled sound but she complied.

Using the viewfinder to align the shot so that the destruction was visible over her left shoulder, Crusher directed her into position with hand signals and softly voiced instructions. "To the right just a bit. A bit more. Okay, now about a half step forward. That's it. Perfect."

Amanda planted her feet, faced the camera, squared her shoulders and tilted her chin at that sultry angle Houston viewers were so accustomed to seeing.

The wind whipped her streaked hair about her head and shoulders in a frenzied dance, and Reilly groaned when the peach sweat suit lovingly plastered her breasts. Still she managed to look like an elegant sophisticate.

"Good evening, ladies and gentlemen. As you can see behind me, this evening an inbound train heading for the Port of Houston derailed on the north side of town, overturning five tank cars filled with what we must assume to be hazardous material. As of this time...."

Amanda made the intro in only one take, staring straight into the camera with her usual panache, her voice clear and concise. When they finished, there was nothing else to do but wait, something Amanda did not do with good grace, Reilly discovered.

With every passing minute she became more impatient. She yelled and waved at several official-looking men hurrying about, but they either didn't hear her or ignored her, along with all the other members of the press. Crackling with frustration, she tapped her pencil against the notepad she had pulled from her purse and shifted from one sneakered foot to the other.

"Oh, this is ridiculous. We can't just stand here all night twiddling our thumbs. We need information. C'mon, Crusher. Follow me."

Before Reilly realized her intent, Amanda ducked under the barricade tape and ran toward the nearest group of firemen. After only an instant's hesitation, Crusher took off after her, with Norman bringing up the rear, struggling to keep up.

"Amanda! Amanda, dammit, get back here!" Reilly roared, but he might as well have saved his breath. She had already scrambled over what was left of the tracks and was firing questions at the group of startled men as she approached them.

Cursing nonstop, Reilly ducked under the tape and took off at a dead run. Damned fool woman.

Reilly's phenomenal patience went up in smoke. He was so furious he literally saw red—bright crimson dots dancing before his eyes as he loped across the uneven ground. His heart clubbed like a wild thing in his chest. In his mind's eye all he could see was Amanda being swallowed up by an explosion.

Just wait till he got his hands on her. He'd kill her.

By the time he caught up with her he didn't give a thought to diplomacy or persuasion.

"So you have no idea what caused this tragedy? Is that right?" Amanda asked, shoving her microphone in the hapless fireman's face.

Crusher moved in for a tighter shot while Norman strained to hold the extra lights trained on the group of men.

"Well, uh, no, ma'am. But, lady, you really shouldn't be—"

"And am I correct in assuming that—" Amanda screamed when Reilly's arms hooked around her waist from behind.

"What the hell do you think you're doing, woman!" he snarled in her ear, dragging her back. "You're not supposed to be out here. You've no more idea than a bedbug what's in those tank cars! Or if they're leaking! You could get us all blown to smithereens, you little idiot!"

"Rei-lly! Let me go," she hissed. Amanda strained forward and pried at his hands but she couldn't budge them. "Damn you, McCall, I said let go! This is none of your business!"

"The *hell* it isn't!"

"Crusher, help! Do something! Stop that laughing! This isn't funny! Traitor!"

Clutching his side with his free hand, Crusher bent over and laughed harder. Norman stared, bug-eyed.

Amanda tried to dig in her heels but Reilly just kept dragging her away like a sack of cement. She bucked and pitched and finally kicked back and landed a sharp blow on his shin. Yowling, Reilly grabbed his injured leg and hopped on one foot. Amanda broke free and darted back to the group of flabbergasted firemen.

"Now, gentlemen, in your opinion—"

She did not get a chance to finish the question. Reilly limped after her with blood in his eyes. At the same time, from the other direction, the fire marshal descended on her like the wrath of God.

"Lady! What the hell do you think you're doing?" the man in the official-looking uniform shouted. "You and your crew get back behind that barricade. Now!"

"Ah, just the man I wanted to see." Without missing a beat, Amanda swung around and stuck the microphone in the fire marshal's face. "Tell me, sir, do you know yet what you're dealing with here?"

The man turned apoplectic. His face darkened to purple and his eyes bulged. His head jutted forward and he jabbed a stiff finger—at the end of an equally stiff arm—toward the barricade area. "You've got ten seconds, lady. If you're not out of here by then, I'll have your butt thrown in jail."

"But, sir, if you'll just ans—"

"Out!"

"Bu—"

"You little idiot!"

Amanda let out a shriek as Reilly spun her around. The sound cut off in a loud "Ooof!" when he crouched and rammed her midsection with his shoulder and hefted her in a fireman's lift.

"She's leaving. Right now. Don't worry, I'll see to it," Reilly hurriedly assured the irate official, backing away. He shot Crusher and Norman a hard look and growled, "C'mon you two, move it."

Reilly headed back for the barricade as fast as he could move, gritting his teeth and hobbling slightly on his throbbing leg. Dangling head down over his shoulder, Amanda objected strenuously.

"Put me down, you cretin! You mindless oaf! I'll skin you alive for this, McCall!"

She pounded his back with her fists and tried to buck and kick, but he held her in place with a forearm across the backs of her knees and ignored her screeching.

At the KLUX mobile unit he dumped her on her feet. Amanda staggered back, gulped in a breath and took a swing at him. He dodged, and the roundhouse right spun her all the way around. Before she could gather herself for another punch, he grabbed her upper arms and pushed her back against the side of the van and held her there.

"Now, just calm down. If anyone here has a right to be mad, it's me. That was a damned fool stunt you pulled, and you know it!"

"That's not the point. You have no right to interfere!"

Her voice rose to a screech that startled even her, wild and raw with emotions. From the corner of her eye she saw the stares of those around them. Amanda knew she was behaving like a shrew and that made her even madder.

Breathing hard, she gasped and gulped and fought for calm, struggling to put a lid on her temper and pull her dignity back into place. She *hated* being bested. She *hated* looking foolish. Most of all, she *hated* losing control in front of her co-workers and colleagues.

She was the unflappable, sardonic, slightly irreverent, always-in-control Amanda Sutherland. The aura of cool savoir faire she projected had taken years to cultivate. Now, thanks to Reilly, she had shattered that image in mere minutes.

Damn the man. Why was it that somehow, without half trying, he always managed to get under her skin?

"If you had used a little common sense and discretion, I wouldn't have had to interfere, now would I?" Reilly fired back. "And if you think I'm just going to stand around and do nothing while you risk your life, think again."

She glared at him, still breathing hard. She noted his heaving chest and flared nostrils and fiery eyes, and for the first time it struck her that Reilly was no calmer than she. Knowing how easygoing he was and how much it took to jar him out of his habitual good mood, she felt somewhat mollified. Good. Served him right.

"And as for you two." Releasing her, Reilly rounded on her co-workers. "What the *hell* is wrong with you? I at least expected you to show some sense, Crusher. Hell, man, you ought to be the voice of reason and stop her when she gets one of these suicidal impulses, not just blindly follow her lead that way."

"Now, wait just a min—"

"You keep quiet," Reilly ordered, stabbing a blunt finger in Amanda's face. "I'm talking to Crusher."

She blinked. The harsh command, coming from Reilly, left her so taken aback she could only gape.

Plucking at a loose strap on the equipment bag, Norman shot Reilly a sullen look and mumbled, "You're an outsider. You don't understand how impor—"

"Don't give me that garbage."

Under Reilly's glacial stare, Norman's boldness crumbled, and he quickly turned his attention elsewhere.

"No, Norman, Reilly's right." Crusher rubbed a huge hand over his slick scalp, wincing with chagrin. "I'm sorry, man. I guess I'm just so used to following her into dicey situations after a story, I didn't stop and think how dangerous it was to get that close. It won't happen again, I give you my word, man."

The temper Amanda had just gotten under control shot skyward again. She opened her mouth to give both macho males a good tongue-lashing, but before she could utter a sound the fire marshal announced over a bullhorn that he was ready to talk to the press.

Amanda snapped her mouth shut, seething. The withering smile she gave Reilly promised retribution, and she had the satisfaction of seeing his eyes flicker with apprehension. As she pointedly sidestepped around him with her chin up, she contented herself with that . . . for the moment.

It was nearly three before they were done. Never able to stay angry or upset for long, no matter the provocation, Reilly was his usual affable self by the time they parted company with Crusher and Norman. On the drive back to Amanda's condo he teased her about her driving, sitting turned toward her with his arm on the back of her seat, playing with the ends of her hair and flirting outrageously.

Amanda merely smiled and remained quiet. She didn't even object when he saw her to her door. As she turned the key in the lock, he put his arms around her from behind and nuzzled her neck.

"At last," he whispered in her ear. "Now, then . . . where were we?"

Amanda opened the door and turned, holding him off with her palm braced on his chest. Batting her eyes provocatively, she smiled a mean little smile and said sweetly, "In your dreams, McCall."

Giving him a shove, she stepped back and slammed the door in his face.

Chapter Nine

Reilly lounged against the wall outside Amanda's apartment. He gave the appearance of a man without a care in the world, relaxed and sunny and full of lazy confidence. Inside, his gut was twisted in a knot.

Had he given her enough time to cool off? Maybe four days wasn't long enough.

Sighing, he leaned his head back against the wall and jingled the change in his pockets. He'd never been this uncertain of a woman before. It was damned uncomfortable.

Maybe he ought to leave and come back in a few days.

Down the hall, the elevator pinged, and he knew even before Amanda stepped off that it was too late.

This time she spotted him at once. She faltered briefly, clutching her mail in one hand, her purse strap with the other. Emotion flashed across her face and was quickly hidden, but that unguarded instant told Reilly all he wanted to know.

Recovered, she sauntered down the hall toward him with her unhurried, hip-swaying walk. He watched her with a lazy grin, excitement fizzing through his system. God, did she have any idea how wild she made him?

Her spectacular leggy figure alone was enough to drive a man around the bend. Add to that her aura of sultry sensuality, beauty and brains, and the woman was sheer hell on a man's self-control.

Amanda raised an eyebrow as she reached the door. "What, again? Do you have a fetish about loitering in hallways, McCall?"

Reilly shrugged. "Give me a key to the place and I won't have to."

Shooting him a dry look, Amanda unlocked the door. She stepped inside and turned back with a dangerous little smile. "In your dreams, McCall."

Reilly chuckled and caught the door before she could slam it in his face again. She scowled, but he wasn't fooled. The attempt had been halfhearted at best, and her sultry drawl had held not a shred of anger.

"What do you think you're doing? You can't force your way in here like that. Get out, before I call the police."

As Amanda retreated, Reilly closed the door and leaned back against it, crossing his arms over his chest. They both knew her huffy protests were nothing more than face-saving. Excitement sparkled in her eyes and a flush bloomed in her cheeks. The rapid pulse at the base of her throat exactly matched the thunderous beat of his own heart.

"Miss me, darlin'?"

Amanda arched one brow. "Have you been gone?"

He laughed, delighted. God, what a woman.

"Aw, Mandy, sugar, you sure are hard on a man's ego."

"Tough. And I've told you over and over, don't call me that." She raked him with a dismissive look and, with a toss of her head, walked into the living room. "Good night, McCall. Don't let the door bump your butt on the way out."

Grinning, Reilly strolled after her.

Pretending not to notice, Amanda went to the small desk in the corner, set her purse on the top and began sorting through her mail.

"C'mon, sugar. Don't be that way," Reilly cajoled. Coming up behind her, he cupped her shoulders and massaged. "I think Mandy suits you. It's kinda sassy and cute—like you." He nuzzled his face into the side of her neck and groaned. "Ah, sugar, you smell delicious. Um, you taste good, too," he murmured, nibbling his way down the slender column. "I've missed you like crazy, woman."

Amanda hunched her shoulder against his caress and snorted. "Oh, really? Is that why you didn't bother to call or come by for four days? Because you *missed* me so much?"

It was a slip, pure and simple. Reilly knew Amanda too well; normally she would cut off her tongue before making such a revealing comment.

The instant the words left her mouth she winced. "Never mind. Forget it. I really couldn't care less what you do. I don't even know why I said that."

"I wanted to call. The only reason I didn't was because I was afraid you'd hang up on me. And I couldn't come by because I've been in Dallas for the last four days."

Amanda craned her neck and looked over her shoulder. "Really?"

Surprise and hope flashed in her eyes. Beneath it swirled that touching vulnerability she worked so hard to conceal, and he felt a sharp tug on his heart.

"Yeah. I attended a home show for R & R Construction. They have 'em all over the country every year, and either Ryan or I try to make all the ones in this area. We usually set up a booth and hand out flyers, but mainly we go so we can get a line on new products and techniques, that sort of thing. I would have told you about it last Friday night but I didn't get a chance. You weren't exactly in the mood to listen when I left."

Actually, he hadn't had any intention of attending the home show. He hated those sorts of things and usually did everything in his power to avoid them, leaving that duty to his brother. The only reason he'd gone this time was to give Amanda a few days to cool off. Remembering Ryan's shock when he'd volunteered for the job, Reilly almost chuckled.

The relief that flooded through Amanda left her weak. She had not known it was possible to miss anyone the way she had missed Reilly these past four days. Though a part of her still simmered over his high-handed treatment, she had been hurt when he hadn't contacted her... and deep down, terribly afraid that this time she had run him off for good. Crusher's daily defense of Reilly had not made her feel any better about what she had done.

Perhaps it was foolish. Perhaps she was setting herself up for heartache, but that no longer seemed to matter. When she'd stepped off the elevator and saw him, joy had filled her, so intense and sweet it was almost painful.

Even now her body quivered with giddy pleasure, though she knew that nothing had changed.

Amanda tilted her chin and gave him what she hoped was a cool look. "As I recall, I had good reason to be angry."

"Well...about that...I'll admit I got a little carried away, but—"

"Carried away?" Amanda arched a brow. Stepping around him, she crossed the room and picked up a folded newspaper from the coffee table. "Have you seen this?"

"If that's a local paper, no. I told you, I've been in Dal—" He stopped and stared as she walked toward him with the newspaper held outward at arm's length. Under the headline, Reporter Dukes It Out With Local Builder, was a picture of Amanda taking a swing at him at the derailment site.

Reilly's mouth twitched. "Not bad. 'Course, your technique could stand some work. You can see that punch coming a mile."

"This isn't funny, Reilly. First that awful picture of us cuddled up on the dance floor, and now this. It just won't do. For people to take me seriously, I have to maintain a certain image of...of respectability and decorum, and being around you is shooting that all to hell. I'm a serious journalist, for Pete's sake."

Amanda glanced at the photograph and winced. What was it about Reilly that made her lose her temper? Until he came along, no one—herself included—had even known that she *had* a temper. With any other man, all it took was a few sweetly cutting words or a cool look, and she walked away leaving them properly chastised; when necessary, even bruised and bleeding.

"Aw, c'mon, sugar, lighten up. You're human first. Hell, even a respected journalist is entitled to a little romance." He glanced at the grainy newspaper photo again, and his lips twitched. "And to cut loose with a haymaker when someone ticks you off. Although, I gotta admit, I sure am glad you didn't connect with that punch. You would've knocked me into the middle of next week."

She had about as much chance of staying angry with Reilly as an ice cube in hell, Amanda realized with a fatalistic sigh. His twinkling gaze not only wilted her indignation, she quickly found herself battling down laughter. Lord, she had sounded so pompous!

"Well...all right...maybe so," she conceded with a sniff, and pressed her lips together to stop their twitching. "But I'm warning you, Reilly. I won't tolerate another scene like the one the other night."

"I know, I know. Look, sugar, I apologize. I went too far, and I really am sorry."

"My career is important to me. You know that. Touch-and-go situations like that are bound to crop up from time to time. I won't stand for any interference—not from you or anyone. I'm a damned good reporter. I do whatever I have to in order to cover a story. If you can't deal with that, say so now."

Reilly rubbed the back of his neck and grimaced. "Look, I'll be honest. The thought of you risking your life scares the living hell out of me. That's because I care about you, Amanda. I care one helluva lot."

For once, Reilly's expression was serious, and his voice held such heartfelt emotion that Amanda felt a queer tightening in her chest. She stared at him, touched and confused. She could not remember a time when her father had ever shown concern for her mother's safety or well-being.

"And because I do care, I'm going to worry," Reilly continued. "That's part of it. But..." He paused and looked away, gritting his teeth, then finally exhaling a long sigh. "Look...I'll do my best to respect your work and not interfere or complain, but I can't promise not to get upset now and then." He gave her a helpless look and shrugged. "I'm sorry. That's the best I can do."

No lies, no evasions, no promises he couldn't keep—he gave her honesty, even knowing the truth might cause her to reject him. Amanda was amazed...and deeply touched.

His offer, she supposed, was all she could reasonably ask. Amanda knew she was more aggressive and daring in her reporting style than most. It was difficult to watch someone you cared about put herself in jeopardy. Lord knew, Tess had been worrying about her for years. If Reilly truly had feelings for her, as he claimed, it had to be hard on him.

He stood just a few feet away, watching her, waiting for her verdict, braced as though he expected the worst, and Amanda's chest squeezed tighter.

She licked her lips. He looked so wonderful. So appealing. And, dear heaven, she had missed him so much. She wanted, very badly, to fling herself into his arms, but she couldn't quite bring herself to unbend that far. Her stupid pride and fears would not even allow her to accept his offer directly.

"I suppose if this, uh—" she wrinkled her nose and gestured self-consciously between them "—this . . . *thing* between us is going to work, it would be best if you didn't go out on assignment with me in the future."

Reilly got the message. Relief flashed in his eyes, followed at once by joy, then amusement. "Mmm. You're probably right. And, darlin', the word you're looking for is romance. Now come here, woman."

As though reading her thoughts, he stepped forward and pulled her into his embrace. Weak with relief, Amanda went willingly, melting against him. With a growl, he wrapped her in his arms, binding her to him with a blatant masculine possessiveness that should have put her back up. Instead it sent a thrill racing through her. With a sigh, she lifted her face for his kiss.

At the first touch of their lips, desire flared. Going up on tiptoes, Amanda clutched his broad shoulders and burrowed closer, greedily seeking more. Their mouths rocked together, open and wet. Hot and hungry. Their breaths mingled, tongues swirled and mated in an orgy of growing passion and need.

Making a guttural sound, Reilly broadened his stance and grasped her hips, bringing her hard against his arousal. Amanda whimpered and plunged her fingers into his hair, her nails lightly scoring his scalp. She squirmed within his embrace and tried to press closer still, unconsciously seeking to blend her body into his.

Reilly's hands roamed with quick, almost jerky movements that betrayed growing desperation. They clutched and kneaded and pressed, sliding over her back, her buttocks, her thighs, her waist. One hand worked between them. His roughened fingers roamed her abdomen, probed her navel, the points of her hipbones. Then, slowly, his hand slid upward, and he cupped her breast. Amanda moaned.

The sound sent a shudder rippling through Reilly. A groan rumbled from his throat, and he tore his mouth from hers. "No," he gasped. He shook his head as though to clear it, his chest heaving. "I can't...do this."

Amanda made a whimper of protest and would have pulled his head back for another kiss, but he grasped her wrists and pulled her arms from around his neck and set her away from him.

"Re-Reilly?" Still trembling, she swayed on her feet. She grabbed the back of a chair to steady herself and watched him back away, hurt and bewilderment slicing through her. She felt bereft and abandoned. "What's...what's wrong?"

"Nothing. Just...give me a minute," he panted.

"But...why did you stop? Don't you want—" She bit her lower lip, mortified.

"Jeez, sugar, of course I...want you. I want you so damned much I'm...almost out of my mind."

"Then, why—?"

"Dammit, sweetheart. Don't you understand? I nearly lost it just now. I can't...let that happen. I *won't* let that happen. Even...if it kills me. And heaven help me, it's beginning to look like it might."

He reached into his shirt pocket and pulled out a peppermint, but his hands were shaking so he couldn't unwrap it. After a couple of fumbling tries, he made a disgusted sound and put the candy back.

It took a minute for the reason behind Reilly's strange behavior to register, but when it did, Amanda's eyes widened. Why...he was trying to do the honorable thing!

He had promised not to seduce her, had given his word that when or if their relationship became an intimate one it would be strictly by her choice. On the surface, she had accepted the offer, but she had not really put much faith in it.

Amanda tipped her head to one side and stared at him, amazed.

Not for one minute would Kyle Sutherland be concerned about keeping his word, especially to a woman. Oh, she didn't doubt that her father would make any manner of promises if he thought they would get a woman into his bed, but he would have no scruples about keeping them. Reilly's integrity came as something of a shock.

A delightful one, Amanda realized.

She was seeing him in a whole new light. Whatever lingering doubts she'd had about allowing the attraction between them to run its course vanished. Reilly McCall might be a terrible flirt and he might lack ambition, but he was an honorable man, and in Amanda's experience, that made him a rare breed.

She watched him struggle for control, and a delicious feeling welled up inside and spilled over, filling her with warmth and bubbly elation. She felt lighter than air, as though a lead weight had been lifted from her shoulders.

Reilly stood with his hands braced on the back of the sofa, his head hanging between his stiffened arms. The flush of passion still darkened his face, and his chest and shoulders heaved with each long breath he dragged into his lungs. Even as she watched, a shudder shook his big frame, and she saw his fingers dig into the upholstery.

That he would deny himself, when she had so obviously been his for the taking, pleased her immensely. That she could arouse a man like Reilly to such a frenzied state filled her with a new and heady sense of power. Amanda suddenly felt delightfully, wickedly alluring.

"Reilly—" She took a step toward him, but he backed away, a look of panic on his face.

"No! Don't! Stay where you are."

She moved closer, a come-hither smile on her face. "But, why? And what're you doing way over there?"

"Oh, God, sugar, don't come any closer. Just give me a min—Amanda! What're you doing?"

Scrambling to escape her steady advance, he backed into a chair and nearly took a tumble. Before he could regain his balance, she reached him.

She moved in close and placed her palms on his chest. "Why do I have to stay away?" Pouting, she walked her fingers up over his chest. "I like it much better here."

"Oh, God, so do I." Reilly shuddered and grasped her wrists. "But, sweetheart, you don't understa—"

He sucked in his breath and halted, narrowing his eyes on her sultry expression. "Why, you little devil. You're doing this on purpose, aren't you?"

She answered with a slow smile.

Reilly made a sound somewhere between a chuckle and a groan. "Mandy, sweetheart... C'mon now, sugar. Fun's fun, but you gotta gimme a break here. I'm trying my darnedest to do the right thi— Hey! Stop that!" he said, jumping when one of her fingers sneaked between the buttons on his shirt and stroked his chest.

He hastily squeezed around the chair and backed away again. Smiling, Amanda continued her pursuit, her hips rolling in an exaggerated slink.

"Hey, I'm serious. You've gotta give me a minute here."

"Not a chance."

"C'mon, sugar, you're not playing fair."

"I know," she purred.

"Amanda! Behave yourself. Stop this. You don't kn— Hey! Now cut that out!" he yelped, slapping her hand away when she reached out and stroked his thigh with her fingertips.

He took another jerky step back. She licked her lips and glided forward.

"You may think this is funny, but you're playing with fire, sweetheart."

"Mmm. I certainly hope so."

"Amanda! I'm serious. It's not smart to torment a man when he's on the edge. You're about to unleash a tiger nei ther one of us can ride."

"Ooo-oouu. Better and better."

"Dammit, Ama—" The back of his calf struck the cof fee table. He quickly sidestepped it, but before he could maneuver around the sofa, she placed both hands on his chest and pushed.

Flapping his arms, Reilly staggered backward and fell flat on his back onto the sofa cushions with a loud "Ooof"! In a blink, Amanda sprawled on top of him.

She propped her forearms on his chest and looked at him from beneath heavy eyelids. "Now, see? Isn't this better?"

They were breast to chest, thigh to thigh, as close as two people could get without making love. She could feel the thunderous pounding of his heart against her breast and his hard manhood pressing into her belly. Slowly, deliberately, giving him a sultry smile, she rotated her hips and mur mured in a throaty voice, "Now, then . . . where were we?"

Reilly sucked in his breath. He grabbed her hips to stop their tormenting movement, his fingers digging deep into the firm flesh. "Ahh-hh, sweet heaven...don't... I can't... Ah God, darlin', you're killing me."

Amanda gave a wicked chuckle. "Why, Reilly, you must be out of practice if that's what you think I'm doing. Maybe this will make it clearer for you."

Framing his face with her hands, she looked deep into his eyes, puckered her lips . . . and blew.

Reilly frowned. "What are you doing?"

A seductive smile curved her mouth. "Don't you re member? You said if I decided I wanted to make love with you, all I had to do was whistle."

Giving him a sultry look, she leaned closer and pursed her lips again. Reilly's eyes widened as tiny puffs of breath struck his face and the wavery, off-key notes fluttered on the air.

He stared at her, not breathing. Lifting a trembling hand, he touched roughened fingertips to her cheek. His eyes blazed with tenderness and fire. And wonder.

"Mandy. Sugar, you're really serious, aren't you?" he murmured in a husky voice. "I thought . . . I thought you were just . . . well, you know . . . pulling my chain a little."

"Now, would I do that?"

"Oh, yeah," he drawled. "Drivin' a man nuts is second nature to you. But don't worry, I kinda like it."

"Oh, really?" Her eyebrows arched, and he laughed.

"Yeah, but I think I'm gonna like being seduced even better."

"Oh, honey, I can guarantee it," she replied in a sexy murmur.

Inching higher, she slid her body over his, watching him. Something hot and wild flashed in Reilly's eyes and his pupils expanded until the vivid blue irises almost disappeared. Amanda smiled.

Then, without warning, everything changed. All trace of amusement vanished. They stared at each other. Pulsing between them was the awareness that the step they were about to take would change their lives forever. Between them, there could be no casual affair, and they both knew it. Longing and fear swirled in Amanda's eyes; hope and passion and infinite patience in Reilly's.

The silence stretched out, thick and throbbing with tumultuous emotions. Hearts pounded, chests grew tight, eyes searched.

"Mandy." Reilly whispered her name with exquisite tenderness, and Amanda shivered.

Finally, with excruciating slowness, she lowered her head, and as her lashes fluttered shut she placed her parted lips against Reilly's.

It was like striking a spark to tinder.

At once the flames of passion erupted, engulfing them. What had started as a soft kiss of surrender and seduction flared into a white-hot conflagration. The longing and hunger that had been building in them for months—for years—broke free to feed a fire that threatened to burn out of control.

They were insatiable. Like greedy children, they pressed closer, bodies rubbing, hands groping and clutching, little moans and desperate sounds tearing from them. The kiss grew hotter, wider, wetter. Tongues swirled, lips rocked and rubbed, teeth scraped and nipped with rough, tender loving that drove them wild.

"Oh, God, Reilly," Amanda sobbed, tearing at the buttons on his shirt.

"I know, darlin'. I know."

With jerky movements Reilly snatched her blouse from the waistband of her skirt. He fumbled with the hidden hooks and eyes, but when they wouldn't cooperate, he snatched the garment off over her head and sent it sailing. Amanda whimpered, torn between assisting him with the fastening on her bra and exploring his body.

She sat astraddle his hips, her fingers buried in the cloud of black hair on his chest, exposed by the spread edges of his shirt. Reilly sucked in his breath when she found a tiny nipple. Watching him feverishly beneath the screen of her lashes, she scraped the nub with her fingernail.

Reilly jerked, and he arched his head back and bared his teeth. His hands grasped her hips and flexed. "Ah, darlin'. Darlin'," he gasped. "Yes. Oh, yes."

Her fingers danced over his collarbone, his shoulders, down through the thatch of hair to his navel. Her expression was rapt. Her breath came in short pants.

Reilly turned his attention back to the front clasp on her bra, his eyes on her breasts. The ivory globes swelled above the lavender lace cups, and through the delicate webbing he could see the rosy areolae. With a growl, he snatched the fastener open and the lush mounds spilled into his waiting hands.

"Oh, sweetheart," he whispered reverently, staring at the voluptuous flesh. Amanda made a soft sound, and he smiled. "Do you like for me to touch you, sweetheart?"

"Ye-yes."

"Like this?"

"Yes. Oh, yes!"

His fingers flexed, lifted, molded and squeezed, and all the while he watched her face. With delicate brushing strokes, he swept his thumbs over her nipples, bringing them to hard peaks. Amanda writhed and moaned, and Reilly smiled.

Raising up, he buried his face in the silken valley between her breasts. He pressed the soft mounds against his cheeks. Inhaling deeply the delicious womanly scent, he traced an erotic pattern on her skin with his tongue. "And this? Do you like this, darlin'?"

"Yes! Yes! Yes!"

Amanda cried out as his lips closed over her nipple and he took her yearning flesh deep into the warm wetness of his mouth. "Oh, Reilly! Oh. *Ohh-hh!*"

She buried her fingers in his hair, clutching him to her. A high, keening sound tore from her throat, and she arched her back as he drew on her with a slow suction and each rhythmic suckle created a corresponding tug at her womb.

He lavished the same attention on her other breast while his hand slid downward to release the button on her skirt and lower the zipper. When the waistband fell loose, his hand slipped beneath the skirt and slid over her abdomen. Amanda whimpered and began to work on the buttons on Reilly's jeans.

"Oh, God, sweetheart!" Gathering up handfuls of the full skirt, he worked it up until it bunched around her waist. He hooked his thumbs into the top of Amanda's panty hose and panties and shoved them down, but her position astraddle his body prevented them from going lower than her hips.

"Ah, hell!" With a frustrated growl, Reilly wrapped his arms around her and rolled with her to the floor.

They landed in the strip of space between the sofa and the coffee table, but neither noticed as Reilly scrambled to his knees and stripped away her panty hose and panties. Breathing hard, he paused a moment to look at her.

The purple skirt was in a twisted wad around her waist and the flimsy bra still hung from her shoulders, the lacy cups dangling on either side of her bare breasts. With her hair in wild disarray and her lips kiss-swollen, her eyes glittering feverishly, she looked wanton and sexy... and unbearably beautiful.

"Oh, sweet heaven." Reilly began to shake, and with frantic haste, he hooked the tops of his gaping jeans and navy jockey shorts and shoved them down as Amanda reached for him.

"Now, Reilly. Love me now," she sobbed, clutching at him. "Oh, please. Please. I can't wait any longer."

"I know, darlin'. I know," he gasped into her ear as he settled onto her softness. "Neither can I."

Amanda felt as if she were on fire. Her restless hands moved over his back and shoulders and her body writhed. She quaked with an urgent need she had never experienced before. There was a wildness in her, a yearning she couldn't control, and when she felt Reilly's arousal nudge the moist petals of her womanhood, her breath caught. She clutched his shoulders tighter, her nails digging into the broad muscles that spanned his back.

His big, work-worn hands slid beneath her hips to lift her into his possession, and she gave a strangled cry of pleasure as he entered her with one powerful thrust.

There was nothing tentative about their coming together. It was a wild mating of two perfectly suited, healthy, young lovers. This first time, neither wanted restraint or gentleness. Neither could have given it. Almost two years of dancing around each other, of thrust and parry, advance and retreat, had built their ardor to an explosive level that demanded power and strength and potency.

Reilly made love to Amanda fast and hard, and she reveled in it, lifting her hips to meet each thrust, matching his power and glorying in the voluptuous, tormenting bliss that was spiraling higher and higher. Nothing in her life had ever felt so perfect or right as their joining.

Reilly thrust deep and sure, sheathing himself in her as though he would make them one forever. The pleasure was so great it was almost pain. Passions built and soared out of control. Their movements grew faster, stronger, more urgent, and the knotting tension drew ever tighter. When it shattered it was exquisite.

"Reilly! *Reiii-leee!*"

"Yes! *Yes!*"

Their hoarse cries echoed through the room, their taut bodies straining together, shuddering with the powerful release.

When it was over they collapsed, utterly drained and replete.

Chapter Ten

Reilly finally stirred himself enough to shove aside the coffee table and roll onto his back. With a groan of satisfaction, he scooped her up with one brawny arm and tucked her against his side, snuggling her head on his shoulder.

Amanda was only remotely aware of the shift in position. Boneless and utterly sated, she drifted in mindless bliss, neither awake nor asleep.

How long she floated in that delicious state, she did not know, but gradually, awareness began to seep in. The faint twinges of uncertainty and self-consciousness, which were inevitable after making love for the first time, were just beginning to prick at her when she felt a vibration beneath her cheek.

Distracted, Amanda frowned, sure at first that she had imagined it. Then the tremor came again, this time accompanied by a deep rumble that was unmistakable.

Her eyes flew open. She didn't know exactly what reaction she expected from Reilly, but it certainly wasn't laughter!

Incensed, Amanda raised up on one elbow and sucked in a hissing breath when she saw his face. "You *rat!* Don't you *dare* laugh! You...you...ohh-hhh!"

Before he could stop her, she grabbed a hunk of flesh along his side and gave it a vicious twist.

"Ow! *Ow!* Hey! That hurts, woman!"

"Good! I hope it does! I hope it's excruciating!"

She doubled up her fist and aimed a blow at his stomach. Reilly was still shaking with laughter, but he managed to catch her arm before the punch connected.

"C'mon now, sugar, calm down," he sputtered coaxingly between chuckles, his eyes twinkling at her.

Amanda was in no mood to be cajoled or sweet-talked. "Let me go, you cretin! Pig! I'll teach you to laugh at me, you lop-eared jackass!" With an enraged snarl, she twisted and squirmed and kicked, until finally, in self-defense, Reilly rolled her onto her back and held her there by main force.

"Mandy, now knock it off!" he ordered in a half-growl, half-laugh when she tried in vain to knee him. "I wasn't laughing at you, darlin'. I was laughing at us. At the situation."

Amanda stilled and eyed him with suspicion. "And just what, exactly, is that supposed to mean?"

"Well, I don't know about you, darlin', but it's been one helluva long time since I got so carried away I made love with my clothes on. In case you hadn't noticed, my jeans are still around my ankles." Grinning, he slid his hand over her shoulder, slipped it beneath the lavender satin strap and lifted the empty bra cup. Pure devilment danced in his blue eyes as he dangled the lacy scrap from his forefinger.

Amanda turned tomato red. Reflexively, she tried to cover herself, but Reilly held her arms firmly at her sides. "Now, sugar, don't go gettin' all shy and skittish on me." Smiling tenderly, he dropped the softest of kisses on one corner of her mouth, on her chin, on the tip of her nose. Then he gave the same sweet attention to each breast. "I think you're gorgeous just the way you are," he murmured against the satiny skin.

Normally she would have had a cutting comeback to that, but all she could think about was the way they had fallen on each other as if they were starving. They couldn't even wait long enough to take off their clothes, for heaven's sake! Amanda was so mortified she wanted to jump into a hole and pull it in over her.

Not so, Reilly. When he was sure she wouldn't bolt and run, he released her and collapsed onto his back with a deep chuckle, one forearm slung over his eyes. "Hell's bells, woman, you make me as randy as a sixteen-year-old. I've still got my boots on, for Pete's sake. Believe me, I've *never* done that before... not even when I *was* sixteen and learning all about the birds and bees with Barbara Buford in the back seat of my '57 Chevy." Rolling his forearm up, he turned his head and waggled his eyebrows at Amanda. "Barbara was the local bad girl."

"I really don't care to hear about it," Amanda said with icy hauteur. Sitting up, she cast about for her blouse, her face stiff. When she couldn't locate it, she untwisted her skirt from around her waist and, as casually as possible, pulled the waistband up under her armpits.

"Back in Crockett, she was known as Back Seat Babs," Reilly added in a wicked whisper, his eyebrows jumping.

Amanda socked him then—hard—right in the chest. "Will you *shut up!*"

Whooping with laughter, Reilly wrapped his brawny arms around her and hauled her down. Amanda squealed but he didn't stop until she was sprawled full-length on top of him.

"Aw, sugar, I'm sorry. I know I shouldn't tease you. But you're just so darned cute when you drop that worldly from-

nd get all huffy and puffed up like a bantam hen that I just
an't resist."

"Reilly McCall, you—"

"Shh. Shh, little darlin'." Clasping her head between his
ig hands, he gazed deep into her eyes with a look so dev-
statingly loving Amanda caught her breath, and every-
hing inside her turned warm and mushy. She felt as though
he were melting, her body conforming to his like hot wax.

"Listen to me, sweetheart. I'll admit I've had my share of
omantic encounters, but I'm nowhere near the Romeo you
eem to think I am. Anyway, that's all in the past. There's
o reason for you to be jealous or upset. There hasn't been
lmost from the first."

"Reilly... what are you saying?"

"I'm saying that I haven't made love to another woman
ince we met."

Amanda stared at him, incredulous. "But... that's been
wo *years!*"

"Tell me about it," he drawled, his mouth twisting in a
vry version of his usual devilish grin.

Almost at once his expression became serious again, and
e gazed at her with such depth of feeling that Amanda
ould barely breathe. He held her face immobile, his fin-
ers sunk deep in her tumbled hair, the silken strands slid-
ng beneath his touch, catching on his callused skin.

"Aw, Mandy. Sweet Mandy. Don't you understand?" he
urmured, and Amanda's entire body tingled with antici-
ation and fear.

"Since we met, I haven't wanted anyone but you, dar-
in'. I never will."

Amanda's heart began to pump like a wild thing in her
hest. "You... you can't be serious."

"Oh, but I am, sweetheart." His hands tightened on her
ead. "I love you, Mandy."

"Reilly." His name whispered through her lips, in awe, in shock. She felt dizzy and disoriented, awash with panic and joy and myriad other emotions too numerous to name.

Reilly? Charming, irrepressible, never serious, devil-may-care Reilly... in love with her? No. Impossible.

Nevertheless, a keen yearning stabbed Amanda. For almost as long as she could remember, her life had been about hard work and responsibilities, about striving to get somewhere, about ambitions and goals and self-sacrifice. Love was something that had been conspicuously absent from her life, and it called to her like a siren's song.

Reilly was all wrong for her. They were all wrong for each other. And yet...and yet...he possessed a combination of strength and tenderness that tugged at her heart. Also, she was enormously attracted to him on a physical level. Amanda wanted—ached—to believe him, but, of course she didn't. She couldn't.

He truly believed he was in love with her, though, she realized. Amanda could see the absolute conviction in his eyes, and deep inside she felt a peculiar twist of longing and sorrow.

"Oh, Reilly—"

"Shh." He withdrew his right hand from her hair and placed four fingers over her lips. "You don't have to say anything. I know you weren't expecting to hear that. Hell I didn't intend to tell you yet myself. I just didn't want you to think that this was merely another casual encounter for me.

"I do love you, Amanda. If I know nothing else, I know that. But I don't expect a declaration from you yet...not if you're not sure. All I want is for you to give us a chance. Let whatever is going to happen, happen." He touched his thumb to the corner of her mouth and gave her a look of such entreaty that Amanda's eyes grew misty. "Please, darlin'."

"Oh, Reilly." She lowered her head and kissed him with all the aching tenderness that filled her being. Her lips rocked over his, soft and quivering with rampant emotions. When done, she laid her head on his shoulder and tucked her face against his neck, sighing. She felt him press a kiss to the top of her head, and she smiled.

"Can I take that to mean yes?"

"Mmm," she replied, her smile inching wider. Was there ever a woman born who could resist a plea like that? she wondered. If so, it would take a stronger woman than she. To be loved—or even almost loved—by a man like Reilly was too delicious a gift to pass up.

Amanda expected more tenderness and cuddling, but once again Reilly surprised her. In a quick move that caught her off guard, he rolled sideways and deposited her on the floor. Jackknifing to a sitting position, he shucked out of his shirt, then yanked off his boots, socks, and the jeans and jockey shorts hobbled around his ankles. When free, he sprang to his feet with a surprising litheness for a man his size.

"Wha—!" Amanda squealed and clutched at Reilly's bare shoulders as he scooped her up and strode naked toward the hallway with her in his arms.

"What do you think you're doing? Put me down," she demanded, but the laughter in her voice robbed the order of its heat.

Reilly grinned. "Not a chance. The next time we make love it's going to be somewhere comfortable. Like a bed. I'm gettin' too old to be rolling around on the floor."

"Oh, really?" Amanda laced her fingers together at the back of his neck and looked at him through half-closed eyes. "And just what makes you think there's going to be a next time?"

Still smiling, Reilly marched down the hall and into Amanda's bedroom with long, confident strides. At the queen-size bed, he tossed Amanda into the air, as though she weighed no more than a pillow.

She shrieked and bounced twice, but before her head stopped spinning, Reilly joined her on the mattress, his body coming down over hers and blanketing it.

Grabbing her wrists, he stretched her arms over her head and held them there with one hand. He used the other to cup her breast while his head swooped down and captured her mouth in a long, hot, thoroughly rapacious kiss that turned Amanda's brain to mush and set her body on fire.

When at last he let her up for air, his expression was so full of blatant male arrogance Amanda would have socked him if she hadn't felt so marvelous.

She lay perfectly still, her tawny hair spread out around her, and stared up at him, her body beginning to tingle again. Her breasts heaved, and her breath rasped through her kiss-swollen lips with every gasping pant.

Amanda's tongue peeked out, and Reilly's gaze dropped to watch the moist tip sweep over her lips. She felt his body quicken, and the throbbing at the apex of her thighs became more insistent. When he looked back into her eyes, his were smoldering.

He released her hands. "Now, then...what were you saying?" he drawled with audacious arrogance.

Breathing hard, Amanda waited for him to kiss her again and continue the seduction, but he merely watched her. Finally unable to stand it a second longer, she flung her arms around his neck and jerked him down to her. "Oh, just shut up, McCall, and kiss me."

Waking up in bed with a man was a novel experience for Amanda. When she opened her eyes and saw Reilly sprawled, magnificently naked, on his back beside her, she barely stifled the scream that sprang to her lips.

The momentary fright passed almost instantly as memory rushed in. Raising cautiously up on one elbow, Amanda propped her chin on her palm and studied him, a soft smile curving her lips.

He was so incredibly handsome. And he looked so adorable, lying there with his lips slightly parted and his features softened in slumber, his black hair tumbled every which way.

If Reilly had a son he would probably look like that, she realized—like a mischievous angel.

Amanda's heart filled with emotion at the thought of dark-haired children with Reilly's devilish grin and twinkling blue eyes. With a small sense of shock, she realized that he would make an excellent father. He adored his brother's children and was patience itself with them. Family was important to Reilly, growing up as he had in the large, close-knit McCall/Blaine clan.

Longing pulled at Amanda, so strong it was painful, but with a sigh, she turned her thoughts elsewhere. It was stupid to dwell on impossible dreams.

Her gaze ran over his whisker-stubbled jaw and chin and down the strong column of his neck, then traced over his broad shoulders and chest, his concave belly and narrow hips. Lord, he was such a beautifully made man. Long, well-shaped legs, narrow hips, broad shoulders and a magnificent chest that seemed to span half the bed. Even his narrow feet, with the little tufts of hair on the arches and toes, and his big work-scarred hands were beautiful to her. Physical labor had corded his large frame with muscle and sinew that not even the relaxation of sleep diminished. He was big and lean and hard, without an ounce of fat on him.

Amanda eyed the inverted triangle of hair on his chest and itched to run her fingers through it, to find the tiny nipples she knew were nestled there. She sighed and resisted the temptation. He was sleeping so peacefully she didn't have the heart to wake him. After the night they had just shared, he needed his rest.

A sensual look came over Amanda's face at the memory. They had been insatiable. And thoroughly wanton. They had made love over and over, in every way possible—fast and hard, slow and gentle, leisurely and urgent. And most of all, with joyous delight. They had indulged themselves to the fullest, making up for lost time, interrupting their loving only long enough to eat the pizza they had ordered, and even that had been consumed in bed between lingering kisses.

For all her femme fatale airs, Amanda had never thought of herself as a sensual woman, but Reilly had shown her otherwise. There was little in her past to which she could compare the experience. Her only other lover had been her fiancé, Brian Atwell, and in all honesty, those long-ago encounters had been less than thrilling. She'd never been able to figure out what all the fuss was about... until now.

Amanda stretched languorously, reveling in her body's slight soreness, her smile as smug as a cat who'd swallowed the cream. She did not need to be experienced to know that Reilly McCall was a wonderful lover. Every cell in her body still hummed with pleasure.

Whatever happened, no matter how long this relationship lasted or how it ended, Amanda knew she would never regret it. Reilly did not merely give her physical pleasure; he wrapped her in warmth and caring, made her feel cherished, and the experience was almost unbearably beautiful. Somehow, with his gentle persistence, Reilly had chipped away at her defenses and worked his way into her heart... *the dirty rat,* she thought, gazing at him with fond exasperation.

Amanda sighed. It was not an easy admission for her to make, but after the previous night, what else could she do? A serious relationship was not something she wanted. It was not part of her game plan right now. In the past, she had managed to avoid any such entanglement. Actually, it had been easy, since no man had interested her in the least ... until Reilly.

Her gaze wandered over him, and she slowly shook her head. Lord knew, she had tried her best to resist him. She had fought the good fight right to the bitter end, but this big, beguiling, thoroughly maddening charmer was an impossible man to resist.

It unnerved Amanda to have her carefully laid plans altered, but she knew it was too late to do anything about it. After last night, she could not possibly give Reilly up. Not yet, anyway.

Amanda was too wide awake to even contemplate going back to sleep, and she knew if she didn't get up she would succumb to the temptation to wake Reilly. Moving cautiously, she eased over to the side of the bed, sat up and slipped her legs over the side. The soles of her feet had barely touched the carpet when an arm hooked around her waist and hauled her back.

Amanda uttered a soft cry, then slumped back against Reilly's hairy chest.

"Going somewhere?" he murmured in her ear. Nuzzling aside her hair, he nipped at the side of her neck.

Amanda made a small sound of pleasure and tipped her head to give him better access. She was so distracted she almost forgot to answer. "I, uh, I was just going to, uh, take a shower."

"Mmm. Good idea." He nipped her earlobe, then traced the delicate swirls with the tip of his tongue. Amanda shivered. "Why don't we take one together?"

"Together?" Her voice came out in a croak as excitement zinged through her like a hot arrow. She looked back over her shoulder at him, her eyes wide. She had never taken a shower with a man in her life.

Reilly grinned. "Uh-huh," he replied, and she wondered weakly how on earth he managed to imbue the simple utterance with such blatant sexuality. "You can scrub my back and I'll scrub yours,'' he drawled wickedly. He curved his big hand around her jaw and turned her face more fully toward him. "But first . . ."

The touch of his lips on hers was so exquisitely gentle, Amanda's breath shuddered out on a long sigh. She leaned into him, weak with longing, trembling with desire. Against her back she felt the tickle of his chest hair and the slow thud of his heart.

His mouth savored hers with a slow, rocking motion, barely touching, his lips soft and seducing, his tongue a darting whisper. The sweet caress drove Amanda wild, and she shivered, her body heating up.

The ring of the telephone on the bedside table made them both jump and spring apart like guilty children.

"What the hell? What kind of jerk calls at this hour? Ah, hell, sugar, don't answer it."

"I have to. It might be the station."

Groaning, Reilly flopped back on the bed.

"Hello?"

"Slut. Filthy whore," came the chilling whisper. "You're going to get what you deserve, you harlot. Soon—"

Amanda slammed the receiver down and jerked her hand back as though it had been burned. Staring at the instrument, she crossed her arms over her midriff and hugged herself tightly, absently rubbing her elbows.

Reilly became instantly alert. "What's wrong? Who was that?"

"Nobody," Amanda replied too quickly. "It was nothing."

"Don't give me that. I saw your reaction. You turned white. Even now you're as pale as a sheet." Swinging his legs to the floor, he sat up beside her on the edge of the bed and put his arms around her. "Hell's bells, sugar, you're shaking."

"I'm fine. Really."

"No, you're not fine. You're upset and scared." He tipped her face up and forced her to look at him. "It was that nut, wasn't it? That guy who's stalking you?"

"No, of course n—" Amanda had started shaking her head before he even finished speaking, but the look in Reilly's eyes stopped her. She sighed heavily. "Oh, all right. Yes, it was him. But no matter what you say, I'm still not calling the police," she added in a rush.

"Don't worry. I've accepted that."

"You have?" Amanda studied him with unabashed shock. She had braced for a fight; his capitulation, though obviously grudging, was the last thing she expected.

"Yeah. I know when I'm beating a dead horse. So, what did the creep say?"

"Why do you want to know?" Her voice reeked with suspicion and Reilly sighed.

"Because I love you, Amanda, and I worry about you," he said so simply her heart did a little skip.

Other than Tess, no one had ever worried about her before. Instantly, Amanda felt like the most ungrateful witch in the world and was flooded with remorse.

"And just because I agreed to play it your way doesn't mean I'm not going to do my darnedest to keep you safe from that psycho." He touched her hair and smiled tenderly. "Don't you see? Last night changed everything. You're not alone anymore, darlin'. Whatever happens, we'll see this thing through together."

Something shifted and cracked open in Amanda's chest. Self-reliance and independence had been forced on her at an early age, until it had now become ingrained. She had never known how comforting it felt to have help shouldering a problem, how wonderful it was to know that your happiness and well-being were important to someone else. That *she* was that important to someone else.

She gazed at him in awe. "Oh, Reilly." Her throat grew tight and her eyes filled with tears. Her chest swelled with sweetly painful emotions.

Misunderstanding, Reilly became anxious. "Dammit, what did that bastard say to you?"

"Just the usual," she sniffed, giving him a wavery smile. "He called me vile names and raved that I'd get what I deserved. That's when I hung up."

"Have you had any other communications from him that I don't know about?"

"Only one. I received another letter a few days before he called the first time. I was going to show it to you, but then we had that fight and... well..."

"Yeah, I get the picture. Is the letter here?"

"Yes. I put it with the others."

"Good. Let me see it."

Only when Amanda started to rise did she remember that she was naked. Horrified, she realized that they had carried on the entire conversation without either of them having so much as a stitch on.

She blushed scarlet and snatched up her robe from the floor, where Reilly had tossed it the night before after they had gorged themselves on pizza. Slipping into the blue satin garment, doing her best to ignore his wicked grin, she quickly tied the belt and hurried across the room to retrieve the letter from the bureau drawer.

"Actually, I've been encouraged lately," she said, pacing back and forth beside the bed as Reilly scanned the single sheet of paper. "He's contacting me much less frequently now. At first I was getting a letter every few days, but in the last month there's only been that one letter and the call this morning. So you see, it's just like I said it would be. He's obviously growing bored with his sick game."

"Mmm. Maybe."

"I know I'm right. Why, give him a month or two and he will have forgotten all about me," she asserted airily.

"Yeah, well . . . until we know that for certain we're not letting our guard down."

"What does that mean?"

Tossing the letter aside, Reilly snagged one of Amanda's hands and hauled her down onto his lap.

"It means, my mule-headed, independent, adorable love, that I'm going to stick to you like pollen on a bee."

Amanda had been fearful the call and the letter would create another rift between her and Reilly, but looking into his twinkling eyes she could feel her taut muscles relax as the tension drained out of her. Emboldened by the flood of relief she felt, she twined her arms around his neck and gave him a sultry look. "Mmm. Now that sounds like fun." She winnowed her fingers through the hair at his nape, lightly raking his scalp with her fingernails. "Kinda kinky, too."

"Mmm, that, too. But for starters, I've decided to teach you how to play."

"Play?" Amanda's eyebrows arched.

"Yeah. I've noticed that you're always so busy working you never take time to smell the roses and have a good time. So I've decided to show you how," he said with a magnanimous grin.

"Oh, really?"

"Yep." Taking her with him, he flopped back onto the bed and rolled, quickly reversing their positions. He propped himself above her on his elbows and cast an appreciative glance over her hair, spread out around her head in wild disarray, before turning his attention back to her face.

The merriment in his eyes gradually changed to something dark and daring, and Amanda felt excitement lick at her. "In fact," he drawled, running his fingers down the wide satin lapel of her robe. A slow, lascivious smile tugged at his mouth when his hand found the belt. As his clever fingers worked at the knot, the look in his eyes grew hotter and his voice dropped to a low pitch that sent goose bumps feathering over Amanda's skin. "I see no reason why we can't get started right now."

Chapter Eleven

Amanda had not believed Reilly was serious about teaching her to play, but she soon learned otherwise. If there was one thing Reilly McCall took seriously, it was having fun.

At first she resisted—partly on general principles, but mainly because she truly did not know how to just let go and enjoy herself, just for the sheer fun of it.

She had spent too many years setting goals and working hard to achieve them. Whether it was making the honor roll in high school, getting a part-time job to help out her mother, earning a scholarship to college, or climbing to the top in her profession, she had zeroed in on each target to the exclusion of all else.

At present, what little social life she had, other than her friendship with Tess, was centered around business. One never knew what dinner or an evening at the theater or a ball game with a sponsor or a network rep might lead to someday.

As Amanda had already learned, trying to resist Reilly was an exercise in futility. He listened patiently to all her complaints and excuses, then brushed them aside and hustled her out to play.

All that weekend, and every chance they got after that, they spent enjoying themselves. Amanda had not had any idea there were so many ways to have fun, but under Reilly's expert tutelage she was soon in the swing of it.

Actually, it had not been difficult to win her over. That first day, he had taken her to play handball, and within minutes of stepping onto the court her competitive nature had kicked in. She had not won, of course, but she had come darn close, giving Reilly a run for his money. After that, she was game for anything.

In the weeks that followed, Reilly took Amanda sailing and waterskiing on the various lakes around Houston, and fishing in the Gulf of Mexico. They went bowling, they played tennis and golf and racquetball. With Crusher and his daughters, they indulged in spirited games of basketball, softball, volleyball and touch football.

Reilly bemoaned Amanda's competitive streak and despaired of ever curing her of it. He tried—telling her over and over that it was just a game, that the object was to simply enjoy whatever they were doing, but she continued to go at everything as if she were fighting fire. As a result, their outings were always vigorous, and at times ended in hilarious disaster—usually for Reilly.

When they went roller-blading on the sea wall at Galveston it turned into a race, and he ended up crashing into a balloon vendor's stand when Amanda elbowed past him. Not only were his cries of "foul" met with hoots of laughter from her—to add insult, he had to pay for twenty-five balloons that, at last sighting, were riding the air currents high over Galveston Bay.

One Sunday afternoon they went to the zoo and had a picnic in Hermann Park. Afterward, Reilly demonstrated to

Amanda the fine art of Frisbee throwing. He had intended for them to spend a leisurely hour or so tossing the disc back and forth, but, as usual, Amanda got carried away and began to throw with such gusto that Reilly had to hustle to keep up. Ultimately, she sent the Frisbee sailing so hard and so far, he had to pour on the steam to catch it, and back-pedaled into the duck pond.

Interspersed with the outdoor fun were other, less hazardous activities—evenings of dining and dancing, movies, plays at the Alley Theater, visits to comedy clubs. They went to museums and art galleries and toured the NASA Space Center, the battleship U.S.S. *Texas* and the San Jacinto Battleground, where Texas's independence from Mexico had been won more than a hundred and fifty years ago.

Working around her hectic schedule, they saw each other as frequently as they could manage. Eventually, Amanda relented and gave Reilly a key to her apartment, and often, utterly exhausted, she would return home late at night to a hot meal and a back rub, the latter of which never failed to lead to other sensuous pleasures. Amanda felt deliciously pampered and well loved, and she hugged the feeling to her throughout the day, no matter where she was or what she was doing.

It was the most thrilling and exhilarating period of her life. Reilly was a wonderful lover and a delightful companion. He was funny and affectionate, and so handsome and sexy it made her weak in the knees. He persisted in calling her sugar and darlin', but even that he did with such genuine charm and sincerity that Amanda was hard pressed to object, though of course her feminist soul demanded that she do so.

Daily, her attachment to Reilly grew stronger. She could not seem to get enough of him. The more she was with him, the more she wanted to be with him. When they were apart she daydreamed about him like a love-struck teenager, and by the time she saw him again she was giddy with anticipation.

There was a bounce in Amanda's step and a sparkle in her eyes that had not been there before. She was happier than she had ever been, a state of affairs that did not escape her friends and fellow workers. The staff at Channel 5 teased her constantly and unmercifully, but Amanda did not care. She was too deliriously happy.

Not even her best friend's frequent interrogations bothered her...at least, not *too* much. Amanda and Tess had been friends so long, Tess had no qualms about asking personal, often blunt, questions.

"You're sleeping with him, aren't you?" she demanded one Saturday afternoon as she and Amanda sat on the patio of Tess's home.

Amanda's lips twitched, but she said nothing. She kept her eyes on Reilly and Ryan, who, with Mike's help, were setting up a croquet game on the back lawn.

"Don't bother denying it. It's written all over you."

"Did I say anything?"

"Then it's true! Ohh-hh, I knew it!" Tess squealed. "I told Ryan I thought you two were lovers, but he didn't believe it." She sat forward in her chair, her wholesome face full of delight and animation. "So it's serious, then?"

"What makes you say that?"

"Oh, please. I know you, Amanda. You wouldn't be sleeping with the man if it wasn't. So tell me...have you discussed marriage yet?"

"Certainly not! Tess, for heaven's sake! Reilly and I are...are..."

"What? Just good friends?" Tess demanded, arching her eyebrows.

"Well...yes. Yes, we are," Amanda insisted.

She shifted on the chair. It made her uneasy to define her relationship with Reilly in concrete terms. She knew that she was getting in deeper and deeper emotionally, but she could not quite bring herself to call it love. Determined to live for only the present, she refused to examine her feelings or think about whether she and Reilly would have a future together. The whole idea was just too scary.

"Hey! We're all set," Ryan called to them. "You two ready for a game?"

"You bet."

Jumping at the chance to escape, Amanda bounded to her feet and headed toward where the three McCall males stood waiting. She had barely gone two yards when behind her she heard Tess mutter dryly, "Just good friends, huh? Right. And pigs fly."

Within minutes of starting, Amanda was totally caught up in the game, Tess's unsettling observations forgotten. She played with her usual fierce determination and drive, approaching each wicket as though it were the eighteenth hole in a championship round of a PGA tournament.

Halfway through the game, when Ryan explained to Amanda that if you struck an opponent's ball with your own, you were allowed to drive that player's ball out of the field of play, her eyes lit up with an unholy light. That drew a groan from Reilly.

"Oh, no. Now you've gone and done it, Hoss. I wasn't going to tell her that. She's already revved up to win. Now she'll go into her killer mode."

The others laughed, but it wasn't long before Amanda proved him right. First she deliberately whacked Tess's ball, sending it halfway across the yard from the wicket her friend had been about to shoot. Next, Mike suffered the same fate. At that point the only player between Amanda and the last two wickets was Ryan. When she took aim at his ball, he gave her a hard look. It had not the least effect on Amanda; she was playing to win.

"Serves you right for telling her, Hoss," Reilly taunted, and when the two wooden balls clacked together he whooped with laughter.

Seconds later, Amanda's mallet cracked again, this time with stunning force, and Reilly's laughter died as his brother's black-striped ball became an airborne missile. In stupefied silence, five pairs of eyes watched the wooden ball shoot through the air and embed itself in the door of Reilly's precious truck.

"I really am sorry, Reilly," Amanda said plaintively for at least the twentieth time as she and Reilly entered her condo a half hour later.

"Yeah, I know, sugar."

"I didn't expect that wooden ball to go flying like that. And I certainly didn't mean for it to hit your truck."

"Look, let's just forget it. Okay?"

"I didn't even know I could hit that hard."

"Neither did I."

He heaved a woebegone sigh and flopped down on the sofa. The woman didn't know her own strength. It had taken him and Ryan ten minutes to pry the damn thing out of the truck door.

"I'll pay to have your door fixed. I promise. A good body shop can have it looking just like new in no time."

"Look, darlin', I said forget it. Hell, what would be the point? The old heap was already battered every way from Sunday. I mean, so what if I've had that old truck ever since I was in high school? So what if it's a '54 Ford with a 460, V-8 engine and it'll go from zero to sixty in seven seconds flat... and it's a collector's dream?" He forced a smile and spread his hands wide. "Hey. So now it has one hell of an interesting crater in the door. It'll be a conversation piece."

"You *are* angry. I can tell from your tone. Oh, Reilly," she wailed, just as the telephone shrilled.

Wringing her hands, Amanda gave him one last distraught look before rounding the sofa and snatching up the receiver.

"Hello? Oh, hi."

Satisfied the caller wasn't the guy who was harassing Amanda, Reilly slumped on his spine and morosely contemplated the toes of his boots. Dammit, the little nicks and dings his truck had accumulated over the years had given it character, but a smooth, perfectly round fist-sized depression was like a gaping wound. And a just-like-new door on a forty-year-old vehicle would be just as bad.

"What? Of course we will! Just hold on. We'll be there in ten minutes. Fifteen, tops."

Something in Amanda's tone captured Reilly's attention. He twisted around to look at her. "Be where? What's going on?"

"That was Crusher. He was calling from the hospital. Josie's having the baby, and he'd like a little moral support. Poor thing—he's a nervous wreck."

Reilly shot off the sofa, his gloomy mood instantly forgotten. "Well, what're we waiting for? Let's go."

"I'll drive my car. We'll get there faster that way," Amanda said, rushing out the door.

Following her, Reilly paused long enough to roll his eyes and groan.

After a hair-raising ride that Reilly was certain had taken at least ten years off his life, they arrived at the hospital to find Crusher pacing the floor of the waiting room. He looked awful. His face was haggard, sweat beaded his bald head and there was a wild look of panic in his eyes.

"Thank the Lord, you're here," he babbled, latching onto Amanda's hands the instant she and Reilly walked through the door. "I've been going crazy."

"Hell, man, after five kids, I'd think you'd be used to this by now," Reilly teased.

"It's taking too long. Something's wrong, I know it."

"Oh, Crusher, no." Amanda gave his hands a squeeze. "You mustn't even think that. I'm sure everything is fine."

"But it never took this long with any of the others."

"Take it easy, man. That doesn't mean anything. They say every kid is different. Try to calm down, buddy." Reilly cuffed the big man's shoulder and grinned. "Maybe you'll get that boy you wanted."

"I don't care if it is another girl. Dammit, I don't care if it's girl triplets, just as long as Josie's okay," Crusher declared fervently. "That woman is everything to me."

Putting his arm around Crusher's shoulder, Reilly grimaced in sympathy. "Yeah. I know what you mean, my friend."

Amanda gave him a sharp look, a funny feeling in her chest.

For the next half hour, Amanda and Reilly did what they could to distract Crusher. Reilly even regaled him with the story of how Tess had given birth to Molly in the back of his brother's Jeep Cherokee during a hurricane, and how Ryan had delivered the baby while Reilly had driven.

It did not help. Crusher merely gave him an appalled look and kept pacing. Reilly didn't really blame him; the episode had scared the living hell out of him at the time.

Crusher was so huge and so obviously distraught, the two other expectant fathers in the waiting room gave him a wide berth, keeping to the opposite end of the room and now and then shooting wary glances his way. Reilly doubted the big man even knew they were there.

By the time the nurse finally appeared in the doorway Crusher was on the verge of tearing the hospital apart with his bare hands.

"Mr. Williams?"

He whirled around and stormed toward her with such a fierce look the woman paled and took a step back. "I'm Williams. How's my wife? Is she all right?"

"Your wife is fine, Mr. Williams. They're taking her to her room now. You may see her in a few minutes."

Crusher sagged with relief and covered his face with both hands. "Praise the Lord."

Responding to his concern for his wife, the nurse's stern expression softened. "You have a son, Mr. Williams. A big, strapping, nine-pound, seven-ounce boy."

Crusher blinked and reeled back a step. "A . . . a boy?"

"Hey, man, that's great!"

"Oh, Crusher, I'm so happy for you and Josie."

Amanda and Reilly crowded around him, giving hugs and thumps on the back and offering congratulations, but Crusher was so dazed he did not seem to notice.

"A boy," he murmured to no one in particular. "I've got a son."

It was almost ten by the time Amanda and Reilly returned to her condo. On the ride home each had been lost in thought. The pensive silence stayed with them throughout the elevator ride to Amanda's floor and all the way into her living room.

Finally, seated side by side on the sofa, Reilly glanced at her with a wry half smile. "Cute baby, huh?"

"Yes. Yes, he is."

"Crusher's about to pop his buttons, he's so proud."

"Mmm. Josie, too, I imagine."

They fell silent again.

Reilly drummed his fingers on his thighs and stared across the room at nothing. He had a funny feeling in his gut and his heart was beating with a slow thud.

They both knew that something had happened to them back at the hospital. Something profound. When the nurse had held Crusher's son up to the nursery room window, Reilly had felt such awe and longing he had barely been able to breathe.

He glanced at Amanda's pensive profile. He was sure she had felt something, too. He just didn't know whether her reaction was the same as his.

Suddenly, quite desperately, he needed to know.

"Amanda..." he began in a cautious voice, keeping his gaze fixed straight ahead. "Have you ever thought about kids? I mean... you know... having any?"

He felt her tense. She didn't answer for a few seconds, and he held his breath. "Of course," she said finally, in a carefully neutral tone. "Every woman has thought about that at one time or another."

He turned sideways on the sofa and put his arm along the back. "And what did you decide?"

"To put the subject on hold. I'm not exactly in a position to start a family right now."

"And if you were?"

"Reilly..."

"I love kids." Picking up a strand of her hair, he rubbed it between his fingers. "I'd like to have three or four."

"Reilly... please—"

"I'd like to have them with you," he whispered.

She closed her eyes and caught her lower lip between her teeth. Then she trembled. "Please...don't." She turned her head and looked at him, and there were tears in her eyes. "You're not being fair. We were both touched by what happened tonight...all that emotion." She shook her head, pleading with her eyes. "Don't do this to me, Reilly. Not now. Please, I can't... I'm not in any shape... I just can't deal with it. Not yet."

She looked so vulnerable, so confused, it made his heart clench. He knew that she wanted the same things he did; he could see it in her eyes. Tonight, when they had viewed Crusher's infant son, he could feel the raw hunger in her. It was the same hunger and wistfulness he sensed whenever she was around Tess and Ryan and their kids.

Aw, sweetheart, for once forget all your careful plans and take a chance. Trust your instincts, darlin', and reach out for what you really want. C'mon, baby. Just this once.

Even as the words went through his mind, he knew his silent urgings were wasted. He could see that she was terri-

fied of what she was feeling, and he simply did not have the
heart to push her any more than he had.

He sighed. "Okay, I'll drop it...for now. Just tell me you
haven't ruled out the possibility for the future."

Leaning in close, she touched his cheek. Her teary eyes
swam with emotion and a smile quivered on her lips. "I
haven't," she whispered. "I promise."

Reilly put his hand over hers and brought it to his lips. He
pressed a kiss to her palm, then touched the spot with the tip
of his tongue. Amanda sucked in her breath and her pupils
expanded, and he felt a surge of fire in his loins. "Come
here, woman," he groaned. He wrapped his arms around
her and pulled her across his lap.

He kissed her hungrily, his body trembling with the intense emotions stirring within him. Amanda returned the
kiss with a longing just as strong, just as tightly drawn. The
only sounds in the room were the rasp of labored breathing
and the soft moans of want and love.

Reilly pulled his mouth from hers and looked down at
her. He felt almost savage. "I want you," he growled.
"Now."

"Yes," Amanda whispered. "Oh, yes. Yes."

He lunged off the sofa with her in his arms and strode for
the bedroom, and Amanda looped her arms around his
neck.

"Oh, my darling," she whispered with aching tenderness, and laid her cheek against his shoulder.

"How do you feel about biking?" Reilly asked over
breakfast the next morning.

Amanda paused in the act of buttering a piece of toast
and cocked one eyebrow at him. "That depends. Are you
talking Harley-Davidson or Schwinn?"

"Oh, definitely Schwinn," he said with a chuckle, casting an admiring glance at the way her satin robe gaped when
she reached for the coffeepot. "You don't seriously think I'd

trust you with a Hog, do you? You'd be out challenging a Hell's Angels gang to a drag race within an hour.

"And while I'm on that subject, I'm not talking about a race or an endurance test. I just thought we'd take a leisurely ride around the neighborhood, maybe pedal a little way out into the country."

Amanda studied Reilly over the rim of her cup. She was continually amazed at how attuned to her he was, how well he understood her and read her every mood.

Last night she had made more of a commitment to him than she had ever made to any man...and it terrified her. Though she'd thought she was hiding it, Reilly had obviously sensed her anxiety. The casual suggestion that they go for a bike ride was his way of returning things to normal, of subtly letting her know that he would not push.

Amanda's heart swelled with love. She could no longer deny the emotion. How could she not love him? And, despite her fears, she had meant what she told him. All her logical, sensible plans for picking a husband were no longer viable. If she married any man, it would be Reilly. Only Reilly.

"It sounds like fun, but I don't have a bike."

"No problem. I have my own and we'll borrow Mike's ten-speed for you. Now that he's sixteen it's 'uncool' to ride anything with pedals. He's working on Ryan for a car."

"I know. He's dropping some heavy hints on Tess, too." She took a sip of coffee and shrugged. "If Mike doesn't mind lending me his bike, I'm game."

"Good." He stood, then leaned down and planted a kiss on her mouth before heading for the door. "I'll go round up the bikes and be back by the time you get dressed."

"This is great. I'm so glad you thought of it," Amanda said as they pedaled down a little-traveled back road. There were only a couple of houses along the road. Most of the land on either side was either woods or cattle pastures.

"Yeah. I thought we'd better take advantage of this weather while it lasted. Before long it'll be hotter than blue blazes."

Spring had hung on for longer than usual along the Texas gulf coast, and Reilly and Amanda were not the only ones out enjoying the balmy weather. They had passed several other bikers and a few people out for a walk. Some were even picking blackberries in the ditches and along the fences.

"Smell that air." Amanda held her face up to the wind and inhaled deeply. "Is that honeysuckle?"

"Yeah, I think so. It—" Reilly heard a car coming up behind them and glanced over his shoulder. "Hell's bells, that guy's driving fast." His eyes widened as the gray sedan bore down on them. "Holy—! Watch out! He's gonna hit us!"

Desperately, Reilly cut his wheel to the right and rammed into Amanda. She screamed, and as they went careening into the weed-choked ditch the sedan clipped the back wheel on Reilly's bike and sent him sailing.

"Reiiil-leeee!"

Amanda landed on her back with the bicycle on top of her. Sobbing and gasping, she fought like a demon to untangle herself from the machine and get to Reilly. By the time she succeeded and scrambled through the waist-high weeds to him, he was on his knees, hunched over, cradling his left hand close to his body.

"Are you all right? Oh, Reilly. Darling." She dropped down beside him and ran her hands over his shoulders and back and arms. "Are you hurt? Oh, God, darling, speak to me. Say something!"

Gritting his teeth, Reilly looked up, and Amanda moaned. A grimace contorted his face, which was white except for the numerous bleeding scratches inflicted by the berry vines. "It's my...hand," he gasped. "I...think something's...broken."

"Oh, no. Oh, my poor darling."

"Are you hurt, young fella?" An elderly couple who had been walking along the road came hurrying over, their wrinkled faces pink with exertion and excitement. "We saw the whole thing. Why, it looked like that dang fool took aim right at you. It was a lucky thing you weren't both killed."

"He's hurt," Amanda cried. "His hand is broken."

"Oh, dear me," the old woman fluttered.

"Not surprised. Here, let me help you outta there, son," her husband said, climbing down into the ditch with them.

Between Amanda and the old man, they managed to assist Reilly up the slight embankment and seat him on the grass verge. Reilly's face looked like bloody parchment, and he was obviously dazed. Amanda's stomach flip-flopped when she saw the way his thumb stuck out from his hand at an odd angle.

"I've got to get him to a hospital. Do you live around here?"

"Sorry, dearie. We live more'n a mile from here in that direction. We were out for our daily constitutional."

Wringing her hands, Amanda looked up and down the road but there was not a car in sight.

"I can ri-ride," Reilly mumbled.

"Not on that bike, you won't," the old man said sagely. "That back wheel, she's busted all to hell and gone."

"Mine's okay, I think. Look, can you stay with him while I ride home and get a car?"

"Sure, little lady. You just go on, we'll watch out for your young man."

"You...you stay. I'll ride back." Uttering the slurred statement, Reilly tried to struggle to his feet, but he was hampered by dizziness and the need to protect his injured hand.

"You'll do no such thing. In fact, I think you should lie down."

"I'm okay," he argued, but Amanda ignored him and put her hands on his shoulders and pushed him down onto his back. When she had him prone she worked her hand into his jeans' pocket.

"Mandy, wha—?"

"I changed my mind. I'm going to go get your truck," she said, pulling out his keys. "That way I can haul your bike, too."

"Mandy, wait—" Reilly began, but she had already snatched her bike from the ditch and was pedaling away for all she was worth.

Amanda paced back and forth in front of the admitting desk in the emergency room waiting area, twisting her hands together. Alternately, she checked the clock on the wall and glanced through the windows in the double doors to the curtained treatment cubicles on the other side.

"How much longer do you think it will be?"

The nurse behind the desk sighed and gave her a censorious look over the top of her glasses. "I told you before, Miss Sutherland—I don't know. The doctor is with Mr. McCall now. You'll just have to be patient."

At first the woman had been flustered and excited when she recognized Amanda, but over the past hour she had gotten over being star-struck.

Amanda gave her a sour look and clenched her jaw. Patient, my eye. She'd *been* patient. Well . . . sort of. What the devil were they doing in there?

Shoving her hands into her shorts' pockets, she continued pacing. The poor darling. Reilly had been in such pain during the drive to the hospital. Although . . . she wasn't sure how much of that had been caused by his injury and how much had been due to the way she'd careened his precious truck through the city traffic. The man was downright foolish about that battered old pile of junk. It did run like a top, though, she had to admit.

The woman behind the desk got up and went to the ladies' room. Amanda stopped pacing and watched her. Then her gaze switched to the wide double doors. She made up her mind in a second and pushed through the swinging doors into the treatment area.

Several people, some in white uniforms and others in green surgical gear, were rushing around, but no one paid any attention to her. She heard Reilly's voice and made a beeline for the cubicle she had seen them take him into earlier. As she reached for the curtain she heard a muffled murmur, followed by Reilly's deep chuckle. Twitching aside the curtain, Amanda slipped into the cubicle—and froze.

Reilly, his left arm in a sling, sat on the side of the treatment table with his legs dangling over the side. Standing between his knees, her arms draped over his shoulders, was Brandy Alexander. They were smiling into each other's eyes with such affection and familiarity Amanda felt as though she'd received a blow to the chest.

At her entrance they both looked around.

"Oh, hi, Amanda."

Reilly grinned. "Hi, darlin'. You remember Brandy, don't you?"

Neither showed a trace of guilt, which incensed Amanda, though the woman at least had the decency to step away from Reilly. To think she'd been out there worrying herself sick for the past hour, and all the while he'd been in here playing doctor with Miss Big Boobs.

Amanda barely spared Reilly a look before turning a tight smile on the gorgeous brunette. "Of course." Slipping her hands into the pockets of her shorts, she sauntered closer with what she personally considered to be remarkable aplomb, given the fact that what she wanted to do was scratch the woman's eyes out. She also had a strong urge to break Reilly's other thumb for him. "Hello, Dr. Alexander. What a surprise to find you here. I didn't realize you still worked emergency once you became a specialist."

"Oh, she doesn't. But when I found out that Brandy was in the hospital I asked for her." Reilly slipped his injured hand out of the sling to display the cast, which encased his thumb and palm and extended halfway up his forearm. He flashed the brunette one of his teasing grins. "I wanted the best."

"Obviously."

Brandy shot Amanda a curious look, then her mouth twitched. Discreetly, she took another step back and put her hands in the pockets of her white coat. "It was a simple fracture any intern could have set, but I was glad to be of help. After all, that's what friends are for."

"Oh, I'm sure. Especially *good* friends."

For the first time since she entered the cubicle, Reilly became aware that all was not quite right. "Mandy? Uh, is something wrong, sugar?"

"Wrong? Why, what could possibly be wrong?" she said in a tone that proclaimed exactly the opposite. She skewered him with a frosty glance before turning to the woman.

"How is he, doctor?"

"Oh, he'll be fine. Other than the thumb, his only other injuries are a few scratches and bruises. I've given him some pain pills and I recommend rest for a few days. And please, Amanda, won't you call me Brandy? I'd like for us to be friends."

Amanda gave her a level look. "I don't think so."

She turned to Reilly, "If you're ready to go, I'll take you home." Without waiting for a reply, she turned on one heel and marched out.

"Mandy! Amanda, wait!" Reilly called, but she kept right on going. She pushed through the double doors, crossed the emergency room lobby and was almost to the exit before he caught up with her.

"Amanda. Amanda, sugar, what's wrong?" Amanda stared straight ahead, her jaw set. "Aw, c'mon, darlin', don't be this way. What's wrong? What'd I do?"

"Oh, don't play innocent with me, McCall. I'm not in the mood."

"I'm not playing anything. What is it I'm supposed to be guilty of? And what happened to all that TLC and sympathy you were giving me on the way to the hospital?"

"You want sympathy? Then I suggest you go back inside. I'm sure your friend Brandy would be only too happy to oblige you."

"Why...you're jealous."

"I certainly am not."

He grabbed Amanda's arm and pulled her to a stop. His eyes widened as he inspected her stiff face. "You are. You're jealous."

"Will you stop saying that," she ground out through her teeth. "I am *not* jealous. I'm angry. Now let me go."

She snatched her arm from his grasp, marched the few remaining yards to the truck, jerked the door open and climbed behind the wheel. Reilly quickly followed, climbing in on the passenger side just as she gunned the motor and slammed the gearshift into reverse.

"Mandy, sweetheart, listen to me. Brandy and I really are just good friends. That's all. There is absolutely nothing going on between us. I swear it."

"Oh, please, I'm not stupid. I saw the way you two were looking at each other. The way you were touching. The body language was pretty obvious."

"I tell you that didn't mean anything. Brandy and I go way back. We're pals, that's all. I swear it."

"Oh, yeah, right. Pals." Amanda made a rude sound. "Are you saying you've never been intimate with that woman?"

"Well, uh, not exactly, but—"

She sucked in her breath and shot him an accusing look. "So you *are* lovers!"

"Ye— No! *Were!* We were lovers once. But that was over years ago. We realized quickly that there was no fire—"

"I don't want to hear about it," Amanda snapped. She turned a corner with a squeal of tires and slammed Reilly against the passenger door.

"Amanda, that was ten years ago," he insisted when he'd righted himself.

"I *said* I don't want to hear it."

"But, Mandy..."

All the way to Amanda's building, Reilly pleaded, cajoled and argued, but she flatly refused to listen. Instead of using the parking garage, she parked in front of her building. As soon as she turned off the engine, she pulled out the keys and tossed them in his lap.

"I'll call Tess. She and Ryan can come over and pick you up and drive you and your truck home."

She slammed out of the truck without giving him a chance to reply, but Reilly stormed after her.

"Go away."

"No. Not until you listen to reason."

"I'll call security."

"You mean that old geezer who snoozes in the lobby? Go ahead."

If looks could kill, he would have crumpled on the spot. "Go away, Reilly. I don't want you here."

"That's tough, sugar, 'cause I'm staying."

The argument continued in the elevator and was still going when they stepped into the hallway on Amanda's floor.

"You're wasting your time. I'm not going to let you in."

"You have to."

"I most certainly do not."

"C'mon, darlin', I have to take a pain pill. That stuff they gave me at the hospital is wearing off."

She pressed her lips together and shot him an exasperated look. "Oh, all right. But then you have to lea—"

They both pulled up short, just a few feet from Amanda's apartment, and stared.

"Oh, my Lord."

"Hell's bells."

Her front door stood ajar, the lock broken, the frame around it splintered.

Chapter Twelve

The fine hair on the nape of Amanda's neck stood up and did the Lambada.

Someone had broken into her home. She stared at the door, unable to take her eyes off the large, dirty footprint just to the left of the knob. A shiver rippled through her.

Reilly grabbed Amanda's arm and pulled her behind him, placing himself between her and the apartment.

"Mandy, do you know any of your neighbors?" he asked in a hushed voice, his gaze fixed on the open doorway.

"One or two. Why?"

"I want you to go stay with one of them until I get back."

"Where are you going?"

"To check out your apartment. That guy might still be in there. He's probably your stalker. If I'm not back in ten minutes, or if you hear anything, call the police."

Amanda leapt forward as though she had been goosed with a cattle prod. "Oh, no, you don't. I'm not letting you out of my sight." She scooted up as close to Reilly's back as she could get, grabbed doubled handfuls of his shirt and hung on tight.

"Amanda, do as I say—"

"Forget it, McCall. Where you go, I go."

He glared at her over his shoulder, but Amanda was too terrified to notice...or care. He couldn't have pried her loose with a crowbar. Reilly cursed and muttered something under his breath.

"All right, dammit. But you do what I tell you, when I tell you. If I say run, you'd darn well better light a shuck outta there. In the meantime, you stick close, you hear?"

Stick close? *Stick close?* Amanda glared at the back of his neck. What a dumb thing to say. Did he think she was going to go wandering off by herself, for Pete's sake? She was practically plastered to his back as it was. If she could, she would climb right inside him.

Reilly edged to the doorway. Holding tight to his shirt, Amanda moved with him step for step, as though her legs were glued to the backs of his. She peered over his shoulder, her eyes huge, her heart galloping.

Reilly eased around the splintered door frame into the tiny entryway. There was no sound from inside the apartment, so he moved cautiously toward the living room. A few feet inside, he halted. "Ho-ly hell."

Amanda sucked in her breath. "Dear Lord," she whispered. Her heart clubbed against her rib cage, and she unconsciously gripped Reilly's shirt tighter.

Her apartment looked like a war zone. Every piece of furniture was overturned. Seat cushions, pillows and curtains were slashed. Shelves were swept bare. Ripped and torn books, smashed pictures, broken lamps and small decorative items littered the floor. Spray-painted on the walls in huge letters were obscenities...and the words I'll Get You Soon, Bitch.

Amanda made an unconscious whimpering sound, and Reilly reached behind him and squeezed her arm. "Take it easy, darlin'. Don't let it get to you," he whispered.

She pressed her lips together and tried, but as they crept through the rest of the apartment it became harder and harder.

A thorough search turned up no intruder, but that was the only positive outcome. None of the other rooms had fared any better than the living room.

In Amanda's bedroom, the mattress, bedspread and curtains had been slashed, and the contents of her closet and all the dresser drawers had been dumped onto the floor. Nightgowns, bras, panties, slips, teddies, garter belts, and stockings were scattered everywhere. Amanda could not be sure, but some of her intimate apparel appeared to be missing. The thought of a stranger, especially that deranged monster, touching her things made her sick to her stomach.

Amanda began to shake. In her job as a reporter she had witnessed gang shoot-outs, gone along on police drug busts, and covered riots. She had even reported from the front lines in a Mideast border war, but nothing had ever frightened her like this. This was personal... and evil.

Cramming her knotted fist against her mouth, she buried her face in Reilly's back. "Oh, God. Oh God. Oh, God."

"Take it easy, sugar. C'mon, now." Reilly pulled her into his arms and held her close. Rubbing his chin against the top of her head, he rocked her tenderly and cooed soft words of reassurance, but the shattered mirror above the dresser revealed the fierce look on his face, so at odds with his gentle tone.

If he could get his hands on the creep who had done this to her he would break every bone in his body. How he hated to see his strong, brave Amanda brought to such a state. Racking tremors shook her body and she sobbed and clung to him like a terrified child.

She moaned and tried to pull away, but Reilly would not release her.

"Oh, please, let me go. Oh. Oh! I'm going to be sick!"

"Ah, hell." Reilly swooped her up in his arms and almost ran with her into the bathroom. She tried to wave him away, but he ignored her and held her head over the commode while she retched and shuddered. When she was done, he tenderly wiped her face with a cool cloth.

He carried her back into the bedroom and sat her down on the edge of the slashed mattress. She wrapped her arms around herself and huddled into a ball, still shivering. Gritting his teeth, Reilly bundled her in a ruined blanket, then quickly set to work.

"Wh-what are you do-doing?" Amanda asked through chattering teeth.

He sorted hurriedly through the clothes scattered over the floor, stopping now and then to stuff items into the suitcase he had located among the jumbled mess. "Packing some things for you. I'm getting you out of here."

The very fact that she didn't argue or even ask where he was taking her told him just how badly shaken she was. When he had finished packing what he thought she would need, and led her down to the truck, she went without a word of protest. Not until he pulled his truck into Tess and Ryan's driveway did she rouse herself enough to question him.

"What are we doing here? I don't want Tess to know about this. I don't want her upset."

"Too late. She and Ryan already know. I told them weeks ago." Amanda started to object, but he reached over and touched her cheek. His voice and expression were tender but firm. "You can get mad at me if you want, but I'm not sorry I told them. Stop trying to protect Tess, darlin'. She's a lot stronger than you think. Besides, she's your friend, she has a right to know."

"I guess you're right." She slumped listlessly against the seat, but her gaze sharpened when it happened to fall on the cast on his left hand. "Oh, my word, I'd forgotten that you're hurt. And you're taking pain medication. Reilly, you shouldn't be driving."

"I managed fine. And I didn't take another pill. Don't worry," he added when she looked concerned. "If I'm in pain, I'm too damned angry to feel it." *And too worried,* he added silently to himself.

Tess and Ryan were appalled when they learned what had happened. Reilly's twin was almost as angry as he was.

"Amanda, I thought it was stupid not to notify the authorities when this thing first started," Ryan stated bluntly. "Now you must see that you have to. Enough is enough. This guy is out of control."

"Ryan is right." Tess gave her friend's hand a squeeze. "You can't just ignore him anymore. The man is obviously unbalanced. There's no telling what he'll do. Let us call the police."

"No! I..." Amanda shuddered. "No. I don't want that."

"Dammit! Can't you see we have to?" Reilly exploded. He had half expected her to refuse, but still it infuriated him.

Jutting her jaw, she gave him a frightened but stubborn look. He exhaled a long breath and pulled both hands down over his face. "All right. All right. If you won't call the police, I'm calling in a friend of mine named Dan Burrows. He's a private detective."

"Reilly—" Amanda began, but he stopped her with a raised hand and a hard look.

"That's it. I've had it. It's the police or my friend Dan. Those are your only two choices."

"Dearest, please. Do as Reilly wants," Tess urged.

Amanda searched his implacable face. There was not a trace of the happy-go-lucky man she knew so well. The amused twinkle in his eyes had turned to a steely glint and his handsome features held only fierce determination.

"Oh, all right. As long as he understands that not one word of this is to leak out."

Reilly placed the call at once, before she could change her mind, and Dan Burrows agreed to come right over. While they were waiting for the detective, Ryan and Mike went to Amanda's and repaired her door and installed a new dead bolt, though Amanda could not imagine that there was anything left in the apartment that anyone would want to steal.

Amanda was surprised when she met Dan Burrows. The ex-police officer was a soft-spoken, serious man who looked nothing like the private detectives on television. He had thinning brown hair, intelligent hazel eyes and nice, evenly spaced but unremarkable features. He was the kind of man most people would pass on the street without seeing. However, he had a way of listening, of asking penetrating questions, and especially of looking a person straight in the eye, that inspired confidence and trust.

He listened intently while Amanda, then Reilly, told their story. Scribbling copious notes, he interrupted now and then to ask questions, but otherwise his expression remained impassive.

"Ms. Sutherland, could this man who is harassing you possibly be someone you know?"

"No. That is...I don't know. I never considered that. It's possible, I guess."

"Do you have any enemies?"

"No. Well...there is Harry Kowalski, my boss. He doesn't believe in equality for women. He especially hates the idea of women reporters."

"Do you think he could be behind this?"

Amanda glanced at Reilly, a wide-eyed, slightly stunned look on her face. "It's possible, I suppose. He's been trying to get rid of me for years. He'd try anything, if he thought it would work."

"How about the others where you work? Any problems there?"

"Not really. Oh, there's the usual competitiveness among reporters—over stories and job opportunities. Perhaps a bit of jealousy. The usual office politics. That sort of thing."

"Mmm." Dan Burrows scribbled something down on his notepad. "And how about the other women at the station? Do you get along with them?"

Amanda thought about the venomous look on Ellen Keyes's face when she had returned the note the woman had put in Reilly's pocket. "Well..."

By the time he finished questioning Amanda about her fellow workers, she realized that the only people at Channel 5 whom she could trust with absolute certainty were Crusher and Bob Donaldson, the station manager. It was an unsettling revelation.

"After the accident this afternoon, when you returned to get Reilly's truck, did you go into your apartment?"

"No. I just got into the truck and drove back as fast as I could."

"So the intruder could have been in the apartment then."

"Oh, dear Lord." Amanda turned pale and shivered.

"Mr. and Mrs. Sweeny, the old couple who witnessed the incident, got part of the license number on that gray sedan," Reilly interjected. "It was Texas plates, EJX4 something. I think if you find that driver, you'll have found the stalker."

"What? Reilly, what are you saying?"

"That was no accident, Mandy. That guy took dead aim at us. He was trying to run us down."

"But...but you never said... I—I thought it was just another of our overzealous accidents. Oh, Reilly," she wailed. "You could have been killed because of me."

"Hey. Don't blame yourself, darlin'. This guy's a nut. Anyway, I think by now he's after me as much as you."

"Oh, no. What are we going to do?"

"My suggestion to you both is to get out of town, or at the very least, hole up somewhere safe for a week or so while I investigate."

"I agree with Dan," Ryan said. "Get out of town and let him handle it."

"Take off from work with no notice? I couldn't possibly. What excuse could I give? And I'm sure not going to tell Harry about this. Even if he's not responsible, at the very least he'd want to make it the lead story on the six o'clock news. That old war-horse would betray his own mother for a hot story. And besides, the whole idea smacks of running away. No top-notch journalist can afford to be labeled a coward."

"For the love of—! For once, will you forget about your career? It's not going to do you a whole helluva lot of good if you're lying in a morgue."

Amanda turned pale, and Reilly grimaced. "Look, I'm sorry, sweetheart. I don't mean to upset you, but this is serious business. I don't like running away, either, but until we know who this guy is, the smartest thing to do is to get out of reach."

"I suppose," Amanda relented grudgingly.

In the end, she called Bob Donaldson at home. The station manager was shocked and concerned when he heard what was going on. He personally okayed her leave time and promised to come up with a convincing reason to cover her absence. Other than himself, no one at the station would know the truth.

After that, things moved so fast Amanda was dazed. Dan gave strict instructions to everyone. Reservations were made. Tess and Amanda exchanged a tearful goodbye. Then Ryan and Mike drove the pickup to Reilly's townhouse and stashed it in his garage while Dan drove Amanda and Reilly to the airport. Within an hour of talking to the station manager, Amanda and Reilly were on a plane heading west.

"Why, pray tell, are we going to Denver?" Amanda asked as the jet leveled off and headed into the sun. "There are places closer to home to hide out, you know, like Dallas or Austin or San Antonio."

"We're not going to Denver," Reilly replied with a hint of his usual teasing good humor. "We just change planes there."

"I see. Well, would you mind telling me where we *are* going? I understand the need to keep our whereabouts hush-hush, but don't you think that I, at least, have a right to know?"

Reilly and Ryan had huddled together and decided on the best place for them to go. Amanda had been too upset and distracted to even ask their destination until now. Other than his twin and Dan Burrows, no one knew where they would be for the next week.

"We're going to the Durango, Colorado, area. My family used to own a cabin in Vail, but a few years back Erin and Elise had a horrendous experience there, and because of the bad memories we stopped using it. So last year we sold the place and bought a house about ten miles north of Durango, halfway to Purgatory Ski Resort. Being far out in the valley, the place has a nice, country feel to it and great scenery, but there are a few neighbors around, so we won't be completely isolated. It's a beautiful spot. You'll love it."

Amanda did. The small cluster of homes nestled in the Animas Valley had a spectacular view of mountains and the Hermosa Cliffs all around. The Blaine/McCall house sat on the shore of a small lake and, like most of the others, was built of cedar and glass. Amanda fell in love with it on sight.

A lavender twilight was beginning to settle over the valley when they drove their rented car into the driveway. Though it was early summer, when the sun went down in the mountains, so did the temperature, and the minute they stepped inside Reilly turned on the heat.

"It'll be cozy warm in just a few minutes," he said. He glanced around the spacious room, his gaze sweeping with pride over the vaulted redwood ceiling and massive beams and the river-rock fireplace. "Well? What do you think?"

"It's lovely, Reilly." The living room, dining room and kitchen ran along the back of the house where the outer wall was almost all glass, giving a panoramic view of the lake and the mountains beyond. The decor was cozy and warm, done in shades of navy, beige and rust, with comfortable furniture and little personal touches that reflected the combined taste of Maggie McCall and her sister, Dorothy Blaine. "Are you sure your folks won't mind if we stay here?"

"Nah. Not a bit. Any of us can use the place whenever we want. Ryan checked with Mom earlier, and she said no one had plans to use it for the next few weeks. She assumed that he and Tess wanted to come up, and he let her think so."

A wan look flickered over Amanda's face at the reminder of why they were there, and the need for secrecy. Her gaze swept the lovely room but her vision became blurry as the fear and emotions she had been holding at bay for hours came welling up and tears flooded her eyes.

"Oh, Reilly." She turned and flung herself against his chest.

"Hush, baby. Hush," he crooned. "It's going to be all right. I promise you. I won't let anything happen to you."

"It's so unfair," she wailed.

"I know. I know. But you just wait, Dan will find our man for us. He's good, darlin'. He's real good. And when he does, it'll be all over."

She sniffed against Reilly's chest and held him tight, needing his strength. He was so good to her, so loving and so caring, so absolutely solid and dependable—all the things she had tried to convince herself he wasn't. Somehow, without her quite knowing it, Reilly had become the most important person in her world, more important, even, than Tess.

He was, she realized with a small sense of shock, the bedrock of her life, the one to whom she could always turn, the one who offered love and tenderness and strength, the one in whose arms she knew she would always find a haven. She also knew, deep down in the very core of her soul, that she could always trust him.

"C'mon, sugar." Reilly grasped her shoulders and turned her, and with his good arm around her waist, he led her into a large bedroom. "All in all, it's been one helluva day. Between all that's happened and a touch of jet lag, I'm bushed. Whaddaya say we put off the grand tour of the place until tomorrow and just take a nice long soak in the whirlpool and have an early night."

"Oh, Reilly, I forgot about your hand again," she cried. "You were supposed to rest, and here you've been traipsing all over the country protecting me."

"Hey, I'm fine. I hardly feel a thing. But if it'll make you happy, I'll take a pain pill while you fill the tub. There's nothing like a whirlpool to take the kinks out and relax you. It'll help get your mind off of things for a while."

Amanda doubted that anything could do that, but she hurried to do as he suggested. She even flung a handful of the bath salts she found in a pretty glass jar on the counter into the five-foot-square tub.

Ten minutes later, sitting between Reilly's outstretched legs in the churning water, with bubbles billowing up to her chin, Amanda had to admit that he was right. Leaning back against his chest, her head on his shoulder, she felt boneless and utterly content, her mind floating free—much too relaxed to worry about anything. Houston and her problems seemed a million light-years away.

She smiled when, beneath the water, Reilly's right hand slid up over her rib cage and cupped her breast. His other hand, encased in the heavy cast, lay on the rim of the tub.

As his callused fingers stroked and flexed around her he nipped at her earlobe.

"Mandy?"

"Mmm?"

"I'll scrub your back if you'll scrub mine."

Arching her neck, she sent him a heavy-lidded look over her shoulder. "All right."

"Of course, you'll have to lather the washcloth for me, since I have a bum hand."

"I think I can manage that."

Though she hated to give up her present position, Amanda got to her knees and turned around. Without taking her eyes from him, she slowly worked up a lather on a thick washcloth.

Like an Eastern potentate, Reilly lay back against the side of the tub, his arms outstretched on either side; his eyes glittered wickedly, watching her watching him. The look on his face was so blatantly sensual she felt her nipples tighten in response. Reilly exuded a raw maleness that tugged at everything feminine and womanly in her.

"You'll have to stand up." Her voice came out so husky she barely recognized it as her own.

Without taking his eyes from her, he heaved to his feet, sending water sluicing down his magnificent body. Gaining her feet, as well, Amanda took a deep breath and began. With languorous strokes she lathered his chest and abdomen, then his neck and both arms before moving around him and washing his back and firm buttocks.

"Raise your foot," she instructed in a raspy whisper when she moved back to his front.

Obediently, Reilly braced first one foot, then the other, against the edge of the tub. When his feet and calves were done, she worked her way up his thighs with tantalizing slowness.

"Saving the best for last?" Reilly teased when the soapy cloth reached the top of his thighs and stroked that tender juncture where his legs met his body.

Saying nothing, Amanda dropped the cloth. It hit the water with a splat, and all trace of humor fled from his face, replaced by taut anticipation as he watched her work up a lather between her hands. When her cupped palms were mounded with thick bubbles, she smiled—a soft, knowing smile as old as Eve—and Reilly made a low sound in his throat as her hands closed around him.

Shuddering, his jaw clenched, he allowed the delicious torment for as long as he could, but finally he grabbed her wrists. "Enough," he said in a gritty voice. "Now it's my turn."

In silence, Amanda soaped the washcloth and handed it to him, and his blue eyes glittered hotly. With excruciating care, he returned the favor, caressing her with the soft terry cloth, stroking the creamy lather over each dip and curve of her body. By the time he had finished, Amanda was trembling.

"Make some more lather for me, darlin'," he commanded in a seductive whisper as the cloth splashed into the water churning around their calves.

As though in a trance, she did as he asked, and when he scooped the mound of lather from her palm she bit her lower lip and watched him with feverish anticipation. When Reilly's cupped palm slid between her legs she moaned and closed her eyes. Swaying, she gripped his waist to steady herself.

His stroking fingers drove her wild and filled her with a voluptuous pleasure so intense it was almost beyond bearing. Amanda's knees were on the point of buckling when at last he growled, "Time to rinse off," and drew her back down into the swirling bath.

The water came halfway up Reilly's chest and barely covered Amanda's nipples. Repeatedly, he dipped up water in his cupped palm and poured it over her shoulders, watching the lather slither down her slick skin like warm wet fingers.

Amanda was on fire, shaking with need, but he took his time.

"Now," he announced with husky satisfaction. "Come here, darlin'." He lay back against the tub, and the sudsy lather coating his chest hair floated away in the agitated current that flowed around him. A hint of his teasing smile played around his lips as he caught her hand and tugged her forward, letting the water support her weight, until she was stretched out atop his body.

They lay still, their gazes locked. Steam rose from the gurgling water and their tortured breaths rasped in unison. His nostrils were flared, his face dark and rigid with passion. Amanda knew her own face mirrored the same primitive desire. Reilly slipped his right arm beneath her bottom and lifted her, sliding her inch by inch up his slick body until she was poised over his swollen manhood. Still watching her, he removed his supporting arm. Amanda threw her head back and bit her lip, and something wild leaped in his eyes as she sank down upon him with an abandoned cry of joy.

"Oh, Reilly. Reilly, my love," she sobbed against his shoulder.

"Yes. Yes. You feel so good, darlin'. So tight. Ah-hh, love."

The water buoyed their undulating bodies, and the pulsing jets incited them to a pagan rhythm that quickly drove them over the edge. Soon their exultant cries echoed through the small room.

Then there was only the sounds of bubbling water and sighs and slow, stertorous breathing.

A short while later, Reilly stirred. "I think we'd better get out, sugar. We're getting pruny."

"Mmm." Amanda felt so wonderful she didn't care if she ever moved, but she allowed him to coax her from the tub with only a minimum of grumbles.

They dried off quickly, and in minutes they lay snuggled together in the king-size bed, naked and sated, and utterly content. Absently Reilly smoothed his hand up and down Amanda's arm. She sighed and rubbed her cheek against his shoulder.

"Mandy."

"Mmm?"

"I may be a fool for bringing this up now...but... well...about Brandy. Sugar, I swear to you, we really are just friends. I don't want you to worry or have any doubts about that. There's nothing going on between us."

Amanda rubbed her cheek against his chest again and smiled. She knew that. Deep down, she had known it all along, even when she had been nearly blind with jealousy. She supposed she had gotten angry because she had been so worried and had felt so frustrated and helpless, and it had hurt that another woman—especially his gorgeous ex-girlfriend—had given him the care that she could not.

Still, Amanda could not resist teasing him just a little. "How can you say that? Not three months ago she was your date at Tess and Ryan's housewarming."

"Only because Tess told me you were bringing a date. I didn't want to stand around looking like a lovesick jerk. Brandy knew how I felt about you, and she agreed to help me out." Amanda felt his chest heave with a big sigh. "Ah, hell, I might as well confess all of it. That passionate kiss you saw between Brandy and Eric down by the lake? It was a setup."

"You mean—"

"There was no way I was going to lose that bet, because Brandy and I cooked up the plan. When she saw us coming she grabbed Eric in a clinch and he reacted just the way we knew he would."

"Why, Reilly McCall, you rat! You ought to be ashamed of yourself," she huffed, and gave a tuft of his chest hair a sharp pull.

"Ow! That hurt."

"Serves you right!"

Amanda was grateful for the darkness that hid her smile. Her sharp tone was pure sham; she could not have been more delighted. It was a dirty rotten trick, of course, and Reilly deserved to squirm before she let him off the hook, but she had to admit, she was delighted with the outcome. She and Dr. Alexander just might become friends, after all.

"Mandy?"

Amanda let several seconds tick by before answering stiffly. "What?"

"Are you angry?"

"I should be."

"Does that mean you're not?" he asked hopefully.

She exhaled an exaggerated sigh. "No. I guess not. I love you too much to be angry."

His hand stilled on her arm, and Amanda's smile deepened. The mattress abruptly shifted and the bedside lamp clicked on. Reilly loomed over her, his expression intense, hopeful. "Do you mean that?"

"Yes."

"Say it again. I want to see your face when you say it."

"I love you."

"Again."

Giving up all pretense of anger, Amanda laughed, a soft throaty sound redolent with satisfaction and happiness. She gazed tenderly into his eyes and laced her fingers together at the back of his neck. "I love you, Reilly McCall," she whispered. "With all my heart."

"Ah, darlin'." Reilly exhaled a long sigh and rested his forehead against hers. "It seems like I've been waiting forever to hear you say that."

Then he kissed her, slowly, sweetly, and there was no more need for words.

During the next week Reilly did his best to keep Amanda occupied. They went horseback riding and hiking. They went white-water rafting down the Animas River. One whole day was spent at Mesa Verde, poking through the museum and exploring the Indian ruins—the pit houses and cliff dwellings of the Anasazi, "the ancient ones," who had lived in the area from the time of Christ to the thirteenth century.

They spent another day at Purgatory on the summer bobsled run. Like a couple of children, countless times they rode the ski lift up the mountain to the top of the run, where they got onto plastic sleds and came zooming down the fiberglass chute that twisted and turned down the slope, simulating the winter sport.

Early one morning Reilly dragged Amanda out of bed and drove to town, where they boarded an antique narrow-gauge train for an all-day round trip from Durango to the old mining town of Silverton, high up in the mountains.

Another day they drove to the Four Corners Monument, which marked the spot where Colorado, Utah, New Mexico and Arizona meet, and Reilly took a picture of Amanda standing on the flat monument with her feet in all four states at once. When the photo session ended she went crazy buying jewelry from the Indians who had set up shop in booths around the marker.

In the evenings they sat in front of the fire and talked, as lovers do, of anything and everything, recounting past hurts, disappointments and triumphs, revealing secrets, sharing hopes and dreams. And afterward they made love—in front of the fire, or in the tub, or on the moonlit king-size bed, with a million stars twinkling down through the skylight overhead.

It was a space out of time, a magical period during which they did their best to suspend worry and live for the moment, and, for the most part, they succeeded. However, the problem was still there, niggling at the back of their minds, and though Amanda enjoyed every minute she spent with Reilly, by the end of the week she grew restless.

"Mandy, sugar, you agreed we'd stay out of the way and let Dan do his job," Reilly said patiently when she broached the subject of going home.

"I agreed to a week. That's all. It's been a week and now I want to go home."

"But you have to give Dan more time."

"Why? We've called him every day, and so far he's come up with nothing."

"He's still trying to run a license check. It's not his fault that his buddy down at the station can only sandwich in bits of time on the computer between official police business. It'll take a while to check out all the Texas licenses that start with EJX4."

"I don't care. I want to go home. I can't live in limbo forever."

Reilly argued with her for hours, but Amanda was adamant. If he wouldn't take her, she would go alone, she told him. There was a high-strung edginess about her that disturbed Reilly, but he knew she meant it. Against his better judgment, he booked them on an early flight home the next morning.

They arrived by taxi at Reilly's townhouse around noon. There was a message on his answering machine from Dan, but when they tried to return the call, no one answered.

"I guess his secretary is out to lunch," Reilly said, replacing the receiver. "I'll try him again later."

"Fine." Amanda paced around the perimeter of the room, too restless and on edge to sit. The waiting was driving her nuts. She needed to be doing something. Anything. She glanced at Reilly. What she wanted to do was call the station to find out what was going on, but she knew he'd have a wall-eyed fit if she even mentioned it.

"Mandy? Sugar, are you okay?"

"I'm fine...that is...well...to tell the truth, I've got a touch of PMS. Would you be a darling and go to the pharmacy for me? Here, I've got a prescription right here," she said, reaching for her purse.

"PMS?" He cleared his throat and shifted uneasily from one foot to the other. "I, uh, I don't suppose aspirin would do?"

Chuckling at his discomfort, she handed him the bottle and gave him a little push toward the door. "No, it won't. Don't be silly. Just give this to the pharmacist and he'll refill it."

"Okay. But you stay put and keep the doors locked while I'm gone. And don't answer the phone. You hear?"

"I won't. Now go."

Reilly stole a kiss and went, reluctantly, leaving through the kitchen door that led into the garage. Amanda listened to the sound of steel rollers as the garage door rose. The instant the purring engine receded and the garage door rumbled shut, she raced to the telephone.

Harry answered on the first ring. "Yeah. Kowalski."

Amanda nervously wound the telephone cord around her forefinger and forced a bright tone. "Hi, Harry. What's up?"

"Sutherland!" he boomed. "Where the hell are you?"

"Here. In town."

"Well, get your butt in gear, Lois Lane. We just got word of a hostage situation in the ten thousand block of Windriver, out in your part of town, and all my other experienced people are already on assignment."

"Where?" Adrenaline was already pumping through Amanda's veins as she grabbed the pencil that hung on a little chain beside the kitchen phone. She looked around for a pad and cursed under her breath when she couldn't find one. There wasn't so much as a scrap of paper in sight. In desperation, she wrote the address down on the wall next to the telephone.

"Crusher was off duty, but I called him at home, and he's on his way out there. I was about to send that green kid we hired last week, but since you're back, you can cover it. Unless, of course, you're too tired from your little impromptu vacation."

Amanda was too wired to let his sarcasm bother her. She was already flipping through the phone book for the number of a taxi company. "No problem, Harry. I'm on my way."

Chapter Thirteen

Reilly heard the telephone ringing as he climbed from the truck. He walked into the kitchen and set the sack containing the prescription on the counter.

"Mandy, I'm home," he called out as he reached for the receiver. "Hello?" He frowned at the address scribbled on the wall in pencil.

"Why the devil didn't you call and tell me?"

"Hello to you, too, Hoss. And just what is it I was supposed to tell you?"

"Dammit, Reilly, you know that Tess and I are worried," his brother complained. "We expected you, or at least Dan, to let us know when they caught Amanda's stalker."

"What? You mean they've nabbed the guy?"

The line hummed with taut silence. "I assumed that's why you came back," Ryan said cautiously. "You mean they *haven't* caught him?"

"Not as far as I know."

"Then what are you doing here? And what the devil is Amanda doing back at work?"

"What're you talking about? Amanda's right here with me." Reilly frowned. "And how did you know we were back?"

Ryan ignored the last. "How the hell can Amanda be with you when I'm standing here watching her give a live news report on television this very minute?"

"*What?* That's impossible." Reilly moved the mouthpiece to one side and yelled. "Amanda! Amanda, where are you?"

"I think you'd better turn on your TV," Ryan said dryly. "And brace yourself."

Cradling the receiver between his jaw and shoulder, Reilly reached out with his uninjured hand and snapped on the tiny portable television sitting on the kitchen counter. When Amanda appeared on the screen against a backdrop of squad cars and men in SWAT-team gear he cursed long and fluently.

"You didn't know?"

"Hell, no, I didn't know. Dammit, we just got here. I left her alone for thirty minutes. *Thirty minutes!* I even told her to stay put and not answer the phone. And what does she do the minute my back is turned?" Reilly raked a hand through his hair and cursed again. "I can't believe this."

His gaze fell on the sack containing Amanda's prescription, and his anger rose another notch. Of all the sneaky, underhanded—!

There was a flurry of movement on the screen, and Reilly's heart nearly stopped when he heard several pops that sounded like gunfire. "What the hell's going on?"

"Some guy in that red brick house went berserk and started taking potshots at passing motorists," Ryan said, and Reilly uttered an obscenity.

"Where the hell are they?"

"I don't know. Somewhere out here on the northwest side. They gave the street a while ago but I can't recall it."

Reilly's eyes fell on the address scribbled on the wall. "Was it Windriver?"

"Yeah. That's it. How'd you—?"

"I gotta go."

"Go wh—?"

Reilly slammed down the receiver and bolted out the door into the garage, the string of swear words streaming from him turning the air blue. When he got his hands on that woman he'd, by damn, skin her alive.

He spotted Crusher first . . . then Amanda, standing just a few feet away.

The sniper had surrendered during the short time it had taken Reilly to get to the scene. By the time he shouldered his way through the crowd to the police barricade the drama was over and the news people were packing up their gear.

"Reilly! Hey, man, what're you doing here?"

He stalked past Crusher without a word, but the greeting alerted Amanda. She whirled around, her face white.

"Reilly! How . . . how did you find me?"

He neither slowed nor hesitated, but continued to advance on her at the same lethal pace, and Amanda prudently backed away, her eyes growing round.

"If you don't want to get caught, next time don't write the address on the wall," he snarled. Never in his life had he experienced such intense anger. He had not known it was possible to feel such extreme emotion—not without going up in flames. He could feel the heat of his fury radiating from him in waves.

"Now, Reilly—" Amanda took another step back and came to an abrupt halt when she bumped into the van. Before she could move, he slapped his palms against the vehicle on either side of her shoulders, trapping her. The cast on his left hand banged so hard Amanda jumped. Bending forward, he brought his face to within an inch of hers.

"Just what in the bloody hell do you think you're doing?" His fury was so great he could not unclench his jaws, and the words grated between his teeth. He'd started out with a menacing softness, but with each syllable his voice gained volume and intensity, in direct proportion to his rising temper, until he ended with a shout that had the whites of her eyes showing all around.

"Reilly... I'm sorry. I know I shouldn't ha—"

"You *tricked* me. You sent me after that damned prescription so you could take off."

"No! Honestly, it wasn't like that. I swear. I just wanted to find out what was going on at the station. But when I talked to Harry, he needed some—"

"You weren't supposed to talk to Harry or anyone else! You knew that! Of all the stupid, reckless, foolhardy—"

"Now just one minute. Who do you think you're talking—"

"Dammit, woman, I told you to stay put!"

"Oh, is that right?" She ducked under his arm and backed away, her expression growing mulish. "Well, let me tell you something, you big, blockheaded Irishman. Nobody tells me what to do. Not your Mr. Dan Burrows, and certainly not you. If you'll recall, I didn't like this whole stupid idea in the first place!"

"Like it or not, that's the way it's going to be. Now c'mon. I'm taking you home."

"In a pig's eye! I'm not going anywhere with you. Just go away and leave me alone." Pivoting on one heel, she stalked to the back of the van, where Norman was doing his best to appear as though he wasn't listening.

Reilly took a step after her, but Crusher put a hand on his shoulder. "Give her a minute to cool off, man. While she's doing that you can tell me what the hell's going on. Where the devil have the two of you been? Donaldson put out the word that Amanda took emergency leave because of a death in her family, but we both know that's jive. The woman doesn't have any family."

Reilly looked as if he was about to explode. Crusher recognized the look.

"Whoo-ee. What's she gone and done now?"

Gritting his teeth, Reilly reined in his temper and in as few words as possible explained to Crusher all that had happened. By the time he finished, the huge black man looked ready to blow himself.

"I knew it. I knew something had happened when you two disappeared," he raged. "I can't believe that creep broke into her place and trashed—"

The van's engine started up. Startled, Crusher and Reilly looked around as Norman drove away... with Amanda sitting next to him in the passenger seat.

"Dammit, Amanda! Come back here," Reilly shouted, but the van merely picked up speed. "I don't believe this!"

"Take it easy, man. I know Amanda. She won't stay mad long. She's got her share of faults, but holding a grudge isn't one of 'em. Fact is, until she started hanging with you, I'd never seen her lose her cool."

"Yeah, well that makes two of us. That woman would drive a saint crazy."

Chuckling, Crusher slapped Reilly on the back. "C'mon, my man. Everything's cool. Go on and catch up with your lady. And don't worry. Take my word for it, by the time Amanda gets home she'll be regretting the whole thing. Hell, she probably is already."

Amanda felt wretched. She tried to hold on to her anger but guilt kept creeping in. Oh, Lord, she might as well admit it; this whole thing was her fault. Reilly was right; it had been a stupid, irresponsible thing to do. He had every right to be in a towering rage. The man had just put his own life on hold and spent a week trying to keep her out of harm's way and the minute she got back in town she blew it. When—*when*—would she ever learn to curb her impulsiveness? It had gotten her into trouble more than once. Old act-first-and-think-later Sutherland. That was her.

The self-deprecating taunt had barely formed when Norman hit a pothole. Amanda bounced, and her purse jostled out of her lap.

"Sorry," Norman mumbled.

"That's okay. I probably needed a little jolt." Amanda glanced at the young man. Norman was never one for small talk, but today he was more withdrawn than usual. He hadn't said a word since they'd got in the van. Amanda shrugged and bent down to retrieve her purse. Just as well; she was too agitated to talk, anyway.

Reaching for her purse, she noticed a scrap of paper lying on the floorboard beside it, and her hand stayed an inch shy of the strap. It appeared to be a grocery list...written in a tiny, precise hand. Amanda stared at the rigidly controlled script, and a chill slithered down her spine. It was the same handwriting as that on the notes she had been receiving.

Norman. Oh, dear God! Norman was the man who had been harassing her!

Panic gushed up inside Amanda, but she fought it. *Take it easy. Don't blow it. He doesn't know that you know,* she told herself. *If you're going to get out of this van alive, you have to stay calm and act normal. And think. Think, dammit!*

Amanda picked up her purse and straightened. Casually—she hoped—she looked out the side window. What should she do? Jump out and run? No, she could be killed or seriously injured. Act normal and hope he hadn't yet worked up the nerve to harm her? She barely stifled a shudder. The chance of that seemed pitifully slim when she recalled the state of her apartment.

One thing was certain; she couldn't let Norman inside her condo.

Reilly would come after her. Of that, Amanda was absolutely certain. Which, she realized with a twinge of guilt, was probably why, subconsciously, she had felt perfectly safe in defying him. She had never expected to see Reilly in such a towering rage. Even his fury at the train derailment was nothing compared with tonight. But no matter how angry he was, she knew he wouldn't let her out of his sight for long.

A tiny flicker of hope stirred inside her. If worse came to worst and she couldn't get away from Norman, she would just stall until Reilly arrived. Amanda glanced in the side mirror and searched the rear traffic for the battered pickup. What was taking him so long?

Reilly and Crusher had almost reached the truck when they heard a shout. They turned to see Dan Burrows shoving his way through the dispersing crowd.

"Reilly! Wait up!" The detective was breathing hard when he caught up with them. "I've been trying to reach you all day," he panted. "When I saw Amanda on the news, I figured I'd find you both here."

"Well, you found me, anyway," Reilly said sourly. "What's up?"

Hesitating, Dan glanced at Crusher.

"Hey, it's okay," Reilly assured him. "This is Crusher Williams. We told you about him. He's a friend, and he knows all about what's going on."

Dan still looked doubtful, but he shrugged. "I thought you ought to know that I finally got a list of all the Texas licenses that start with EJX4, and one very interesting possibility turned up."

"What? Who?" Reilly demanded, instantly alert.

"A '78 gray Chevy sedan that belongs to a Mrs. Ida Lee Krupps. It turns out, she's the mother of one Norman

Krupps, who just happens to be an apprentice photographer for Channel 5."

Reilly and Crusher exchanged an alarmed look.

"Norman. Oh, God, no—"

"Why that little—"

Both men exploded into action at once.

"C'mon! Let's go!" Reilly ordered, making a dive for the truck.

"Go wh—?"

Wasting no time on civilities, Crusher clamped his giant hand around Dan Burrows's arm and practically jerked the man off his feet as he made for the other side of the pickup.

"Hey! Wait just a—!" Crusher shoved him inside and piled in after him as Reilly cranked up the engine and peeled out with a squeal of tires and burning rubber. "Holy—!" The detective braced one hand against the overhead and held onto the seat edge with the other as the truck careered around a corner. "Dammit! Would someone mind telling me where we're going?"

"After Amanda. She left here with Norman just a couple of minutes ago."

"Where do you think he's taking her?" Crusher asked.

Reilly's mouth thinned. "I'd like to think she asked him to drive her to my place, but I doubt there's a prayer of that. I'm guessing she'd have him take her to her apartment. She was angry enough to do something that foolish."

"Yeah, you're probably right," Crusher said.

Dan nodded his agreement, as well, but in the eyes of all three men was the knowledge that Norman could have driven Amanda anywhere. By tacit agreement, none voiced the chilling thought as Reilly floor-boarded the gas pedal and headed the truck toward her condo.

Amanda tightened her grip on her purse and cast one last glance in the side mirror as Norman turned into the Ushaped drive at the entrance of her building. *Where are you, Reilly? Please, hurry. Please.*

Norman brought the van to a stop in front of the double glass doors. He did not speak, but Amanda could feel his gaze on her. Her heart was pounding so hard she was sure he could hear it. *Act calm. Play it cool. Don't let him know you suspect a thing.*

Forcing a smile, she glanced at him and reached for the door handle. "Well, thanks for the ride, Norman. I appreciate it. Good night."

He nodded, still watching her. Amanda snatched open the door and scrambled out with more haste than she had intended.

The urge to run was almost overpowering but she gritted her teeth and forced herself to walk at her usual languid pace. Feeling his gaze on her back, she pushed through the double doors and walked into the lobby. Mr. Emory, the elderly security guard, was nowhere in sight, but she nearly whimpered with relief when she spotted an empty elevator waiting with its doors standing open.

Amanda headed in that direction, her heart caroming with hope and fear. Almost there. Just a few more steps and she would be safe.

Two feet from the open cubicle, she reached out a hand to prevent the elevator door from closing. At the same instant she heard the ominous squeak of sneakers against the marble floor, coming up behind her.

Fear grabbed her by the throat. Unable to resist, she glanced back over her shoulder...and opened her mouth to scream.

Norman's rough, two-handed shove caught her just below her shoulder blades, cutting off the sound and knocking her into the elevator and down to her knees.

The last thing Amanda wanted was to be trapped inside the tiny box with Norman. Gasping, she tried frantically to scramble out on her hands and knees, but before she could, he hit the button and the doors closed.

"Nor-Norman, what're you doing?" she demanded shakily when he hauled her to her feet. "Have you lost your mind?"

"Don't play games with me," he whispered, sneering at her feigned bewilderment. "You know. Don't pretend you don't. I saw your face when you spotted that list. Did you think you could fool me? Huh?" he demanded, jerking her closer. "Jezebel. Creature of Satan. I should have known. I should have seen it in you. Mama warned me about women like you. But I will purify you. Then...then you will be mine again. Only mine."

His fetid breath struck her face, making her stomach clench. That close, she could smell his dirty hair and the faint stench of body odor that clung to him. Amanda knew it was pointless—maybe even dangerous—to argue with him. He was too near the edge. He had a crazed looked in his eyes and his rambling words were sinister and chilling.

The elevator dinged when they reached her floor. The doors slid open and Amanda drew a breath to scream to her neighbors for help but he clamped his dirty hand over her mouth. She mumbled a strenuous protest against his palm and strained to dig in her heels, but though Norman was skinny, he was wiry and strong, and he forced her down the hallway.

"Give me your keys," he demanded outside her door.

Amanda shook her head, and with a curse, Norman dug through her purse until he found the ring of keys.

Keeping his hand over Amanda's mouth, Norman thrust her inside and locked the door behind them. "Stop fighting me, bitch," he snarled in her ear, and shoved her ahead of him into the living room.

Amanda gave an instinctive cry of alarm and stumbled forward. Grabbing hold of an overturned chair, she barely managed to save herself from falling. When she recovered her balance, her first instinct was to run, but one look around her and all she could do was stare. She had not been in the condo since the night Norman had broken in and vandalized it, and the wanton destruction shocked her anew.

"You're frightened." Norman snickered. Amanda swung around as he moved toward her. His eyes glittered with malicious glee. "Good. You should be. What's the matter? Don't you like what I've done to your place? This is nothing compared to what I'm going to do to you. Your precious Reilly won't recognize you when I'm through."

Amanda groped behind her and backed away. "Norman...please...don't do this. You'll only make things worse. You need help, Norman. Let me go, and I'll see that you get it. I promise."

"No! I'll never let you go. You betrayed me, and now you have to pay! I warned you!" he screeched.

His face crumpled and tears filled his eyes. "Why? Why did you do this to us?" he sobbed. "I loved you. I loved you so much. You were different from other women. Mama didn't believe me when I told her, but I knew you were. You talked to me, and you were nice to me. You belonged to me, Amanda. You were mine. And then...then you gave yourself to *him!*"

In desperation, Amanda tried the teasing charm she usually employed to keep men in line. "Now, Norman," she said, forcing a smile. "You know I didn't mean anything by that. I was just being friendly. That's all."

"No! You loved me." His eyes turned wild again. "I hate you for what you've done. Do you hear me? I hate you!"

"Norman, listen to me. I never—"

"No! I won't listen to your lies!" He gasped for breath and his eyes went out of focus as he slowly shook his head. "I won't. I won't. You must pay. When you're bad you have to pay. That's the rule. Mama said so. I must make you pay."

Amanda's stomach roiled with sickness. She was both unnerved and saddened by his pathetic ravings. He was mad—beyond reach. As much as she wanted to believe that he would not really do her harm, she could not take the chance. Time was running out.

The logical, reasoning side of her said her best chance was to stall until Reilly arrived, but when push came to shove, fear overrode intellect and logic every time, and when Norman made a move toward her, she bolted.

He caught her before she had taken three steps. Amanda fought and struggled like a wild woman. Finally she managed to stomp on his instep with her spiked heel.

"Arr-rrgh!" Norman released her and hopped around holding his injured foot, and Amanda made another dash for the door.

Whimpering, she fumbled with the unfamiliar dead bolt but she was so terrified she could not seem to make her fingers work right. Before she could retract the plunger, she felt a sharp pain in her scalp and her head was jerked back cruelly.

Amanda screamed as Norman slung her away from the door by her hair. Instinctively she grabbed her stinging scalp. Norman moved in close and tried to take hold of her but she struggled like a woman possessed, twisting and gasping and moaning, clawing at his face, his eyes, his neck—anyplace she could reach. She squirmed within his hold until she was facing partially away from him. Clasping her hands together, she rammed her right elbow back into his bony chest with all her might. Norman's breath left him with a loud "Ooof"! and he staggered back against the door, doubled over.

Unable to go through him or around him, Amanda took off the other way. She tore, willy-nilly, through the apartment, her only thought to escape the madman stumbling after her. With every breath, little gasping whimpers of fright tore from her throat.

In her panic, she instinctively ran into her bedroom. Not until she skidded to a halt in the adjoining bathroom, just as her bedroom door crashed open, did she realize she was cornered.

Turning in a circle, Amanda looked wildly around for a weapon, and grabbed the first thing at hand. A second later when Norman charged through the door, she raised the aerosol bottle, depressed the nozzle, and sprayed her favorite perfume into his face at point-blank range.

Norman screamed and clutched his face.

"My eyes! My eyes! You've blinded m—ah...ahh-hhhh..."

Amanda grabbed the companion box of scented bath powder, snatched off the lid and threw the contents over him. Instantly a dense cloud of talc filled the room...and Norman cut loose in a sneezing fit.

"Ahhh-*choo!* Ah-*choo!* Ah-*choo!* Ah-*choo!*"

The cloud of talc was so thick Amanda could barely make out Norman's shape. Holding her hands cupped over her nose, she back away. Covered head to toe with powder, he stumbled around like a ghostly Frankenstein, groping and flinging his arms out and "ah-chooing" every breath.

In his flailing around, one of Norman's arms got tangled up in the shower curtain. He struck out blindly, twisting and turning, but only succeeded in wrapping the curtain around his body. The more he fought to free himself, the more enmeshed and more panicked he became. To Amanda's astonishment, he struggled so hard he lost his balance and took a header into the bathtub, wrapped like a mummy in the plastic sheet.

Seeing her chance, Amanda grabbed the heavy porcelain lid off the toilet tank and dashed over to the tub. Visibility in the bathroom was severely limited. Peering through the roiling cloud, she could barely distinguish one end of the plastic-wrapped lump writhing in the tub from the other.

Amanda had never deliberately inflicted physical harm on anyone in her life, but she knew this was a do-or-die situation. Screwing up her courage, she raised the heavy lid and brought it down on one end of the thrashing lump. It connected with a satisfying *conk*. A groan sounded within the roll of plastic, and the frantic struggles ceased.

The heavy lid shattered into a dozen pieces when Amanda dropped it on the marble floor and ran. She had every intention of running like hell, but another groan from the bathtub stopped her before she reached the door. Biting her lip, she stopped and turned back, squinting through the white cloud. She hadn't hit him hard. It was doubtful he would be out for long. Still...she couldn't just leave him like that; he might suffocate.

Reluctantly, Amanda eased back to the tub. It was a struggle, especially since she could barely see or breathe, but she finally managed to unwrap Norman's upper body. Almost at once, he cut loose with a tremendous sneeze. Startled, Amanda shrieked and jumped back, and landed hard on her bottom.

Oh, Lord, now what? she wondered frantically as he began to stir. Waving her hands in front of her face, she looked around, her heart pounding. Then, through the swirling powder, she made out the eerie shape of her stockings draped over a towel rack. With a glad cry, she scrambled to her feet and snatched them down. They were her best French silk stockings, and Amanda experienced a brief moment of regret, but it couldn't be helped. Quickly, she crossed Norman's wrists over his back and bound them with the stockings. She was tying the last knot when she heard a tremendous crash from the front of the apartment.

Reilly silently cursed his brother's thoroughness as he charged into the apartment with Crusher and Dan on his heels. Ryan had put such a sturdy lock on the door it had taken his and Crusher's combined efforts to kick the damn thing in.

In the living room he screeched to a halt, his gaze searching through the shamble of broken furniture. "Mandy! Mandy, where are you?"

The sight of the Channel 5 van parked in front of the building had flooded him with hope and terror, and now his heart was pounding so hard it felt as though it would burst right out of his chest.

From the rear of the apartment came a noise that sounded strangely like someone choking and sneezing at the same time. Reilly took off.

A few feet inside Amanda's bedroom, he skidded to a halt, and an instant later Crusher and Dan did the same. Bewildered, they gaped at the white cloud billowing out of the adjoining bathroom.

"Holy—" All three men began to cough and sputter and wave their hands in front of their faces. "What the hell happened here? This place smells like a French whorehouse," Reilly choked.

"I don't know, but— Great jumping—!" Crusher's eyes bugged out and he took a step back as a wheezing, ghostly apparition, covered in white from head to toe, stumbled out of the billowing cloud. "Man, what is *that!*"

"What the—?" Reilly's head jutted forward. "Mandy? Mandy, sugar, is that you?"

"Oh, Reilly," Amanda wailed. Stumbling forward, she flung herself against Reilly's chest, and the impact sent up another miniature cloud of powder.

Reilly's bewilderment quickly gave way to relief and concern, and his arms clamped around her like a vise. Holding her tight against his chest, he laid his cheek against the top of her head and squeezed his eyes shut. "Oh, God, sugar. Are you all right? Did he hurt you?"

Until that point, Amanda had done a credible job of keeping her head, but in the safe harbor of Reilly's embrace the shock of it all came crashing in on her, shattering her control. "Oh, Reilly. The stalker was Norman. H-he's crazy."

"I know, darlin'. I know."

"He was going to ki-ki-kill m-me," she sobbed against his chest.

"Shh. Shh, darlin'. It's okay now. You're safe," he crooned, but Amanda continued to cry and cling to him for dear life. She was shaking so hard her teeth were chattering.

"Amanda?" Reilly murmured, rubbing his hands soothingly over her back. "Sugar, I know you're upset, but, uh, can you tell us... Where is Norman?"

Burying her face more firmly against him, Amanda made an agitated sound and gestured toward the bathroom. Immediately both Crusher and Dan sucked in deep breaths and plunged into the miasma of swirling talc.

Seconds later, surprised exclamations, followed by a burst of laughter, erupted from the bathroom and both men came staggering out, holding their sides and whooping.

Reilly scowled. "What the devil is so funny?"

"Ah, man, you won't believe it," Crusher sputtered. "She's got him hog-tied and trussed up like a mummy in there. An' he's got a knot on his head you could hang a hat on."

"And to think," Dan added between guffaws. "We came charging in here like white knights to the rescue. Oh, man, that's rich. That's one helluva lady you've got there, McCall."

Reilly looked down at the delicately built woman quaking in his arms, and his chest swelled with pride and love. "I know," he said softly. "I know."

Chapter Fourteen

It was almost two hours later before Amanda and Reilly returned to his townhouse. The interview with the police, going over and over everything that had happened, seeing Norman hauled out in handcuffs, ranting and screaming threats, had been a harrowing and seemingly endless ordeal that strained Amanda's overwrought nerves to the limit. By the time they reached Reilly's place she was wound so tight she was almost vibrating.

The instant Reilly closed the door she launched herself at him, flinging her arms around his shoulders and burying her face against his neck. "Make love to me, Reilly," she gasped, between scattering frantic kisses over his neck and jaw. "Oh, please. Please love me now."

"Oh, God, Mandy. My sweet Mandy," Reilly groaned. Driven by the same demons of fear and anxiety that bedeviled Amanda, he abandoned all pretense of control and clutched her tight, needing to feel her against him, warm and whole and alive.

Making desperate little sounds, Amanda snatched at the buttons on his shirt. "Oh, please, hurry. Hurry! I can't wait any longer."

Thought and reason no longer existed; she was driven by instinct, by a primal need so great nothing else existed. Nothing else mattered. After the terrible ordeal of violence and terror, Amanda desperately needed Reilly's loving touch. Her soul craved—*demanded*—to experience again the shattering pleasure that only their oneness could bring, that reaffirmation of beauty, of life, of love.

Consumed by the same need, Reilly pulled her blouse from the waistband of her slacks. Buttons, hooks and zippers were dealt with swiftly. Neither could wait to disrobe completely, and clothes were shoved aside. In a frenzy of emotion, they sank together to the carpet.

There was no time and no need for foreplay. The fright and uncertainty of the past few hours had driven their desire for one another to a fever pitch. They kissed deeply, their hands clutching, bodies straining together, and as Reilly rolled Amanda onto her back, her legs came around his hips, and, in a move as natural as breathing, they were one.

Their loving was swift and intense and immensely satisfying. Each movement, each touch, brought a pleasure greater than any they had ever known. And the end, when it came, was so sharply sweet, so perfect, it was shattering.

They collapsed in each other's arms, breathing hard, sated and content, at peace. When at last they gathered the strength to move, they rolled apart. After a moment, Reilly sat up and turned to reach for Amanda—and promptly burst out laughing.

"What? What's so funny?" she demanded, struggling up on her elbows.

Reilly couldn't catch his breath long enough to speak, but an answer wasn't necessary. One look around at the blobs and smears of bath powder on the carpet, and Amanda dissolved into laughter and collapsed against him.

Several minutes passed before they regained enough composure to speak, and even then their eyes were streaming with tears.

"Oh, Lord, I forgot about the powder," Amanda sputtered. "I must look a fright. No wonder that policeman was giving me such peculiar looks."

Reilly gasped and clutched his side. "If you think *he* looked spooked, you should have seen Crusher's face when you staggered out of the bathroom. I thought for a second he was going to pass out."

Still chuckling, Reilly got to his feet and reached for Amanda. "C'mon, you wild woman. Time to hit the showers."

Neither Reilly nor Amanda had eaten since the breakfast snack they'd had on the airplane early that morning, but after a long, leisurely time beneath the warm spray, and another bout of lovemaking, they barely had the energy to call Ryan and Tess and fill them in on the day's harrowing events before tumbling into bed. Within seconds of cuddling up together, they were both sound asleep.

The sun was streaming into the bedroom windows the next morning when the telephone on the bedside table shrilled. Amanda sat up with a start, and Reilly groaned.

"Good grief! It's after ten." She bounded out of bed and began searching through her suitcase for something to wear. "I should have been at the station over an hour ago."

Reilly rolled over and stretched. "Relax, sugar. After what happened yesterday, I doubt they expect you to show up today," he mumbled over a yawn, groping for the telephone.

After muttering a sleepy hello, he held out the receiver to Amanda. "It's for you. It's Bob Donaldson."

"You're kidding." Amanda hurried back to the bedside, her eyes wide with surprise. "Good morning, Mr. Donaldson."

"Good morning, Amanda. I apologize for disturbing you after all that's happened, but I have some news I think will cheer you up. We received a call this morning from..."

Five minutes later when Amanda hung up the telephone, she was so dazed she was speechless. Then her gaze met Reilly's, and her face lit up. "I don't believe it. My story was picked up by the network."

"Don't tell me you're surprised?"

"Actually...yes."

Amanda had not wanted the story aired at all, but there had been no hope of that. Knowing that as soon as they called the police, the other TV stations in town would get word of what had happened, she had sent Crusher to the van for the camera, over Reilly's protests. By the time the police arrived, Crusher had already called in the story to Harry and had exclusive, on-site coverage—including his own firsthand knowledge and involvement—on tape, ready for voice-over dubbing. Amanda's career goals might have been down the tubes, but she had been determined to at least have the satisfaction of Channel 5 scooping the other stations.

Somehow, though, she had not considered that the story would be picked up by the network.

"I thought when this got out it would hurt my chances of landing a network job, but I was wrong."

Amanda shook her head, trying to take it in. She was so amazed and preoccupied she failed to notice the wary look that came over Reilly's face, or the stiff way he rose from the bed and pulled on his jeans.

"They not only liked the story, they were so impressed by the way I handled myself, Mr. Donaldson says they're considering me for the position of co-host of Wake Up Call. That's their network early morning news show," she said with rising excitement. "Oh, Reilly, can you believe it? They actually want me to fly to New York tomorrow to discuss a deal!"

"I take it you're going."

"Of course I'm—" The flatness in his voice got through, and when she saw his shuttered expression, her elation began to fizzle. Until that moment, she hadn't thought about what the career change would do to her personal life. "Oh, Reilly... I..."

Reilly went to the closet, took out a clean shirt and shrugged into it. He left it hanging open and looked at her across the width of the room as he slowly rolled up the cuffs. "I gather you're going to accept the job. This is what you've been shooting for, after all."

The pain in his eyes, his wooden expression, tore at Amanda. The thought of leaving Reilly was unbearable. Yet...how could she not? This was the chance she had been waiting for. Working for.

She stared at him, unable to answer, and Reilly's jaw tightened. "I see," he said tonelessly.

"No! That is...I—I don't know." Amanda spread her hands wide. "But don't you understand? I have to at least go to New York and hear their offer. That doesn't necessarily mean..."

She stopped and bit her lower lip. She felt as though she were being torn in two. "Look, it's only an interview. And Bob Donaldson did offer me the anchor position on the six o'clock news if I decide to stay here."

Reilly just looked at her. His steady blue gaze held a world of sadness and pain—the same pain that was twisting Amanda's heart.

"Don't look at me like that!" she cried. "I've worked hard for this opportunity! I deserve it! I—" She made a frustrated sound and shot a bitter look at the ceiling. "Why am I even bothering to explain this to you? You don't understand. You'll never understand. You haven't an ounce of ambition in your whole body, so how could you?''

''Is that what you really think? No, never mind. I can see that it is.'' Reilly gave a humorless chuckle and shook his head sadly. ''Well, you're wrong. I'm not like your father, Amanda. I have ambitions, all right,'' he said quietly. ''Not as grand as yours, maybe, but they're goals that are important to me. I want a wife and a home and children. I want to live with dignity and honor and to work at a job that I can take pride in. I want the respect of my neighbors and the loyalty and trust of my friends. I want to always live close to the people who are dear to me. Not alone among strangers in a dog-eat-dog world where people claw and scratch and climb all over one another's bloodied backs to reach some illusionary success. I want my children to have the security and the joy—and yes, sometimes the aggravation—of being part of a close family, so they will always know that in a world that's not always kind or easy or safe, there is a place where they will be welcomed and people will care about them. In other words, I want to have a happy, productive life surrounded by the people I love. Those are my ambitions, Amanda.''

The words tugged painfully, insistently, at something buried deep inside her—all the secret dreams and desires she had long ago set aside in pursuit of success. Amanda gazed at him, riddled with longing, but she ruthlessly suppressed the yearning ache.

''I love you, Reilly. I do. But this is my big chance. You can't ask me to just throw it away.''

''I'm not. If this job is what you really want, if this is what it takes to make you happy, then—'' he closed his eyes briefly ''—then I think you should take it.''

He walked to her and took her hand. Staring at it, he gently rubbed his thumb over her knuckles and the fine bones and delicate skin on the back. At last he looked up into her eyes, his own gentle and infinitely sad. ''You have to do what is best for you. Only you know what that is. All that I ask—all I've ever asked—is that you follow your heart.''

"You will have use of the network's suite at the Plaza for as long as it takes to find an apartment. I've been instructed to help you with that, but I've got to warn you, it could take months to find something suitable.''

"Months?'' Amanda lifted one eyebrow.

"Hey. That's life in the big city,'' Teresa Tortoni cracked in her cocky Brooklyn accent, shooting Amanda an impudent grin.

Amanda acknowledged the barb with a droll look. If she decided to take the job, Teresa would be her assistant. Yesterday had been spent in meetings with the network brass, and she had been given a VIP tour of the studio and offices. Today, she had been handed over to Teresa for a bit of practical grounding, to give her a "feel" for their operation. The young woman was quick, savvy, blunt, funny, and thoroughly likable, in a cheeky kind of way that Amanda found refreshing.

"I hate to break this to you, Teresa, but Houston isn't exactly Hicksville. Why, we even have running water and electricity.''

"Yeah, yeah. That's what they all claim. Anyway, about the apartment, it'll help that you won't be needing a parking garage.''

"What do you mean? Of course I'll need a parking garage.''

"No, you won't. You'll be driven to and from the studio by limo. You won't need a car at all.''

"But I have an almost new car that I love.''

Teresa waved an imperious hand. "Take my advice and sell it. A car in New York is nothing but a headache. Not to mention a horrible expense. Anyway, you don't want to be driving yourself to work at four in the morning.''

"Four!" Amanda groaned. God, she detested keeping early hours. She hated getting up at seven. She couldn't imagine stumbling out of bed early enough to be ready at four. That was the middle of the night, for pity's sake.

"Hey, you'll be home every day by one."

Yeah, but to do what? Amanda wondered. She didn't know a soul in New York. And being driven to and from work in a limo didn't sound all that great, either. One of her biggest pleasures in life was zipping around in her little sports car.

As Teresa nattered on about Amanda's daily schedule and what she could expect, Amanda turned the leather desk chair partway around and gazed out the twelfth-floor window of the office that was to be hers if she accepted the network's offer. It was raining outside and all she could see was gray—gray rain, gray sky, gray buildings everywhere. Just like her gray mood.

What was the matter with her? She ought to be ecstatic. On top of the world. The past three days had been the fulfillment of every dream she'd ever had—the first-class flight to New York, the limo to the studio, the suite at the Plaza. Her meeting with the network execs had been a roaring success. They had been effusively complimentary about her past work and made no secret of their eagerness for her to accept the job. The salary and perks were beyond her wildest hopes. Heck, with a decent run, she could be a wealthy woman in just a few years—a successful, wealthy woman.

Success. The word had been her lodestone for almost half her life, pulling her, drawing her. She had always told herself it was worth any sacrifice. But was it?

Was it worth sacrificing love?

Amanda went absolutely still. Her father had loved her mother, in his own selfish way, yet he had sacrificed that love for the sake of money and the easy life. Was what she was doing so very different?

Oh, dear Lord. Had she been so determined to prove to the world that she was nothing like her father that she had blinded herself to the fact that she was behaving exactly as he had?

She had convinced herself that achievement, a sense of purpose, a career marked by a steady climb up the ladder of success would bring happiness and give her life meaning.

Well . . . she had made it to the top, all right, but the truth was, with no friends and no family to share it, success was empty, and New York seemed a cold, lonely, alien place.

What was she doing there? Everyone and everything she loved was back in Houston—Tess, Ryan, Mike, baby Molly. Even Crusher. And most important of all . . . Reilly.

Ryan glanced up from the blueprint he was studying when she entered the construction site office. At once his face lit up with surprise and delight. "Amanda! What are you doing here? When did you get back? I thought you weren't due until the day after tomorrow."

Amanda laughed, and when he came around the desk she returned his hug. "I made my decision, so there was no reason to stay longer."

"I see," he said cautiously, but as he studied her, a look of relief entered his eyes and a slow smile cut grooves into his lean cheeks. "You don't know how relieved I am to hear that. That brother of mine has been a bear to be around ever since you left."

"Reilly? In a bad mood? Impossible."

"Yeah, right. That's what I used to think, but for the past three days he's been about as easy to get along with as a grizzly with an impacted tooth. So why don't you do us all a favor and go put him out of his misery. You'll find him with the construction crew at the new house going up down by the lake."

Grinning, Amanda went up on tiptoe and kissed his cheek. "Thanks, Ryan."

* * *

Amanda spotted him at once. Her heart began to boom as she climbed from her car and approached the half-constructed house. Reilly and another man were standing out in front, talking, their backs to her. She stopped several yards away and waited. A sweet, achy feeling filled her at the sight of him. He was so dear to her, and he looked so wonderful, so rugged and beautifully male in his jeans and chambray work shirt.

The other man laughed and went inside the unfinished house and Reilly started to walk away. Amanda took a step forward, her nerves jumping. "Reilly?"

He wheeled around. In quick succession, shock, joy, then wariness flashed across his face. The last pricked Amanda's conscience as she realized fully how much pain she had caused him. It saddened her to see that even now he was keeping a tight rein on his emotions, not daring to read anything hopeful into her early return.

"Amanda. What are you doing here? You weren't due back for another two days." He remained where he was, his expression shuttered, his posture stiff, as though braced for bad news.

Amanda's heart squeezed. *Oh, Reilly, my love, what have I done to you?* Smiling tenderly, Amanda picked her way toward him over the rough ground. "I found out everything I needed to know. I didn't see any point in staying."

"I see."

She stopped in front of him. She had hoped for a response of some kind, but he neither spoke nor made a move to touch her. He simply watched her, his vivid eyes intent on her face.

The first niggle of doubt snaked through her. Was she too late? "Aren't you happy to see me?"

"I don't know. I guess that depends on why you're here."

"Oh, well...I just came to do this." Gathering her courage, Amanda stepped closer, put her hands on his chest and gave him a sultry look from beneath her lashes. Slowly, provocatively, she puckered up her lips and blew.

He frowned, and with a throaty chuckle, she slid her arms around his neck. "Don't play dumb with me, McCall. It's too late to change your mind. You know perfectly well you said if I ever wanted you, all I had to do was whistle."

Reilly sucked in his breath. In the depths of his vivid blue eyes she saw the sudden flare of fierce elation. As she watched, his wary expression changed to one of unbounded joy, and Amanda's heart squeezed painfully.

He let out a whoop, and his arms came around her, lifting her clear off the ground. Amanda squealed, but the sound was cut off as he crushed her against his chest and caught her mouth in a long, devouring kiss. The hard cast on his left hand pressed painfully against the small of her back, but she did not care.

Remotely, Amanda heard the shrill whistles and catcalls that erupted from the workmen swarming over the half-finished house, but neither she nor Reilly paid them any mind. Clinging together, they kissed endlessly, their hearts soaring.

When at last they drew apart, Reilly framed her face between his uninjured hand and the one encased in the stiff cast, and looked intently into her eyes. "Tell me. I need to hear you say it."

"I'm staying. I'm going to take the job Bob Donaldson offered me as anchor on the six o'clock news. You should like that." She wrinkled her nose at him. "It means very little fieldwork in the future."

"Good," he said succinctly. A concerned look shadowed his face. "Are you sure you're happy with this? No regrets?"

"None. I discovered that I didn't have to actually take the job. I realized that just getting the offer meant I'd made it to the top. Now that I have, I'm free to do as you suggested and follow my heart. And my heart is here ... with you."

"And you'll marry me?"

"Yes. Oh, yes," she said, half laughing and half crying. "I'm all yours, my darling. For as long as you want me."

A primitive passion darkened Reilly's face and his eyes grew heavy-lidded. "Forever," he whispered against her lips. "I'll want you forever."

*   *   *   *   *

HARDHEARTED
Bay Matthews

Chantal Robichaux would rather die than call on Dylan Garvey again, but now she desperately needed his help. Chantal's newborn baby—a baby Dylan didn't know was his—had been kidnapped. If anyone could find their son, it was tough cop Dylan. Dylan's heart, on the other hand, would be hard to reach...and only Chantal's love could soften his defenses.

Share Chantal's loving reunion in Bay Matthews's HARDHEARTED, available in January.

THAT SPECIAL WOMAN! She's friend, wife, mother—she's you! And beside each Special Woman stands a wonderfully *special* man. It's a celebration of our heroines—and the men who become part of their lives.

Silhouette

SPECIAL EDITION™

WHAT EVER HAPPENED TO...?

Have you been wondering when a much-loved character will finally get their own story? Well, have we got a lineup for you! Silhouette Special Edition is proud to present a *Spin-off Spectacular!* Be sure to catch these exciting titles from some of your favorite authors.

FOREVER (SE #854, December) *Ginna Gray*'s THE BLAINES AND THE McCALLS OF CROCKETT, TEXAS are back! Outrageously flirtatious Reilly McCall is having the time of his life trying to win over the reluctant heart of Amanda Sutherland!

A DARING VOW (SE #855, December) You met Zelda Lane in KATE'S VOW (SE #823), and she's about to show her old flame she's as bold as ever in this spin-off of *Sherryl Woods*'s VOWS series.

MAGNOLIA DAWN (SE #857, December) *Erica Spindler* returns with a third story of BLOSSOMS OF THE SOUTH in this tale of one woman learning to love again as she struggles to preserve her heritage.

Don't miss these wonderful titles, only for our readers—only from Silhouette Special Edition!

SPIN2

Also available by popular author

GINNA GRAY

Silhouette Special Edition®

#09722	A GOOD MAN WALKS IN	$3.29	☐
#09792	BUILDING DREAMS	$3.39	☐

Silhouette Romance®

#08826	STING OF THE SCORPION	$2.59	☐

(limited quantities available on certain titles)

TOTAL AMOUNT	$
POSTAGE & HANDLING	$
($1.00 for one book, 50¢ for each additional)	
APPLICABLE TAXES*	$ _____
TOTAL PAYABLE	$ _____
(Send check or money order—please do not send cash)	

To order, complete this form and send it, along with a check or money order for the total above, payable to Silhouette Books, to: **In the U.S.:** 3010 Walden Avenue P.O. Box 9077, Buffalo, NY 14269-9077; **In Canada:** P.O. Box 636, Fort Erie, Ontario, L2A 5X3.

Name: _____

Address: _____ City: _____

State/Prov.: _____ Zip/Postal Code: _____

*New York residents remit applicable sales taxes.
Canadian residents remit applicable GST and provincial taxes.

GGBACK1

Silhouette®